RIVERS MUST RUN

To Tom & Karen
For memories of
great times!

Paul Kending

Paul Kending

Waubesa Press
The quality fiction imprint
of Badger Books Inc.
P.O. Box 192
Oregon, WI 53575

© Copyright 1997 by Paul Kending
Published by Badger Books Inc. of Oregon, Wis.
Editing/proofreading by J. Allen Kirsch
Color separations by Port to Print of Madison, Wis.
Printed by BookCrafters of Chelsea, Mich.

First edition

ISBN 1-878569-46-5

Acknowledgments

I wish to thank members of the Lac Vieux Desert Band of the Chippewa for inspiring creation of this work. Others deserving my gratitude include: Bill Swensen for involving me in the history of hydroelectric development in Wisconsin, Dana Grams and Marshall Buehler for checking historical and cultural accuracy, Andi Wittwer and the Sawyer County Historical Society for photo research, Jo Stewart, my daughter Katheryn Senn and my wife, Candy, for reading the manuscript and providing criticism and encouragement.

Prologue

The first hydroelectric dam in North America was constructed in Appleton, Wisconsin in 1882. It was built to run the city's new trolley cars, but its impact signaled a new era for the men who worked the woods and waterways of the north. Wisconsin was timber country and before the railroads had reached the north woods, great log jams driven by burly men in checkered wool flannel, floated from the virgin forests to saw mills. Rivers were the thoroughfares of transportation and the lumberjacks claimed them as their own. Power dams posed a threat to their territorial rights. Had Wisconsin still been a frontier when the popular press was born, the untamed world of the lumberjack might have rivaled that of the cattleman and battles that ensued when power dam and logjam met would have been the stuff of nineteenth-century fiction. Such was not the case. Media attention had turned to the territories west of the Mississippi long before the rivers in the northern forests were dammed to provide electric power.

Dams were nothing new. The Pilgrims had harnessed the streams within ten years of landing on Plymouth Rock to grind their corn, but on the wide Wisconsin, millers were content to build *wing dams* and skilled burlers poled the logjams past them. Accidents happened in the swift current, of course, but the fights that broke out as a result were brief and of no serious consequence.

Power dams were different. To turn the giant turbines that produced electricity, water had to be held back above the dam; and that meant the flow of the whole river was blocked. The promise of side channels to float logs past the dam provided little consolation to men who saw not only their livelihood but their way of life in jeopardy.

The lumberjacks were a diverse lot, some immigrants themselves, most no more then one generation from their European roots. They were proud of their ancestry and ethnic terms that a century later would be seen as derogatory were expressions of both identification and affection. It was common for men to be known only by their country of origin, such as the big lumberjack referred to simply as "Swede." The friendly jibes could get out of hand of course, especially when loose talk was mixed with whiskey, and even the closest friends might exchange a few blows, but any differences were quickly forgotten when a threat came from beyond their ranks.

Hydroelectric company people were outsiders who challenged the loggers' dominion over the waterways of the north woods. The lumberjacks were determined not to give in, but when the state sponsored a plan to harness the power of the mighty Wisconsin River, the loggers had a far more serious challenge to face. It was a challenge they could not meet without some unexpected help.

Chapter 1

The old Indian had spotted Jotham when he started to chase the cottontail. It was just curiosity at first. He had seen young boys around the logging camp, but this was the first time he had seen any as young as Jotham. He stayed far enough behind not to be observed. A white boy roaming alone in the woods could be as dangerous as a bear cub with its mother nearby. The Indians in Wisconsin were at peace with the white man, but he knew that battles still raged in the west and while there was no open conflict between his people and the whites, the war would continue for many years in men's hearts. He knew that most settlers did not trust Indians. To approach a child in the woods, if he was seen by other white men, could invite the flash of a high-powered rifle. Some lumbermen he feared would not simply shoot to scare the red man. He had heard them say, *the only good Indian is a dead Indian*, and he was determined not to be that kind of good.

Jotham had run into the woods to get away from his older brothers. They had been teasing him. It was his name again, Jotham. Why did his mother insist on the name Jotham? Nobody named their kids Jotham anymore. The boys and girls at school had teased him too, but that was mostly last year when he was a little second grader. This year he was in the third grade and he wouldn't be pushed around. His older brothers were Gino and Dominic. Now those were real names. Names for boys who would grow up to be real men, not Jothams.

Now Jotham Marichetti was lost. He could no longer see the small lopsided building they called their house, but it was still early so he hadn't even thought about how he would find his way back. The sun had only crossed the mid-point of its path across the April sky. He also hadn't heard the quiet moccasin-clad footsteps that followed just far enough back to escape notice.

With no brothers or sisters his own age, and almost no kids at all in the lumber camp, Jotham played alone a lot. He liked to play in the woods. Usually he stayed closer to the house, but it was such a beautiful day that he had gone a little farther into the forest. No one had told him about the Indian village up at the north end of the lake. He had seen a rabbit, a baby cottontail and followed it. It would run ahead for a while, then stop as if it were waiting for him to catch up. Pretty soon it had run off into some thick brush and Jotham couldn't see it any more.

The sun was still high in the sky, but it was past noon and Jotham was hungry. Under the trees he found clusters of small plants. Wintergreen. Hiding beneath the waxy green leaves were the tiny red berries with a sweet, minty taste. The old Indian watched from behind a small cedar as Jotham picked a few and ate them. The sharp tang was refreshing, but a few wintergreen berries were by no means enough for a meal. Even at eight years, Jotham knew it was too early in the spring for ripe blueberries or blackberries. He continued to walk, unaware of the silent feet that followed him, through the grove of pines and down toward the water.

It occurred to the old man that there might be other white people in the woods that he didn't know about, perhaps settlers — homesteaders he had heard them called — but the longer he followed the more he became convinced the boy was alone. He began to feel concerned for the boy's safety. The big woods was a dangerous place for one so small. The boy didn't look like he was lost. A lost boy would be looking around, trying to find his way. This one just wandered from one discovery to another, but he didn't look like he knew where he was either. If that was the case, the old Indian knew it would be up to him to take him home. It made no difference that it was a white boy;

he was a child and grown people were expected to watch over children. That's what grown people do. He wondered where the boy's mother was and why she would let him go so far into the woods by himself. He could not understand the ways of the white people. No Indian mother would let her child wander off like that.

Jotham never really knew his mother. She had died during the winter of '86, his pa said. Pneumonia. That was a bad winter, pa said. Lots of people died because of the cold weather.

Jotham was only three then. Gino and Dominic stayed with his dad, but Jotham had to go to Wausau and live with his Aunt Sarah, his mother's sister. Gino and Dominic weren't really his brothers anyway. Their mother had died when they were very small, before Jotham was born.

They had lived someplace in Europe, *Italy*, Jotham thought. He didn't know where that was, but next year he would study geography in school and then he would learn all about Europe. Anyway, that's what Gino said. In the fourth grade you learn geography. His father had come to America where he married an English woman, then sent for Gino and Dominic. Soon after Jotham was born. She had insisted that her son be named after someone in the Bible so she named him after Jotham, whoever that was. It didn't even go with Marichetti.

They lived in Minnesota then, close enough to a town where Gino and Dominic went to school for a few years. When they moved to Wisconsin and his papa started the lumber camp up by Michigan, Gino and Dominic quit school and went with him. Neither one of them had a chance to finish eighth grade, but at least they learned how to read a little and to figure some. Jotham didn't know how far his brothers went in school, but he thought Gino must have at least finished fourth grade if he knew that was where Jotham would learn about geography.

Dominic and Gino were a lot older and could stay in the camps with his father. Dominic was five years older than Jotham and Gino was three years older than that. Besides, Aunt Sarah didn't want to take care of Dominic and Gino because they weren't really her sister's kids, and Gino, having learned to talk in another country, had an Italian accent. Jotham didn't know what difference that made. He never had any trouble understanding Gino and, as near as he knew, all the other kids understood him too, but Aunt Sarah didn't seem to like people who had a foreign accent. Only Jotham was sent to Aunt Sarah's. Of course that meant that Jotham had to go to school, living in Wausau.

There wasn't any school close to the camp so now that Dominic and Gino were older they worked with the men in the lumber camp on Lac Vieux Desert, over in Michigan. It seemed to Jotham that the camp should be a long way off, over in another state, but it was really just a few miles, so Pa and his brothers lived in their own house in Wisconsin. Jotham went to school in Wausau so he only got a chance to come up for vacations. This week was Easter vacation, so he took the train as far as Rhinelander and his dad had picked him up there. Now that he was eight he got to stay for the whole summer after school was out.

The old Indian waited just a short distance behind and watched as Jotham crept down the shallow bank to the water's edge. The creek was small, even with the spring run off, but farther to the south Jotham knew it became the Wisconsin River. His father had told him it was the same river that he followed to and from school. He found that hard to believe. This was just a brook, bubbling over the rocks, not wide and still like the river flowing past his school in Wausau. Jotham had also been told that the creek came out of Lac Vieux Desert, but he had no idea how far to the east that might be. There, close to the water he found what he was looking for; a cluster of ferns that took advantage of the warmer earth along the creek bed and started to spread across the sunny bank. He pulled one up and peeled the hard, dark, outer surface of the root away. Then he reached in and dug the soft meat out as he had seen his brothers do. They called it a banana fern because the meat, once removed from the root, looked like a tiny banana. Jotham put it in his mouth and began to chew. *It sure doesn't taste like banana*, he thought. It really didn't have much taste at all, certainly not sweet, but it didn't taste bad either, not bitter or anything, and it was food.

The fern root left Jotham's mouth feeling dry and he really wanted something to drink. He thought about drinking from the river, but in early spring the water was flowing very fast and crawling down the bank looked a little too scary. Besides he really wanted something sweet. A boy growing up in the woods in the 1890's knew a lot about survival, though no one at the time would have called it that. Jotham took his brand new pocket knife, the one his father had given him for Christmas, and opened the big blade. He'd had the pocket knife for only a few months, but already he had become an adept whittler. He searched the hardwood growth that bordered the river until he found a small maple sapling. Being careful to push the knife away, his father had said you should never draw it toward yourself, he peeled away a small section of the sapling's bark. Jotham was careful not to cut too deeply. He wanted to taste the sweet maple sap that ran just under the bark of the tree. He made the cut low, less than a foot off the ground where the sap would run more freely. Jotham dropped down on his hands and knees and put his lips to the white surface. He had just started to savor the sugary liquid when he heard a sound. At first Jotham thought it might be a bear and he could feel his heart jump against his chest. Yet it didn't sound like an animal. It sounded almost like a man laughing, or more likely trying not to laugh. Jotham remained frozen in place, his lips still against the tree, but he was no longer sucking the sweetness from the sapling. The sound grew softer, just a chuckle, and he heard the crunching of branches as whatever it was came up behind him. Jotham turned and what he saw was almost as frightening as a bear. He was facing a real, honest-to-gosh Indian. Now he was scared, but it was too late to run.

"What you tellin' me, you lost Jotham?" Enrico Marichetti yelled at his son Dominic.

"I didn't lose him, Papa. He ran off. I went in the house for a drink of water and when I came back he was gone."

"Where'd he go?"

"I dunno," Dominic stammered, "off in the woods I guess. I'm sorry, Papa."

"That's all right. It's not your fault," his father consoled. "You go get Old John and the Polack to help look and tell Gino to come too. We find Jotham. Don't worry." The elder Marichetti tried to sound confident. Dominic was shaking with fear, not so much of his father, but fear for his little brother. Both he and his father knew how easily a little boy from the city could become confused in the deep woods around the Wisconsin River headwaters. He didn't doubt that Jotham would be found. He would get the whole camp of lumberjacks out to look for him if necessary, but it could take all day, maybe even longer and he could imagine how frightening a night in the woods would be for a boy like Jotham.

Dominic turned and ran to get the men his father had asked for. Old John and Stanley Rodzaczk were two of the most faithful workers in the logging camp. Both had worked for Enrico Marichetti in Minnesota and when the timber began to run out there, they moved with him to Lac Vieux Desert. They were like part of the family and could be counted on to drop whatever they were doing to help look for the boy. Marichetti watched his son run off toward the camp, then sat down to wait for help. It would be a while before Dominic could find the men and get a party together and there was little he could do until then.

Jotham waited, scared the Indian was going to run off with him like in some of the stories Dominic had told him, but Old Eagle Feather just kept laughing. Jotham saw that the Indian wasn't wearing war paint and he didn't have a tomahawk or anything. Maybe Indians weren't so scary after all. This one didn't even look mean.

The old Indian just chuckled. "Ahmeek," he said, his chuckle turning into an uproarious laugh. "You are Ahmeek." Old Eagle Feather could not help himself. Jotham, down on his hands and knees, his rump in the air and his lips pursed over the maple sapling, looked more like a beaver felling a tree for his dam than a little boy.

Whatever fear Jotham felt began to vanish in the twinkle in the old man's eye. "Ahmeek?" he asked, not having the slightest idea what Eagle Feather was talking about.

"Ahmeek. You are the beaver, chewing on a tree."

"Ahmeek?" Jotham asked again.

"Your people call him beaver. Indians call him Ahmeek," Eagle Feather said. "He chews tree to build dam."

"I wasn't building a dam," Jotham said, still not at all sure what the old man was talking about.

The old Indian laughed again. Of course he knew what Jotham had been doing. As a boy he too had sliced into the soft maple sapling, the *a'nina'tig* and he too had tasted the sweet nectar that ran in the early spring.

"No, but you looked like the beaver. Beaver build dams. Beaver chew trees."

Jotham thought about that. For several seconds neither of them spoke. Finally Jotham broke the silence.

"Ahmeek is the Indian word for beaver?" he asked.

"Chippewa," the old man replied.

"What?"

"Chippewa. Ahmeek is Chippewa word for beaver."

"Why do you call him Ahmeek?" Jotham asked.

"Why do you call him beaver?"

"I don't know," Jotham replied. "Because that's what he is."

"Okay."

"Why do they chew on the trees?"

"Why do you?" Eagle Feather asked.

Jotham laughed. "I wasn't chewing on the tree. I was just licking the maple sap. Do beavers eat wood?"

The old Indian smiled. This white boy had so many questions. "No," he said, "beaver eat roots, like you."

"I don't eat roots" Jotham replied as indignantly as an eight-year-old could manage.

"Yes, you do. I saw you."

Jotham remembered the fern. "Oh, that. We just do that when we're in the woods... and we get hungry."

"And you can not find enough berries?"

"Yeah."

"Okay."

Again neither of them spoke. Jotham studied the old man. *Indians know a lot about the woods and animals and stuff,* he thought. Finally he returned to his question.

"You didn't answer me. Why do the beaver chew the trees?"

"To build dam," Eagle Feather answered. He knew what was coming next.

"Why do they build dams?"

The old Indian smiled. He paused and looked right into Jotham's eyes. Then with a note of finality he said, "because that is what beaver do."

That didn't seem like a very good answer, but Jotham knew from the tone of the old man's voice that the questioning was over.

"You are hungry?" Eagle Feather asked.

"Yes. I should go home, but I'm not sure where home is."

"Come, little Ahmeek. I will take you."

The old Indian walked with Jotham through the woods back toward the Marichetti lumber camp. Eagle Feather was careful to lead the boy along paths that would keep them well out of sight of the loggers. As they walked, he talked about the woods and all the wood's creatures. He talked too about the river. "The river very important," he said, "It brings life to all that is in the forest."

"But it's such a little river," Jotham said, "hardly even a creek."

"Even small rivers give life," the old Indian said. "Small rivers run to be part of bigger river, like little Ahmeek will some day be a big brave." Jotham could see that Eagle Feather thought of the river as something very special. He liked this old man and couldn't understand why people in the logging camp hated the Indians so much. They walked past the south end of the lake and just outside the lumber camp they turned onto the trail that led across the state line to Jotham's father's house.

When Old Eagle Feather and Jotham approached the clearing where Gino and his Papa planned to plant a small garden and they could see the house on the other side, he stopped.

"I go no closer," he said.

Jotham didn't speak, just smiled up at the old man.

"We will talk again of woods and river. Goodbye, little Ahmeek."

"So long," Jotham whispered. His smile broadened, then he turned and started to run. After only a few steps he stopped and turned back. Wait!" he called. "I don't know who you are."

The old man paused and brought his hand to his chin for a moment's thought.

He waved as he called back, "I am Eagle Feather." Then he disappeared into the forest. Jotham looked until he could no longer see Eagle Feather before walking across the clearing to the house.

By then it was late afternoon and the sun hung low over the trees. Gino and Dominic were waiting outside while their father, Old John and Stanley prepared to start the search. Gino was the first to see Jotham, looking back into the woods, as he stumbled across the meadow.

"Jotham, where you been? Your papa, he's worried about you."

"You shouldn't run off like that," Dominic chimed in. "Pa's gonna tan your hide good when you get in the house."

"Will he really?" Jotham looked up at Gino for support.

"He maybe will," Gino said. "That's pretty dumb, you stayin' away all day like that. You know there's Indians in those woods, don't you?"

Jotham didn't say anything. He even kept the smile that was trying to form on his lips inside. They would be mad enough about him running into the woods alone and staying all day. He was pretty sure they would really be mad if he told them about Eagle Feather and they probably wouldn't let him play in the woods again. He wanted to go back. He wanted to find the old man and talk some more about the animals and plants and the lake and the river, but that would have to wait until summer. Tomorrow he had to return to Wausau and to school.

"Yeah, real dumb," Dominic added, "but what you expect from a kid named Jotham?"

Jotham spun around and stuck his chest way out. "I'm not Jotham," he said. "I'm Ahmeek."

Chapter 2

Jotham was daydreaming. He could see the kind, gentle face of the old Indian he had met in the woods near his father's lumber camp. In another six weeks summer vacation would start and he would go back. Maybe he would see the old man again and be able to ask him more about Indian things. He thought about the beaver and what the old man had said, *"beaver build dam because that's what beaver do"*. He wasn't just sure what to make of all that, but it did seem to make sense. After all, beavers didn't go to school and if they didn't go to school where did they learn how to build dams? Jotham had never heard of a beaver that didn't know how to build a dam. He didn't suppose anyone had. But if all the animals and all the birds and the trees and rivers and everything had their purpose like Old Eagle Feather said they did, what about people? What was their purpose? Jotham didn't think going to school had much to do with his purpose. There ought to be something that he just knew, didn't have to learn, but just knew, like the beaver.

It was almost too much for his eight-year-old mind to think about and after a few minutes his head started to hurt and he thought he felt a little dizzy. If he could see the old Indian when summer vacation started, he'd ask him about those things. It seemed to Jotham that Indians knew far more than white people about a lot of things. He never heard his teacher, Miss Merriweather, talk about anything so important. What grade did you have to be in before they started to teach you about things like that, about how each animal just knows what it's supposed to do and what people are supposed to do? Of course he knew a lot of people, living in the city, and they did a lot of things, but maybe that wasn't the important stuff. Mr. Putnam ran the general store, and there was Orville Norton, he was the sheriff, and of course there was Miss Merriweather, the teacher, but was that what they were supposed to do? How did they know that they were supposed to be a general storekeeper, or a sheriff, or a school teacher? Was that what was natural for people or had people somehow got out of touch and lost their place in nature?

Pretty soon he could hear Miss Merriweather's voice coming back into his consciousness. She was talking about subtraction and how when one of the numbers was bigger than the number you were subtracting it from you had to borrow one from the number next to it. Jotham understood all this. He could do those complicated subtraction problems easy. He was more anxious to get to next year and learn long division. He did have one question about subtraction though. He couldn't understand why the teacher kept saying you should borrow one. If you were trying to subtract seven from two and you had to borrow one from the nine next to the two — well then, you were changing that number from a ninety-two to an eighty-two — so weren't you really borrowing ten? He'd asked Miss Merriweather about that one day, but she just said, "Do it the way I tell you to and then you won't get confused, Jotham." Jotham didn't think that was a very good answer.

It was a good thing he had started to listen again though, because just about the time he had figured what Miss Merriweather was talking about she asked the class a question. She wrote the figures on the blackboard as she spoke.

"What is one-hundred and twenty-six minus ninety-four?"

Jotham didn't even bother to write the problem on his paper. He could figure that one out in his head. His father had been teaching him arithmetic since he was four and his father had a lot of shortcuts that probably even Miss Merriweather didn't know about. His mind worked quickly.

He figured that ninety-four was only six less than one hundred, so the difference between the two numbers was really the same as six plus twenty-six or thirty-two. You didn't need to put a problem like that on paper and you really didn't need to worry about borrowing numbers. His father couldn't write or read English, but arithmetic was the same in English as it was in Italian and papa was real good with arithmetic. So was Jotham. He sat quietly, hoping the teacher wouldn't call on him, but of course she did. He hated it when she called on him in arithmetic. He liked knowing the right answer, but after class, at recess, the other kids would call him the teacher's pet and tease him about being so smart.

"Jotham," he heard Miss Merriweather say.

Jotham didn't answer.

"Jotham!" The voice was more insistent.

Still he didn't answer.

Miss Merriweather walked right over to Jotham's desk. The room became very quiet and the eyes of all the other students were turned toward him. "Jotham," she repeated, this time with just a tinge of anger in her voice.

Jotham straightened up. "I'm not Jotham anymore, Miss Merriweather. My name is Ahmeek."

Everything was quiet. Then there was just a little giggle from the back of the room. It was Rebecca Morgan. She was in the fourth grade, and in the one-room school that was only one row away from Jotham. Jotham used to like Rebecca. He thought she was the prettiest girl he had ever seen, with her long, curly, red hair. Rebecca was embarrassed to have a second grader wanting to be her boyfriend, so she was pretty mean to Jotham. He still thought she was a pretty girl, but when he came back last fall for the third grade he decided he didn't want Rebecca to be his girlfriend. She quit being so mean, but she still thought of him as a baby and made fun of him whenever he made a mistake. A minute later all the boys and girls in the school were laughing out loud. Even Miss Merriweather couldn't help but smile a little and Jotham thought he might have made a mistake. He had been thinking about Eagle Feather and the Indian name the old man had given him, but that was up in the woods, not here in school. Somehow he hadn't imagined that the kids might tease him as much about calling himself Ahmeek as they did about being named Jotham. After all, they didn't know Ahmeek was a Chippewa word for an animal. They thought it was just a silly word Jotham made up. Jotham didn't have time to decide whether he should be firm about this or just pretend it was a silly joke because just then the big clock on the wall by the cloak room chimed and Miss Merriweather dismissed them for recess. Just as Jotham was starting to cross the room to slip out the door, Miss Merriweather stopped him.

"Would you come here a minute, Jotham?" she asked.

She didn't sound angry, so Jotham walked right up to her desk. "Yes, Miss Merriweather," he said.

"Jotham, tell me about your new name."

Jotham told her about meeting the old Indian in the woods at his father's logging camp and how the old man had called him Ahmeek. He told her that everybody always teased him about being named Jotham and that he thought since Old Eagle Feather had given him a new name, and since it was an Indian name, maybe they wouldn't tease him as much.

Miss Merriweather was genuinely sympathetic. She knew how they had teased Jotham, though she suspected it was more because they found it hard to keep up with him in school than anything to do with his name. "I'll call you Ahmeek, if you want," she said.

"Really?" Jotham expected more resistance to his new name than that. Dominic said that his teacher would never just let him change his own name and both Gino and Dominic were sure Aunt Sarah would object.

"We'll see how it works out for a little while and if they keep teasing you and you want to change your name back to Jotham again, well that will be all right too."

She had a kind smile on her face as she said it. Jotham thanked her before he went out into the schoolyard to play with the other children.

As soon as Jotham came out the door he could hear the giggling start again. For some reason it didn't bother him as much as it had when they teased him about his real name. A fourth grade boy approached him.

"Ahmeeek," the boy said, drawing the last syllable out. "What kind of a name is that anyway?"

Jotham might have been hurt by the way the question was asked if it hadn't been for the way the boy looked. The fourth grader's voice was intentionally taunting, but Jotham could only laugh at the look on his face. Of course the boy didn't know what the word *ahmeek* meant, but when he said it, the way he drew out the last syllable — meeeeek — he stuck his chin out and curled his upper lip to display two protruding buck teeth. Jotham could not help himself. *He looks like a beaver,* he thought, and he just started laughing. He wondered if that was how the beaver got that Chippewa name. Maybe someone a long time ago made a face to show what the animal looked like as he was making a sound that came out "ahmeek." Everyone around began to laugh too and it seemed that only the fourth-grade boy failed to see that it wasn't Jotham they were laughing at.

After a few minutes some of the boys started teasing again, but Jotham didn't care. After all, he knew what *ahmeek* meant, and he had decided that would be his secret. And it was a secret he didn't plan to tell them, at least not the ones that teased him. These kids, after all, had never been in an Indian village and they probably wouldn't understand the significance of having a name like Ahmeek. If they knew that it meant "beaver" they would probably tease him even more.

"Ahmeek, Ahmeek!" one of the boys cried out, laughing. "Hey everybody, this is my friend Ahmeek. What do you think of his name?"

"I think I like it," answered Rebecca Morgan. "It's kind of cute."

Wow, Rebecca Morgan thought Ahmeek was a cute name. He sure didn't expect Rebecca Morgan to be on his side, but he was sure that if she was, they wouldn't tease him about his new name for long. Maybe he had decided he didn't want to be her boyfriend, but she was still the prettiest girl in the whole school. He was right. In a few minutes the girls started to drift off to one side of the playground while the boys stayed on the softball field. They started a game of work-up, but Jotham was too small to play softball with the older boys. He and some of the other second- and third-graders stood on the sideline and watched.

"How did you come up with a name like Ahmeek?" Michael Barry asked. Michael was a fifth-grade boy. He was standing near home plate waiting his turn to bat.

"An Indian chief gave it to me," Jotham said.

Michael started to smile. A friendly smile, but one that said he didn't believe it.

"Up in Michigan." Jotham added quickly to make the story more believable.

"Jotham goes to Michigan a lot," the voice of a third grader standing next to them piped up. "His dad has a logging camp up there."

Of course Jotham didn't know if he had been in Wisconsin or Michigan, when he met Old Eagle Feather, but it sounded more impressive to say that it was in Michigan. Few of the boys and girls in his school had been out of Wausau, much less out of the state, and the tribal village was in Michigan so it wasn't a very big fib. He guessed that it might not be totally truthful to refer to Eagle Feather as an Indian chief either, but he was, after all, an old Indian and Jotham was not sure he wasn't a chief. It was a small addition to the story and it might help to prevent a lot more teasing about his name. He guessed that having a name given to you by an Indian chief was pretty important stuff and with that information the other children would be much more likely to accept him.

He was right. It was only a few days until most of the boys and girls at the school stopped teasing him. Some of them started to call him Ahmeek and, since the children accepted his Indian name, Miss Merriweather seemed to accept it too. At least she did at the beginning, but that would soon change.

"What is this Indian name nonsense?" The question was firmly stated by the stern-looking lady who stood over Miss Merriweather's desk. Jotham stood by her side with a look that said to his teacher, *I'm sorry I got you into this.* Aunt Sarah was well-known and well-respected in the community. Her husband, Oliver, was the county surveyor, at that time one of the more highly salaried men in government service. She was tall for a women, almost five-foot-eight, and she wore her brown hair in a tight bun that added to the severity of her appearance. Aunt Sarah had heard some of the children near her home playing with Jotham and calling him Ahmeek. At first she thought it was just part of a game and paid little attention, but when they turned to leave and she heard, "See you tomorrow, Ahmeek," she stopped one of the boys to ask about it. He said it was his new name, given to him by a real Indian chief when he was in Michigan. "Everybody at school calls him Ahmeek," he said, "even the teacher." That was it. Children could do what they wanted to on the playground, but a teacher should not be fostering that kind of behavior. If her sister had wanted her child named Ahmeek, she would not have had him christened Jotham, she told the young woman sitting in front of her. Miss Merriweather tried to explain how the other boys and girls had teased Jotham about his name and how much better he was able to mix with them at recess now. That just made matters worse. Jotham was a perfectly good name and if the children teased him then it was Miss Merriweather's job to put a stop to it.

"His baptismal records and his school records list his name as Jotham, Jotham Marichetti," Aunt Sarah said with a tone that signaled the end of the discussion. "You, Miss Merriweather, will refer to him by his given name and see that while he's at school the other children do the same." She meant, though she did not say it, given name only. She would object to the name Marichetti if she could. It sounded so foreign. She never understood why her sister Elizabeth married an Italian and she blamed Enrico Marichetti for taking her to a place that had eventually led to her death. Aunt Sarah continued, "I'll take care of the situation when he is at home." With that she grabbed her nephew by the hand and turned on her heel so rapidly that Jotham thought his arm would come right out of his shoulder. On the way home Jotham tried to reason with Aunt Sarah, but she wouldn't listen.

Jotham decided he wasn't going to let Aunt Sarah bully him. No one else had much objected to his new name. Why should she? His father and Gino had laughed and said that if he wanted to be called by an Indian name that was all right with them. Even Dominic, the one who had said that his teacher and Aunt Sarah wouldn't allow it, the one who teased him most of all and who objected to almost everything he said or did, agreed to call him Ahmeek. Why did Aunt Sarah have to be so difficult? Well, he knew how he would deal with her. He just wouldn't answer to Jotham anymore. She'd have to call him something and sooner or later she would give in to Ahmeek. He would put his plan into action starting with supper tonight.

"Jotham," Aunt Sarah asked, "would you like some chicken dumplings?" She held the bowl in one hand and the ladle in the other as she always did, waiting for an answer.

Jotham did not respond.

"Jotham?" she repeated.

Jotham remained quiet.

"Oh," she said, "I guess Jotham isn't eating with us to-night." And with that she turned and went into the kitchen, taking those delicious chicken dumplings Jotham liked so much right along with her. A moment later she returned and took the dishes from in front of him and returned them to the sideboard. It was going to be a long, hard, all-out war, but Jotham resolved not to give in.

"A little hard on the boy, weren't you?" Jotham heard Uncle Oliver say as he started up the stairs to his room. Sarah had told her husband about the incident on the playground and about her talk with Miss Merriweather.

"Sometimes it takes a hard lesson for a stubborn child," Jotham heard Aunt Sarah respond.

The struggle went on for more than a week. Jotham refused to answer to his given name and Aunt Sarah re-fused to acknowledge any other name for him. There were many nights without supper, usually when something Jotham especially liked was being served. His school lunch, however, was always prepared and at school he wouldn't have to answer to Jotham in order to be allowed to eat it. Now and then, after the evening meal he would hear a tap on the door to his room and find Uncle Oliver standing there with a bowl of soup or a chicken wing.

When Jotham was out in the yard playing, many of the children referred to him by his Indian name. Aunt Sarah would come out and ask where Jotham was and it would take a moment for some of them to remember who she was asking about. Aunt Sarah was as firm as ever when Jotham was in the house, but when he wasn't there she began to think she was fighting a losing battle.

Ahmeek might have been firm in his convictions, but Jotham was getting very hungry. His daily school lunch wasn't enough to get along on and Uncle Oliver wasn't home every day. The surveying job sometimes kept him way over on the other side of the county for two or three days at a time. Just about the time Jotham had decided he couldn't take it any more and that he would give in and answer to his real name, Aunt Sarah came to his room.

"Ahmeek," she said, "I think it's time we work out a compromise."

Ahmeek!, he thought, *does this mean she's ready to give in? What,* Jotham wondered, *is a compromise?*

"What's a compromise?" he asked tentatively.

"It means neither one of us wins, but we each give in a little bit," Aunt Sarah explained.

"Okay."

"I'll agree," Aunt Sarah offered, "for you to be Ahmeek with your friends at the lumber camp if you'll agree to answer to your given name, Jotham, when you're at home or in school."

"What about the playground? They all call me Ahmeek now. I don't want them calling me Jotham and teasing me again."

"Yes, I've heard some of them call you Ahmeek, but a lot of them still call you Jotham too, don't they?"

"Yes," Jotham admitted, "some of them, the ones that don't know me so well."

"I can't stop them from calling you Ahmeek if they want to, but you'll have to answer to Jotham too." Aunt Sarah was sure the children would soon forget all about calling him Ahmeek, but just to make sure she added, "They can call you Ahmeek on the playground, but you have to tell them that they must call you Jotham when they come to the house."

"And the playground at school, too," Jotham added.

"We agreed that at school and at home you should use the name Jotham," Aunt Sarah responded.

"Just on the playground with my friends. They're the same friends that I play with here." Jotham thought it would be difficult for his friends to remember two names for him and he was sure sooner or later one of them would make a mistake in front of Aunt Sarah and then he'd be in trouble again.

Aunt Sarah finally agreed. At the logging camp and on the playgrounds he could be Ahmeek if in the schoolhouse and at home he would be Jotham. She guessed it would be all right for him to have an Indian name as long as it was only for playtime, just so he didn't start acting like an Indian. Of course he would, but not in Wausau, at least not at Aunt Sarah's house.

Chapter 3

Jotham could think of nothing but the coming summer vacation as he and the other children walked home from school. It was already the 15th of May and in only two weeks he would be able to go the Lac Vieux Desert lumber camp for the whole summer. Because he was a little older this year — he would be nine in July — he would have to stay at the camp more. He would have some chores to do around the house, but he hoped he would be able to find Old Eagle Feather and spend some time with him in the woods too. He liked the way the old man talked about the animals and plants, almost as if he knew them all personally. Jotham wondered about that. Was it just because Eagle Feather was so old, or was it because he was an Indian that he knew so much about nature? The old white men he knew didn't seem to have such a close personal knowledge of animals and birds, of trees and rivers. Jotham thought there must be something special about being Indian. If that was true it made him feel a little bit bad, because the only thing Indian about him was the name, Ahmeek, and he didn't want to believe that he couldn't learn to be more like the old Indian. He decided it wasn't so much being Indian as how the Indians lived and for that reason he was going to always try to live just a little like the Indians do, very close to the woods, with all the animals and birds and other natural things that you found there.

The children walked along the dirt road that led from the schoolhouse to the town. Actually it wasn't really much of a town anymore. Oh, it was still part of the city and there were streets and lots of houses, but there weren't many stores or hotels like in the main part of Wausau. The school was located about half a mile away from the general store and the saloon, but when the big paper mill went in about five miles downriver, it seemed like the whole town started to move. A lot of people built houses down there and they put up a new, bigger store and a big hotel. Some people who had houses along the river didn't want to move, but when the power company bought them out to make the lake, those people went to the new town too. Now the place where Jotham lived had houses for the people who worked along the river, but just one general store, a feed mill, a livery, a blacksmith shop and, of course, a saloon.

The children weren't permitted to leave the school grounds during recess or at lunch hour, but when they went home in the afternoon they could go past the store. Sometimes Jotham or one of the others would have a few pennies, earned for some extra chore, and they would stop at the general store to buy some hard candy. That was not the case this time, but they had to go past the general store to get home anyway.

Jotham looked to his left and saw the place where he and some of his friends came to fish on Saturdays. People said it was part of the river, but Jotham thought it looked more like a lake. Especially when he compared it to the rivers up north, at the logging camp. He couldn't even hear the water running in this river, unless it was a windy day, and even then it didn't sound like a river, just waves hitting the shore. Up at the lumber camp he could remember the way the water bubbled over the rocks, sometimes so many rocks and so much water that the whole river looked white. This river never looked white and it never bubbled. It just wandered through the town. That looked right, but some places it was way too wide for a river and other places it looked just about the size Jotham thought a big river ought to be. The problem was that the water was always too still. If you threw a stick into it, it would drift slowly downstream, but that was the only way you could see that the water was moving at all. Jotham decided this was something he would have to talk to Old Eagle Feather about. If the old Indian was right in saying that it was the job of a river to run, then this one wasn't doing its job very well.

Some of the old-timers would tell how they used to have to walk for almost a mile to get to the fishing spot, but that was a long time ago before they put the dam in. Now the water covered a large area between the school and the town and the road ran right along side it. The dam had been built when they put the first paper mill in, just south of Wausau, and it supplied power for making paper. Jotham had heard that a paper mill took a lot of electricity. He also knew that it took a lot of wood. That was all some of the men in the lumber camp talked about, it seemed, how much timber the paper companies were going to need. They didn't even seem to worry about making lumber anymore. Jotham knew that paper was important, but it was lumber that built houses and bridges, and churches. He thought lumber was more important than paper.

As they got closer to the town, almost to the big pine trees where some of the older boys occasionally met to "settle their differences", Jotham could hear a lot of shouting. *Sounds like a big argument going on someplace,* he thought.

"Sounds like a fight," one of the boys said, and with that they all started to run toward the town.

As Jotham got closer he recognized one of the voices. It was the one they called the Frenchman up at his father's logging camp. He was talking very loud and Jotham thought he was swearing, but since he was swearing in French, Jotham couldn't be sure of that. The Frenchman — Jotham thought his name was Frank, but he couldn't remember for sure — was somewhat of a legend in the lumber camp. Frank liked to drink. When he drank he liked to fight. He was tall and thin. He wore a thin black mustache and his hair was cropped short over his long angular face. He didn't look like a fighter at all with his narrow shoulders and less than muscular arms, but a number of loggers who had judged him to be no challenge, based on his appearance, had ended the night in a ditch outside some saloon. Frank was one of those sawyers common to many logging camps who would drift in, get an advance for a grubstake, work hard until the first payday, then disappear for a week or two. Before he came to the Lac Vieux Desert camp Frank drifted from one camp to another, building up quite a reputation as a fighter, a drinker, yet an honest worker during the sober days when he worked. He always stayed long enough to pay back the grubstake before he went on a drinking binge and when he left the camp he took nothing with him that wasn't his. He had worked for several jobbers who wouldn't have him back, but Marichetti always let him return to the job when he sobered up, even if he had to vouch for him to get him released from the county jail. Jotham wanted to get to know Frank because he also had the reputation of being an expert whittler. When Enrico Marichetti gave his son the new pocket knife for Christmas, he said that he would get Frank to teach him how to whittle. Frank had made all kinds of things out of wood. He had a cross bow carved from cedar and a regular bow and arrow. He also had carved a number of chains out of hardwood, beechnut or black walnut. That was something Jotham wanted to do, carve a chain out of wood. Of course there wasn't anything you could use a wooden chain for without breaking it, but Jotham knew it was very difficult to carve one and it was considered the mark of an expert whittler. All the really good whittlers had at least one wooden chain hanging by their bunk.

"Don't you come after me about your son-a-bitchin' dam," Frank was yelling between the French cuss words.

"I don't care what you wanna call the dam, ya stupid Frenchman, you're gonna pay for what you did to it, you and yer damn logs."

Jotham recognized the second man as Mr. Obermeister. Mr. Obermeister was the owner of the feed mill. It was one of those mills that were common along the river. It was located out of town about half a mile where the river still ran freely. There, enough current could be harnessed to turn the stones that ground the grain farmers brought in for processing. It was what was called a wing dam. It didn't block the whole river, but was constructed like a wing that extended out from the shoreline, angled slightly upstream, so that it caught enough current to operate the mill wheel. It was not at all uncommon for a logjam being floated down the river to the paper mills to drift too far to one side and ram a wing dam. The dams were built from piling and planking and were not impossible nor all that expensive to replace, but either a fight or a lawsuit was a common first step to rebuilding.

Jotham heard another barrage of what he thought must be French cuss words before he again recognized "yer dam?" tossed in as a question at the end. He saw the Frenchman take a step toward the miller. "How about my logs?" Jotham knew Frank was talking about his father's logs. The Frenchman continued, "Your cockeyed contraption wrecked the boom. The logs are scattered all over hell's half acre."

Obermeister responded that he had put up a good sum of money to have his dam built. The loggers were responsible for tearing it down and he was going to see that they paid to have it put back.

Jotham could hardly understand Frank, his thickly accented words separated by long streaks of French profanity, the madder he got the thicker the accent and the more profane the language, but he thought he said something about Obermeister deserving to have a dam that blocked a river used for commerce "broke." It was obvious that Frank wasn't at all sympathetic to the miller's point of view and was getting hotter and hotter as the Dutchman pressed his case.

Obermeister screamed something about getting his lawyer to sue Marichetti. That wasn't Frank's concern. Jotham could tell from what they said that the logs were already lost and there would be no chance of recovering most of them. Nothing Frank could say or do would make things better for his father, but getting even was the way of the lumberman and the argument would not stop until one way or another that end was served. Obermeister interrupted with another threat to call his lawyer.

"You would be better off callin' your doctor," Frank yelled as he took another step and raised his fist in a threatening gesture. "I'll make you pay with your hide, ya damn Kraut. Half our logs are lost and it will take most of the night to fix the boom on the other half."

"It's coming." Jotham said to the boy standing next to

him. "If Obermeister gets much closer..." He didn't get a chance to finish the thought. They heard Obermeister again yell something about paying for his dam, but this time he included a few choice words about the lumberman. He called them a bunch of lechers. He said the town would be better off without a bunch of savages with their drinking and whoring. They caused more trouble when they came in with one of their damn logjams than all the lumber in the state was worth. As he talked he seemed to become more animated, more excited and Jotham knew something was about to start. The Dutchman swung his thick arm and caught Frank square on the cheek. Obermeister was not a big man, but his portly frame put some authority in the punch. The Frenchman rolled onto the dusty street. Obermeister looked surprised and a little scared, Jotham thought, and with good reason. There was just the hint of a smile forming on Frank's bleeding lip. They all knew what was coming next, and Jotham was sure the miller knew it too.

"Uh-oh," Jotham said to the boy next to him. "That was a big mistake."

Frank got up and walked toward Obermeister, his fists already moving around in front of him. Jotham had heard his father and Gino talking about Frank. They said he used to be a prize fighter, but his drinking kept him from training properly and he started to lose. When he couldn't get a manager anymore he moved west, traveling with a carnival where they would offer a prize of fifty dollars to anyone who could box against him for three rounds. He didn't lose against the farmers or even the other lumbermen who went up against him. Few of them realized that no matter how big and tough they were, they were no match for a trained fighter, but as Frank got older his drinking got worse and he would fail to show up on carnival nights. The carnival owner had fired him and just left him there in Minnesota. At least that's what Jotham had heard his father say. That's when Frank started to work in the lumber camps.

Obermeister kept backing up as Frank, hands in constant motion, kept stalking him. The Dutchman struck something behind him and could back up no farther. His heels were pinned against the horse trough that bordered the street in front of his mill.

It seemed to Jotham that he couldn't even see the punch that caught Mr. Obermeister and sat him down in the watering tank. He'd never seen Frank actually fight before but he'd heard that he was lightning fast. That brought a loud cheer from the boys watching. None of them liked Mr. Obermeister. He always yelled at the children for playing near the mill and once threatened to call the sheriff when he caught two of the older boys diving off his dam. Obermeister crawled out of the tank and lunged at the Frenchman. By force of his excessive weight alone he took Frank with him sprawling onto the dirt street. Frank skittered away and got quickly to his feet. Obermeister got up clumsily and tried to resume the fight, but it seemed that each time he swung the Frenchman would dance away. Then, out of nowhere, he would dance back in and land a solid punch to the miller's midsection. It was obvious that Obermeister was getting very tired when Frank began a flurry of punches. First to the face, then when the miller raised his hands to protect his face he felt a hard left to the solar plexus. For a moment he couldn't breathe and he began to double over forward when Frank's right uppercut caught him square on the jaw and stood him up again.

Jotham thought Frank would have killed Mr. Obermeister if the sheriff hadn't arrived just then and stopped the fight. It looked like the Frenchman was in real trouble, but when some of the witnesses told the sheriff that Obermeister had thrown the first punch and when Frank apologized for causing the disturbance and said he had to get the crew together to go out and try to salvage as many of the logs as he could, the sheriff let him go. The sheriff said that if Frank ever got into a fight like that in town again, he was going to spend the night in jail.

A couple of men helped Mr. Obermeister to his feet and took him into the office of the feed mill. The sheriff left and the last Jotham saw of Frank was when he walked across the street toward the saloon. Jotham knew that the logs would likely stay in the lake and it would be a couple of weeks before his father or anyone else at the logging camp saw the Frenchman again.

Chapter 4

Jotham ran across the school grounds and down the road past the lake toward Aunt Sarah's house. Of course he was happy that school was out. He liked school now that the other children didn't tease him so much, but summer meant vacation and vacation meant that he would soon go to the lumber camp. He couldn't wait to see Old Eagle Feather again and to learn more from the old man about the woods and the animals, the river and the lake. When he got home, he found that Aunt Sarah had everything packed and ready for him to take on the train the next morning. He felt a little guilty about wanting to go so bad. It wasn't that he didn't like Aunt Sarah and Uncle Oliver. They really had been very good to him. Aunt Sarah was the closest thing to a mother he had ever known and she had really been a good sport about his new name. He would miss them while he was away for the summer, but he knew that his father needed him at the camp too. After all, he was going on nine years old and there were things for him to do to help out. He had supper and hurried to bed. If he went to sleep fast, then morning would come sooner. Dominic had told him that one Christmas when he was anxious for the morning to so he could open his presents. Of course the problem was that he wasn't tired when he went to bed and instead of morning coming sooner it took forever. He lay awake for hours just thinking about the summer and all the things he would do. He didn't remember going to sleep at all, but he must have because the next thing he heard was Aunt Sarah's voice calling him and saying that if he didn't get up pretty soon he would miss his train.

The farther north he went, the more beautiful Jotham thought the country looked. It wasn't anything like when he went to the camp for Easter. Then the trees had no leaves and everything looked gray with an occasional patch of white snow lingering on the north side of a hill that protected it from the sun. Now everything was green. The grass was one shade of green, the poplars a slightly lighter shade and the giant oaks a darker one. Darkest of all were the needles on the big Norway pines that seemed to cover most of the land along the way. The ice was gone from all the lakes now and Jotham thought he had never seen them looking so blue. Now and then the train would pass a small farm and Jotham could see the cattle and pigs. Many of the farmers were out with their teams of horses, pulling a plow through the soft ground. Jotham knew that plowing a field was hard work, but all the farmers looked happy. Spring was a good time for everyone. It seemed to him that the whole world was new in the spring and he wondered what Old Eagle Feather would think about that.

Jotham could hear the puff of the engine pulling the train cars along the track and the clackety clack of the steel wheels as they passed over the joints in the rails. He looked up to see the smoke from the mighty steam engine drift over his head. After a while he heard the train whistle. He always liked to hear the train whistle, even when he was lying in his bed at Aunt Sarah's. Here, riding on the train, the whistle sounded different somehow. Jotham thought about that and wondered why that should be. When the engineer blew the whistle it was all one consistent tone. When he was lying in bed, the whistle would start out at a higher pitch and then change to a lower one as the engine passed the crossing near his house. He thought of asking Eagle Feather about that, but then he remembered that there were no train tracks around Lac Vieux Desert and the old Indian probably wouldn't know what he was talking about. He decided that he should ask

Gino instead. Gino had heard trains and he knew about stuff like that, especially since his whole life's ambition was to get on a train and go someplace far away.

The train started to slow down and for a minute Jotham thought they must be in Rhinelander. He saw the conductor in his dark blue uniform with its stiff collar and its shiny brass buttons coming down the aisle. He was a kindly old man with a big white mustache. Aunt Sarah had talked to the conductor when she put him on the train and explained that *Jotham* would be traveling alone and "would you please watch out for the boy?" He supposed the conductor was coming to tell him it was time to get off, but the old man just winked at Jotham as he walked by . Then he heard him call out "Merrill, next stop Merrill". The puff of the big engine got quieter and Jotham heard the squeal of the brakes as the train pulled to a stop and let some passengers off. Then there were slow puffs as it pulled ahead and stopped again. Jotham looked out the window and could see that they were putting water in the engine's boiler and taking on a load of dry oak wood that had been split and piled on the siding for the trainmen to refuel. Jotham was fascinated by trains and the people that ran them. He didn't know if he wanted to work in the lumber camps with his father and brothers when he grew up or be an engineer on a train. He knew engineers were nice people because they always smiled and waved at the children when they were waiting at the crossing for the train to pass.

Jotham had his eyes closed. He wasn't sleeping, just resting his eyes, he told the conductor when the old man shook him to tell him that they were approaching Rhinelander. He checked his satchel to be sure he wasn't leaving anything on the train. Aunt Sarah had said he should be sure to take everything with him when he got off, because she was sure there wouldn't be a general store at Lac Vieux Desert or even in Land-O'-Lakes. She wasn't even sure there would be a place in Eagle River where he could buy things if he happened to lose something on the way. Of course Jotham knew that there was a big general store in Eagle River, but Aunt Sarah never came to the lumber camp so he could understand how she might make such a mistake. Besides, if he did lose something and have to buy new, it would be a long way back to Eagle River. Pretty soon the squeal of the brakes and screeching of the steel wheels along the railroad tracks told Jotham that the train was stopping. Even before he got out of his seat he could see Old John waiting on the platform.

Old John was a Norwegian who had worked for his father ever since Jotham could remember. Unlike the others in the logging camp, who stayed in the bunkhouse and had their meals in the cook's shanty, Old John had his own shack on a small plot of ground not far from the Marichetti house. He did odd jobs around the lumber camp and also helped out at the house, clearing brush, taking care of the small garden, and gathering firewood for winter. As he got older he did more work around the house than he did at the camp and that was why Jotham's father had helped him build the shack close by. Sometimes he would work as a sawyer, especially if they were breaking in someone new in the camp. At other times he would help the skinners load the scoot to pull the logs out of the deepest woods, but he was more a handyman than a lumberman. Jotham's dad said he didn't know how he could get along without Old John and it was probably true.

Old John stood leaning against a post waiting for the train to come to a complete stop. He was small in stature, thin for a man of his age with a full head of gray hair and a large gray broom mustache. He walked over and took Jotham's satchel as the conductor helped him down from the train.

From Rhinelander to the lumber camp was a long trip and even with Old John trotting the horses a good bit of the way it took almost all day. As usual, Jotham was full of questions and the old man tried to answer them as well as he could. Were the little ducks back on the lake? Did they still hear the loon call at night? What kind of chores would Jotham have to do now that he was older and Papa said that he would have to learn to help out? John had more answers for that one than the boy wanted to hear. He would have to haul water from the well and carry in the wood for the cook stove and probably help some at the cook's shanty in the camp. They had a nice big garden that was almost ready for the cultivator and Jotham was old enough now to lead the horse while Old John walked behind. Cultivating the corn rows was something they did with only one horse. A singletree, made from stout oak with metal hooks at each end, was attached to the cultivator. The hooks connected the harness to the singletree and the old man would guide the implement between the rows while Jotham kept the horse on a straight path and tried to prevent her from stepping on any of the small plants. There would be a few other things; he would have to talk to his father about them. "That's about it," Old John said.

"Next year you won't have to drive so far to get me," Jotham said. Uncle Oliver said that they're going to run the railroad all the way to Eagle River."

Old John laughed. "Well, let's hope not," he said. "Building a railroad takes time. Maybe we be lucky and it takes more than a year."

"That wouldn't be lucky," Jotham said, scowling at the old man as he spoke.

"Oh ya. It would be for the lumbermen," John said. "We don't want a railroad."

Jotham questioned this odd conclusion. Everybody he'd ever heard talking about railroads wanted to see more of them, but the old Norwegian explained the problem as he saw it. The railroad they were planning to bring into Eagle River was what he called a spur. It wouldn't have fancy passenger trains like Jotham rode to Rhinelander on. It would just be box cars and flat cars to take the saw logs to the saw mills and the hardwood used in making paper — pulp sticks — to the paper mills. Jotham thought that sounded all right but the old man told him why it wouldn't be. As soon as they got their railroads for the logs to go out to the mills, then those "electricity people" would start building more dams on the rivers. The whole river was going to be just a series of dams and lakes and all the trees would have to be sent out by rail. It would cost a lot more to run a train and it would take two or three trains to haul as many logs as they could take to the mill with just one logjam.

The way they moved timber now, he said, was to cut it in the winter time when they could haul it with horses, sometimes eight horses to a team, pulling sleighs over the icy roads. They piled the logs by the lake or by the rivers. Then when spring came, they cut the pilings that held them in place and let them roll down the hill into the water. "Then they make a long boom," he said, "to keep all the logs together while they're in the water." The boom was made by chaining a series of logs together and stringing it along the outside of the logjam. They pulled the whole thing across the water to the place where the river started. There the booms were released and the logs were floated one at a time to a place downstream where the river was wider. At that point the booms would be assembled again for the trip to the mills. Some of the bigger logs, those that would go to the saw mill at Eagle River, were floated alone or in smaller jams. At Eagle River the ones that were too small for saw logs were put into another jam and sent on down the big Wisconsin River to the paper mills. On the lake, horses were used to pull the log booms with ropes stretching to the shore, but once in the river the current was all the power that was needed. The old man felt that was a lot more efficient way to move logs to market and river power was a lot cheaper than railroads.

"Railroad is just an excuse to build more dams" he said.

"Why not just haul the logs to the railroad in the winter when you put them on the sleigh instead of taking them to the lake?" Jotham asked. That seemed like a logical solution and it would cut out one step in the process, but Old John explained that, when the railroad went in, the only place that you could haul logs would be to the end of the spur. When you use the rivers, logs could be dumped into the lake anyplace, and rivers could be found almost anywhere in the woods. There would be only one railroad spur and that would be a long way from where the timber was cut. "By then all the rivers will have dams so we won't be able to use them either," the old man concluded.

Jotham wasn't sure that railroads wouldn't be as good as rivers for transporting logs, once they built enough of

them, but he decided it wouldn't be a good idea to continue that discussion with Old John. The old Norwegian
sounded like he was getting mad about it and the madder
he got the faster he drove, and this road was getting kind
of bumpy for the steel-wheeled wagon they were riding in.
Besides it didn't seem like it was the railroads that John
was worried about. It was the dams. He decided to ask
about them.

"Why are they building all those dams?" Jotham asked.

"Electricity, everybody now wants electricity."

"We have electric street lights in Wausau now," Jotham
offered.

"Ya, Wausau." Old John grunted. "That's okay, but do
we need electric street lights in the woods?" The old man
conceded that electricity was good. It had helped the timber industry when the dam was put up on the lower part
of the Wisconsin River, around Ripon, to run the new
Fourdrinier paper-making machines. But since they built
that first power dam in Appleton, "ten, twelve years ago,"
John said, "to run their street cars, everybody wants a dam
and wants to use electricity for everything. The wing dams
and mill wheels, they were bad enough and they only built
them where the rivers are wide. The power dams, they
build right across the river."

"Yeah," Jotham agreed. He told Old John about the fight
he and the other kids saw in Wausau when Frank's logjam
hit the millers wing dam.

"Is he in jail?" Old John asked.

"Naw, he went to the saloon." Jotham responded as
though that were the other obvious choice.

"So that's what happened." The old Norwegian shook
his head. "Ya, he's been gone for two weeks. He'll be back
tomorrow or the next day."

Jotham didn't respond. He knew that the old man had
it timed about right.

Old John chuckled. "Those dam makers better think
again before they get the Frenchman mad at them."

The news about Frank settled John down a little bit and
he pulled back on the reins and yelled at the horses to
slow down. Jotham was glad he did, because his rump
was getting sore from all the bouncing.

They drove on for quite a while with neither of them saying anything. Jotham didn't want the older man to get excited and let the horses start running so he wasn't going to take a chance on starting John off again. He just sat quietly and watched the scenery. Maybe later the old man would let him drive the team. He knew he wouldn't be able to do that here, where it was hilly and the road was narrow, but he knew that farther on there was a long meadow they would have to cross and he would ask then if he could drive.

Chapter 5

The logging camp was bustling with activity. The men were building another logjam, working just a bit harder to make up for the one that was lost. There were still some logs piled on the shore of the lake, left over from the winters hauling, but many more had to be brought out over the ground. With no snow and ice, moving the timber was more difficult. The big saw logs were dragged out one or two at a time chained behind teams of giant Belgian or Percheron draft horses. Many of the logs were so big the loggers couldn't even lift them. Instead they rolled them into place with what Jotham's father said were cant hooks, long poles with a metal spine hinged on one end so that it would grip the log and at the same time provide the leverage needed to turn it over. A few were so big that it took four or five men with cant hooks to roll them. Smaller logs were hauled out on what Jotham heard his father call a scoot. It was like a sled, with two heavy oak runners almost a foot thick, that four horse teams pulled over the bare ground. Although there was no snow or ice to make the scoot move easier the big horses could pull a load with as much as two cord of pulp wood for the paper mills or three or four of the smaller saw logs.

Jotham watched Old John and Gino working the nine-foot two-man crosscut saw that was about halfway through a big Norway pine.

"Why does Gino look so mad?" Jotham asked Dominic. Dominic, not too happy himself, had been assigned the task of watching after Jotham while he was in the cutting area. A lumber camp was no place for a little boy to be by himself when lumberjacks were in the process of felling trees, even if he was going on nine years old.

"He wanted to ride the logjam this time, but Pa said he couldn't do it." Dominic answered. Jotham was not surprised that Gino would want to ride the logs. Gino always liked excitement, which was one of the reasons Jotham liked Gino so much, and from what little Jotham had seen of them, riding the logjams was about as exciting as anything in the logging camp ever got. He thought he would like to grow up to be just like Gino. Of course the other reason Jotham preferred Gino over Dominic was that Gino was a lot older and didn't tease him all the time.

As they wandered around the camp Jotham watched the men work and noticed almost everything that was going on. He was most impressed by the teamsters — skinners his father and Old John called them — because the logs were once pulled by mules and the mule drivers were referred to as skinners. The men, yelling commands and sometimes profanities to the giant horses, stood atop the big loads of logs. Some of them, like the older sawyers, had heavy black beards and most of them wore a red, woolen, checkered shirt tucked into beltless black flannel pants with wide suspenders strapped over their brawny shoulders. His eyes darted back and forth between them and the sawyers, occasionally turning his attention to a distant wail of "timber" before he saw a tree topple in another section of the camp. He asked why the sound of a falling tree could be heard so long after he had seen the tree hit the ground. Dominic couldn't answer that for him. He asked why the men sprinkled the saw blade with water from a bottle while they were cutting down a tree. His brother said that wasn't water. It was kerosene and they did it to keep the pitch in the pine trees from sticking to the saw so they would be able to pull it. Dominic thought he asked questions about almost everything that was going on.

"When I grow up I want to drive the horses," Jotham

said, "unless I get a chance to be an engineer on the trains."

"You?" Dominic replied, teasingly, "you ain't gonna be nothin'. Yer always gonna be a little runt, like you are now."

Jotham smiled. He didn't mind when Dominic teased him like that. That was a friendly tease, not like some of the other times.

"Timber!" he heard Old John yell. He felt Dominic tighten the grip on his hand, then he heard Gino repeat "Timber!" and Jotham saw the giant pine they had been sawing begin to fall. It seemed to move so slowly at first, gracefully, as though it would take a long time to come down, then he could hear the swish of the wind, as it picked up speed, followed by the loud crash as the crown of the tree hit the ground. This was the first tree he had seen fall close up and he noticed that he heard the sound of the crash right away this time, just as the tree hit the ground.

"Wow!"

"You have to keep your eyes and ears open when you're in the logging camp," Dominic said. "You never know when one of those big trees is coming down."

Jotham didn't answer. He just stood beside his older brother with his mouth open, an expression of both awe and fear. Dominic took him by the hand and they walked over to the stump where Old John and Gino were resting for a few minutes before attacking the job of cutting the big tree into saw logs.

"You cut down a big one," Jotham said, looking up at Gino with admiration.

"Yeah," Gino answered. "Your big brother, he gets the big ones, yes Jotham."

"My name is Ahmeek," the younger boy reminded him.

"Oh, ya. Ahmeek." Gino answered with a slight laugh. "You been gone so long I forgot."

Jotham beamed. "That's okay, Gino," he said.

They watched as Old John and Gino leaned the big two-man saw against the trunk of the tree and picked up their axes. John worked on one side of the big tree while Gino worked on the other side, chopping away at the limbs to clear them from what would soon become big saw logs. When they cut some of the branches that the tree was resting on, the trunk would roll and lurch as it dropped closer to the ground and they would have to scamper away. Gino cut most of the branches underneath because Old John couldn't move as fast and could have been caught if the trunk settled too suddenly. Dominic explained that it was a big tree, so they would make lumber out of it instead of paper pulp. They sat and watched for a long time. When almost all of the limbs had been removed, Old John sighted up from the butt of the tree, explaining to Gino all the while how they would decide where to make the next cut. From the butt he could see where the tree started to curve. That was where they would have to make the first cut.

"They want straight logs for lumber," Old John said. "You have to read the tree to find out where the cuts will be."

The first cut was sixteen feet long. The tree was about two feet in diameter and Jotham heard Old John say that first log would make about four-hundred board feet of lumber. Jotham wondered how the old man knew that. He thought about asking Dominic, but then decided Dominic wouldn't know either. Maybe he would ask his pa when they got home.

That night at the house Jotham couldn't stop talking. He was full of questions for his father. Mr. Marichetti tried to explain what a board foot was, but that was a little too difficult for the young boy to understand. All he could grasp was that it had something to do with how much lumber there was in a log. The big question, though, the one Jotham asked over and over, was when would he be able to work in the logging camp like Dominic and Gino? His father said that would be a long time because he wanted Jotham to finish school. Working in the logging camp was hard work, he said, and if Jotham finished enough school maybe he could get a better job where he would make more money and wouldn't have to work so hard.

"Maybe I can be an engineer, on the trains," Jotham said, and his papa seemed to think that would be all right. With that, his father said it was time for Jotham to go to bed.

"Okay," Jotham responded, "but what am I going to do tomorrow? Can I go to the camp again?"

"Not tomorrow," his father said. "Tomorrow I need

Dominic to help me. Tomorrow you can play in the woods, but don't go too far away and get lost."

"I won't, Papa," Jotham said. He smiled and gave his father a big hug, then went to his bed. Tomorrow he could go back to the creek. Maybe he would see Old Eagle Feather again.

Jotham shared a bedroom with Dominic. It was a small room, walls of rough pine lumber, and no ceiling, just open rafters that ran the full width of the house, holding the walls in place. He remembered watching Dominic and Gino standing on their beds so they could reach the rafters, reaching up and taking one in each hand and swinging themselves up into the space between them and the roof. He had been too small to reach, but in another year he would be big enough to try it for himself. It really looked like fun. The room had one window and there was just the faintest light from the half moon slipping through it. His bed, like Dominic's, was a single bunk built out from the wall with one-inch pine boards. It had slats running cross-wise, each about a foot apart and over that a hay tick for padding. On top of the tick was a hand-sewn quilt that had so many shapes and colors that Jotham couldn't even count them all. Sometimes, especially late in the summer just before it was time for him to return to Wausau, he could hear the call of the wolf in the distant woods, but this night it was quiet outside.

Jotham tried to go to sleep, but there were too many thoughts flitting around in his head. He thought about the ride on the train and then about the long trip in the wagon to the lumber camp. He thought about what Old John had been saying about the dams and how they were changing the river and making it difficult for the loggers to take their timber to the mills. Jotham wasn't just sure about that. They had talked about the dams in school and all the things they could do with electricity. It seemed to Jotham that if people were going to have all the things they seemed to want to make life easier and better, then dams were just something they would have to learn to put up with. The first power dam ever, his teacher had said, was to run the streetcars in Appleton. Until they put the dam in Appleton in 1882 all the electricity had come from batteries and it was only good for little stuff. If the big dams could produce enough electricity to replace horses for pulling streetcars, maybe someday they could use power from the dams to run the railroads and then they might not cost so much, like Old John said, and they could ship their logs out by train.

His thoughts were interrupted when the door opened and Dominic came in. He must have been lying there a long time, he thought, because he knew Dominic was allowed to stay up a lot later than he was.

"How come you're coming to bed so soon?" Jotham asked.

"'Cause I'm tired," was all Dominic said in answer.

"But it's still early isn't it?"

"I said, I'm tired."

"Why?"

"Cause takin' care of a little twerp like you all day is hard work," Dominic answered. "Now shut up and let's get some sleep.

Jotham smiled to himself and curled up under the many-colored patchwork quilt. Even in June the nights were cold this far north. Just as he was starting to doze off, he heard loud voices. It sounded like Gino and his father were having an awful argument.

"But why can't I take the logjam, Papa?" he heard Gino ask. "I worked the jam on the lake. I'm as good on the logs as the Polack and Frank hasn't come back from the last one yet."

Gino wanted to ride the logs. He always talked about doing exciting things. He also wanted to travel. He would tell Jotham stories of all the places he wanted to go. Whenever a new lumberjack came to the camp, Gino would ask him where he was from and what parts of the world he had lived in. Many of them were born in other countries, like his father had been, and came to the United States to find work, so Gino heard a lot about other places from the lumberjacks. Most of them had come from Norway, Sweden or Finland, but Jotham knew of one who had come from Russia and even one from China. The one who came from China was the cook. Jotham didn't see him much, because he spent all his time working in the cook's shanty. Gino asked the cook a lot of questions. He was especially interested in China, but the cook didn't speak much English and he acted mad most of the time so he was more likely to chase Gino away than to tell him anything.

Gino hadn't been as far away as Wausau since they moved here from Minnesota. The logjam would go all the way to Rhinelander this time. The mill in Eagle River wasn't big enough for some of the trees they had cut so they would have to go to the bigger mill in Rhinelander. From there, after it was sawed into lumber it would be strapped together and floated to the big cities to the south, but there were river men to do that. Those were workers whose job was to ferry the boards down the river. The river men would steer the lumber with poles and a rudder just like it was a river boat. Jotham had seen lumber floats going downriver when he came up on the train, but getting the logs to Rhinelander was the job of the loggers, the men that worked for his father, and even if it wasn't as far as Rome or Paris or some of those other places Gino wanted to go, it was away from the logging camp. Gino always talked about going to the big cities. He said that when he got older he was going to leave the logging camp and maybe become a sailor so he could travel to big cities all over the world.

"Gino, Gino," Jotham heard his father say, "you got lotsa time. You don't be in such a hurry. You only sixteen years old. Maybe next year."

"I don't want to wait 'til I'm an old man, Papa," Gino said. "Frank, he's tellin' me about the city. He said the city's where young people should go to have fun."

"Fun, huh? The fun you have inna city with Frank is no good for young people or old people. Where is he, huh? Maybe in jail again, or he sleeps in some ditch with an empty whiskey bottle, or worse."

"Why won't Papa let Gino go on the logjam, Dominic?" Jotham asked, his voice just above a whisper.

"You heard him. 'Cause he's too young."

"How old do you have to be?"

"Old enough."

"How old is old enough?" Jotham insisted.

"How should I know?"

"Gino's old enough." Jotham asserted, "Old John said he's as good as anybody on the logjam, even better'n some of the older lumberjacks."

"Papa's not talkin' about how he works the logjam."

"Whaddya mean, Dominic? That's what Gino's askin' about."

"Gino works the logjam real good," Dominic admitted, "but that's not why he wants to go downriver."

"Huh?" Jotham was confused.

"Papa means he's not old enough to go to town with the others," Dominic said. "With Frank or the Pollack."

"Why not?"

"You're just a dumb little kid," Dominic said at last. "You really don't know, do you?"

"Know what?"

"Why do you suppose Gino wants to go to Rhinelander so bad?"

"So he can start to see the cities," Jotham answered confidently.

"Nope."

"What then?"

"Jotham," Dominic said trying to stifle a giggle, "I think maybe Gino wants to find a girl."

"A girl? What for?" Jotham heard Dominic giggle, now clearly audible. "Oh, you mean..." Jotham was glad Dominic couldn't see his face. He could feel the way his eyes were bugged out and his cheeks felt real hot. He'd heard the men in the lumber camp talk about going to the cities, and he had a pretty good idea what Dominic was saying.

Chapter 6

Jotham started into the woods along the Wisconsin River that wound its way north and west of the Marichetti home. At first he looked back every few steps to make sure he could see the house and would not get lost again. He came to a cluster of birches that he remembered from his earlier adventure. He recognized them because there were five big, white trees that all seemed to rise from the same knoll and spread as they reached toward the sky. From a distance they reminded Jotham of a giant ice cream soda with a foamy green top. Jotham had only seen an ice cream soda once. That was when Aunt Sarah and Uncle Oliver took him to the main part of Wausau for a special treat when he got such good grades on his first third-grade report card. Uncle Oliver said they were something very new and not many kids in Wausau had ever had an ice cream soda.

A little more confident, Jotham pressed farther into the woods, but he was careful to remember everything he could about the trail so he would know how to get back. Mostly he followed the river. He knew that when he went back upstream, sooner or later he would come to the birch cluster and he could easily find his way home from there. When he reached another landmark, a big boulder covered with moss, he turned north. The trail he followed was well-worn and Jotham was sure he could go a little way without worrying about being able to make his way back to the river. He wondered why the path was so wide there, but that didn't make much difference. The important thing was it would keep him from getting lost like he had the last time. He had barely reached the top of the first small hill on the trail when he heard a noise beside him in the woods. He turned to see Eagle Feather sitting beside the path on a big log.

"You go far into woods, little Ahmeek. You lost again?"

Jotham tried not to let the excitement he felt at seeing the old Indian show. If he wanted to talk to Eagle Feather and learn about all the interesting stuff Indians seemed to know he had to act as grown up as he could. "No," he answered, "I know how to get back this time."

"That is good." Eagle Feather paused a long time, then asked, "Where you go?"

Jotham shrugged his shoulders. "No place special." Jotham looked down and shuffled from one foot to the other. After a while he looked up at Eagle Feather and admitted, "I was, kind of, looking for you."

"Why?"

"I don't know. I wanted to ask you things. You know, about the woods and the river, like before."

"Oh. Okay," Eagle Feather answered, "but first we talk about you."

Jotham was surprised and not sure what he was going to say, but he reluctantly agreed. "Okay."

"We talk before — one, two moons — months ago."

"Sure," Jotham answered. "Don't you remember?"

"I remember," Eagle Feather said. "I gave you name. You remember it?"

"Sure," Jotham responded proudly, "You said I'm Ahmeek," He paused and looked down. "But my Aunt in Wausau says I still have to be Jotham."

"Jotham? What is Jotham?" Eagle Feather asked. "It is your white man's name?"

"Yeah," Jotham answered

"Jotham. What this name, Jotham, mean?"

"I don't know," Jotham said. "It's not an animal or anything like that. I guess it's just a name."

Eagle Feather thought about that for a long time. Jotham thought he looked a little confused that he would have a name that didn't mean anything special.

" My mom got it out of the Bible," Joham added.

"Oh."

Again Eagle Feather fell silent. Jotham thought maybe the old Indian didn't know what he was talking about. "You know about the Bible, don't you?" Jotham asked.

"Indians know about Bible," Eagle Feather answered. "Missionaries come to village. Tell us all about Bible. Tell us about Jesus. Missionaries not tell about Jotham."

"I know," Jotham said. "Maybe they never heard of him either."

Again neither of them spoke. *Indians sure do think a lot before they speak,* Jotham concluded. He thought that might be a good idea. Maybe he should have thought about it a little more before he told Miss Merriweather his name was Ahmeek. Finally the old Indian spoke. "You like the Bible name?" he asked.

"I like Ahmeek a lot better," Jotham answered, "but I got in trouble when I tried to be Ahmeek in Wausau."

Eagle Feather shrugged. "Then you be what white mother named you," he said.

"I guess so," Jotham reluctantly agreed. "But I don't like that name. I like Ahmeek."

Eagle Feather brought his arm up as though to rest his chin on his hand with his forefinger extended over his lips. Jotham could tell the old man was thinking hard and he waited a long time for Eagle Feather to answer.

After a while Eagle Feather dropped his arm and smiled. He looked right into Jotham's eyes. Then he spoke. "Here, you are Ahmeek. In Wausau, you are..." He stopped as though he had trouble remembering.

"Jotham," Ahmeek prompted. "Why are you here?" he continued. "Did you know I was coming?" He had suspected that somehow, he had no idea how, the old Indian would know he was coming. Jotham thought it must just be one of those Indian things that white people could never understand. Just like the Indians knew things about nature, maybe they also knew when things were going to happen. He had heard about Gypsies, mysterious people from someplace in Europe that lots of folks said could tell the future. Maybe Indians were a lot like Gypsies. Only

thing was, Aunt Sarah had said that she didn't trust Gypsies. He remembered one day when one of her friends
came to the door and said the Gypsies were in town, Aunt
Sarah had locked all the doors in the house and told him
not to answer the door for anybody. It hadn't made any
difference because nobody came. Jotham didn't know
about Gypsies, but he was sure that Indians could be
trusted. At least Old Eagle Feather could be.

"Indians have special, secret ways to know things before they happen, don't they?" Jotham asked.

"No secret."

"Yes there is," Ahmeek persisted. "You Indians know
about things before they happen."

"No. The animals and the birds, they know, but
anishnabeg..."

Ahmeek looked confused.

"...people," the old man continued, "not know what will
happen, so we watch the animals. When the great Eagle,
migizi, begins his flight south we know winter is close, even
when we think it not yet time. When *adjidaumo* work very
hard to store many nuts, we know it will be long and cold
with much snow."

"Adji..adji..," Ahmeek tried, but could not seem to form
the word.

"You call him squirrel," Eagle Feather offered anticipat-
ing the question. "When *Gitchi Manitou* make animals and
trees and people, he give animals special gift, to see tomorrow, but to people he not give such gift."

"Then you didn't you know I was coming today?"
Ahmeek asked again.

"No," the old Indian answered. "Maybe *wabasso* knows,
but not Eagle Feather."

Ahmeek giggled. He knew Eagle Feather was joking,
though there was no smile on the old man's face. "Then
why did you come here?" he asked.

"*Wabasso,*" Eagle Feather said. Then he stood up and
gestured to indicate that they should walk. Ahmeek followed the old man along a narrow path through the woods.
The Indian said it was a deer trail. The path sidled along a
steep hillside, so steep that Ahmeek thought for a time
that he would slide down the hill. If that happened he

didn't know what would stop him until he got to the bottom. Beyond the hill they went through a grove of large Norway pines that completely blotted out the light of the sun. At last Ahmeek could see where Eagle Feather was taking him. Over the crest of a knoll he saw the waters of Lac Vieux Desert. They walked to a place on the lakeshore shaded by a grove of small Norways.

The old Indian crossed his legs and sat resting his back on the trunk of a pine tree. Ahmeek tried to sit like Eagle Feather did, but he had a great deal of difficulty getting his legs to cross that way. After two or three tries he decided he was close enough. They sat quietly for a long time, just looking at the water. The lake picked up the blue of the summer sky and mingled it with the deep green reflections of the pine forest. Ahmeek thought this must be just about the prettiest place in the world. He told Eagle Feather so and that started the old Indian talking.

He talked about his people, how they had come to this land many years before, to escape the cold winter that had caused the death of many of the tribe at Manitou Island. "That, of course, was long before I am born," he said. Ahmeek didn't know where Manitou Island was, but the old Indian made it seem a long way, not only in distance but in time as well. "When we came," Old Eagle Feather said, "the woods full of deer and the lake full of rice." He said that the eagle nested freely in the big pine trees and even the warm skin the bear provided for the Indian to build his wigwam was plentiful. When the white man came it all started to change. All the food the Indian needed could be found right near the village in the old days, but after the white man started to cut the forests, the Indian had to go out many, many steps to find the deer or the bear.

"When you were little," Ahmeek asked, "did you have to go to school?"

"School?"

"You know. The place where boys and girls go to learn about things."

"No," Eagle Feather replied. "Indians had no school then. Now some Indians have school. They learn to speak white man's tongue."

"But you know about everything. How could you learn so much without school?"

"We learn," the old man answered, "but no school. The old ones, they tell us stories. They tell us all we need. When we get old, we tell. Now you listen."

Ahmeek took that as a sign that he wasn't to interrupt with questions. He listened intently throughout the afternoon as Eagle Feather told stories that Indian parents told their children. He talked about the animals as though they were more than animals, Ahmeek thought, almost as though they were people. He told how each animal had its own special powers, all except the wolverine. He said that each animal had to ask the *Gitchi Manitou* for its special gift: the eagle's keen sight, the bear's strength, the vulture's patience, the dog's capacity for loving. He looked Ahmeek straight in the eye when he got to the beaver and said that the beaver had received the gift of peace. The wolverine, Eagle Feather said was not satisfied and asked for more power than any of the other animals. Because of his selfishness *Gitchi Manitou* took away all his powers and made him wander alone and feed on what other animals had left in the woods.

Ahmeek was especially interested in what the old man said about the snakes. Ahmeek had never liked snakes, but Eagle Feather said they were very special. They had been given less than any of the other animals, no arms, no legs, yet they never complained, but simply continued to do what snakes do, keep the little plants in the meadows safe from the other animals that would destroy them.

Eagle Feather told how, in the early times, the *wabasso*, the rabbit, the most mischievous of all the animals became too plentiful for the snakes and threatened to destroy all the plants. Then, he said, *Gitchi Manitou* bestowed upon the snakes another gift, the fangs of venom, so they could keep even the rabbits from destroying the meadow.

"But watch the snake," he said. "This gift they will not use for evil, but only when they must. Even then, some will rattle their tails as warning."

Every once in a while Ahmeek could hold back no longer and would interrupt the old Indian to ask why something was as it was. The response was always the same. "Because that's the way it is, the way the Manitou made it."

"But can't we change it?" Ahmeek asked.

Old Eagle Feather smiled, "My turn," he said. "Why?"

"Huh?"

"My turn to ask."

"Oh! Okay."

"Why'd you change it?"

"I don't know. Because we want something to be different."

Eagle Feather was quiet for a long time, then he shook his head. "That is the trouble with the white man's way. The Indian lives with all, the way the Manitou made it. The white man always wants something different. See them?" the old man raised his hand to shield his eyes as though looking far in the distance. "They come with their plows and their axes and saws. Where there is woods, they want to make a field. Where there is a meadow, they put trees. They put dam on river to make lake. They dig ditch by lake to make river. Never leave alone. Better they learn to live with the world the way *Gitchi Manitou* made it. They are..." Eagle feather paused, rolling his tongue around as though to find the right word, "fighting with the world. Why? They cannot make the land better. Things Manitou made cannot be wrong. The Indian does not fight. The Indian knows he is only part of the land. White man thinks he own the land. Man cannot own what he is part of. He is part of..." Eagle Feather paused, unable to think of the white man's word, "...what is white man's word for all..." he spread his hands and looked from side to side. Ahmeek shrugged his shoulders. He didn't know what the old man was asking.

"You know," Eagle Feather explained, again gesturing in all directions, "trees, sky, land... all?"

"The whole world?"

"No, No... all. Lake. River. Tree?"

Ahmeek thought and thought as the old man waited patiently, his lips parted and his hands out as if to help the young boy think of an appropriate word.

"Nature?" he offered, somewhat timidly, seeing the old man's agitation.

"Yes nature." the Indian smiled. "Nature, everything

dances its own dance. The clouds must cross the sky. The moon gives us the time. The pine tree gives resting place for the eagle, because that is what pine trees are for. You cannot change it. It has always been so and it will always be so. It is the Manitou. Each thing has its Manitou and Manitou cannot change. Manitou is forever."

Eagle Feather told how people were the last to be created. How they were not given the powers of the animals or the plants, but were given the greatest gift of all, the power to dream.

"All that the *Gitchi Manitou* created had to follow the great laws, what you call nature," Eagle Feather said. "Each thing has its own place, but all work together to fulfill *Gitchi Manitou* vision."

When Eagle Feather told of the great flood that destroyed all but the birds and the water animals, Ahmeek thought of the stories he heard in Sunday School, about Noah and the Ark. He wondered if it was the same flood. It didn't seem reasonable to him there could have been two floods and he thought he might ask Aunt Sarah about it when he got back to Wausau.

The old man told Ahmeek about the sky woman, *Nakomis,* who had survived, how the animals, especially the muskrat made an island for her from the turtle's back, how that island, *Michilimackinac,* could still be found just a few weeks' journey to the east. On that island, he said, the sky woman breathed life back into all the plants and animals that had been killed in the flood.

As the afternoon went on Ahmeek thought his head would explode with all the new ideas and information he heard. It was only the beginning. As he spent time with the old man, he would hear more. Over the next few summers he was to learn much about the Indian way and beliefs. He wanted to remember every story, every name — the Indian name — for every animal and the story that went with it, but already he was forgetting much of what had been said. He remembered the *Gitchi Manitou.* That, whatever it was, was obviously very important. Ahmeek thought it sounded a lot like it might be the Indian name for God, but all those other Manitous were a mystery. It seemed to Ahmeek that the Indians had a Manitou for just about everything. If the *Gitchi Manitou* was as great and powerful as Old Eagle Feather made him sound, what was the reason for having all the others? Ahmeek wanted to ask, but he sensed that the Manitou was a very serious subject and he would have to be very careful how he approached it. He decided to keep quiet and maybe the old man would tell him some day.

Eagle Feather had finished what he had to say so they sat for along time, neither one of them speaking. Ahmeek wondered what was going through the old man's mind as he looked across the valley. He felt the Indian's hand touch his shoulder and saw Eagle Feather pointing to the sky with his other hand. Circling above them was an osprey. Ahmeek's eyes followed the giant bird as it glided so smoothly over the lake. Over and over it circled, then it dove straight down toward the lake, struck the water with a big splash and emerged holding a flopping fish in its beak.

"Wow!" exclaimed Ahmeek. "Didja see that?" He continued to watch as the big bird flew off to a grove of trees on the opposite shore to enjoy its meal.

Eagle Feather didn't answer, but the smile on his face said more than any words could. It was nature in action, an example, as though it had been planned for just that moment, of all they had been talking about. They sat silently again, the ripple of the waves washing against the lake shore, the chirping of small birds, the occasional croak of a bull frog were the only sounds to be heard. Ahmeek watched the old man, but he said nothing, just stared out over the water, a satisfied look on his face, waiting for just the right moment to resume talking. Suddenly there was a rustle of the brush a short distance from where they were sitting. Ahmeek looked at Eagle Feather. The old man's face was still expressionless, but Ahmeek could see the glint of a smile in his eyes.

"Come," Eagle Feather said as he got to his feet. "I'll show you why I came to the woods today."

Ahmeek followed as the old man very quietly walked to the place where they had heard the sound. He leaned over and pulled back some brush and much to Ahmeek's surprise, there was a small cottontail rabbit. The animal crouched in fear as Eagle Feather reached down and picked it up in his big hand. With his other hand he gently re-moved the tiny rawhide noose that had tightened itself around the rabbit's hind leg. Ahmeek could see that the other end of the chord was attached to a small willow stem. Eagle Feather explained how the snare is placed to catch the foot of an unwary *wabasso*. He said that he had set the snare for a bigger animal, maybe a snowshoe, but since they don't need such a little rabbit for food, nor do they need the fur for mittens right now, he will set it free. Ahmeek wanted to keep the rabbit and suggested that they could build a cage. Then the rabbit would be there when-ever they decided they did need it for food or for mittens.

"We could feed it and it will grow bigger. Then you won't have to make a snare every time we want a rabbit," he said. "It'll be right there waiting for us."

"That is white man's way," Eagle Feather answered. "Here you are Ahmeek. That is your Indian name. You learn Indian way."

"What's the Indian way?"

"It is what *you* say is nature. Indian way is nature way." He opened his hands and the little cottontail hopped to the ground and scampered off into the brush. "The *wabasso* is free. White man pretend to own the animals because he can make trap and cage. You can not own nature. *Gitchi Manitou* put *wabasso* here for us to catch when we have need, not to keep all the time. . . in a cage. All things here to do what Manitou put them here to do. *Wabasso* is...," Eagle Feather paused for a moment to think of a proper comparison, "...like a river. *Wabasso* must run."

Chapter 7

The cook shanty was unusually noisy when Jotham and his brothers got there. Frank had returned. Of course he told about losing the logjam when they struck the wing dam at the Wausau feed mill. "But I taught that damn miller a lesson," he added. No one doubted that he had. Frank's reputation was well-established.

"Hell, a few years ago it was just the one dam and that one way down by Port Edwards," Stanley said. Stanley Rodzaczk shared an area in the bunkhouse with Frank. He was a stocky man with a head of jet-black hair, thinning just a little, combed straight back. He had a full set of natural teeth, yellowed from years of smoking cigarettes that he rolled from a supply of papers and a metal can of Prince Albert. He wasn't big, but had broad shoulders and muscular arms earned through years of manning the nine-foot crosscut. He was one of the older lumberjacks at the camp, not in age, which was slightly more than half that of Old John, but in the years he had been with Enrico Marichetti. Stanley liked working outdoors and wasted little time moving to the timberlands of Wisconsin after his arrival from Poland.

Most lumberjacks worked in a camp for only a short time, perhaps a year or two, then moved on. Often they were trying to outrun some trouble they had managed to get into on a weekend in town at their last location. Occasionally some woman in a nearby saloon was getting a little too close and they weren't ready for that kind of commitment or they were just looking for that new forest with tall straight trees, few limbs to clear, and five or six cuts to a tree. The sawyers who cut pulp for the paper mills, rather than saw logs, were paid by the stick, so when the best timber in the forests started to run out and it took longer to make their count, they would move on looking for better cutting someplace else. In addition to cutting the trees, limbing, and cutting them into pulpwood lengths, they had to swamp them out. Swamping required them to carry the bolts out to the logging roads that had been cleared, for the sleighs in the winter or the scoot in the summer, to haul the pulpwood to the landing. A thin forest meant harder work for less pay so when the forest began to thin, so did the seasoned lumberjacks.

"Now they're talking dams all up and down the river," Stanley continued. "Gets so it's too dangerous to take a logjam down to the mill anymore."

"Could be worse," came a response from across the table. "Down by Port Edwards, on the lower end of the river, they built a dam that goes all the way across the river. No sluiceway for logs to go through at all."

"Ya, it does," came a response with a heavy Scandinavian accent, "but nobody floats logs past Port Edwards so it don't make no difference anyhow."

"Sure, that was the first big paper mill. They used the river to run the grinders that chewed the logs into pulp. But the Swede's right. After that mill went in nobody floated logs farther down river anyway."

"It's not the old water-driven paper mills, it's these damn electric projects, that's the trouble," Frank chimed in.

"What do you mean, electric projects?"

Stanley supplied the answer. He was and avid reader and had kept up on the development of hydroelectric power. "They call them power dams, because they make electricity," he said. "First one was built back in '82, down in Appleton, to run the streetcars. Ever since then they been puttin' 'em in all over the country."

"Ya," the Swede added, then they put the dam in south of Wausau for the new paper mill. But it don't run the mill.

It makes electricity and the electricity runs the mill."

"And I hear they're planning a dam way up by Toma-hawk," Frank said. "They put that in, then we got trouble."

"I heard about that," came a gruff voice from the back, muffled by the heavy beard. "Somebody said that when that dam is finished the river would be dry for two miles. They said they plan to make the lake way up at the top, above the rapids, then pipe the water to a power station farther downstream."

That information was not just a rumor. The dam opera-tors needed more power to operate the turbines than the river would provide in places where there was no water-fall or where the water flowed over relatively level land. Since the power provided by the water is dependent on the height of the water between the turbine and the sur-face of the lake, the companies were designing dams with long, overland, penstocks — giant tubes that carried the water far downstream to a lower elevation. The water would then be diverted from the lake above the dam and carried to turbines in the power station at a lower eleva-tion downriver before being returned to the river channel. During the rains in the spring, the spillways sent the ex-cess water down the original river channel, but in the late summer, that channel often dried up completely.

"Well, we can't do much about it," the elder Marichetti said. "The lumber companies can't afford to buy up all the land along the rivers and even if we could, it's the cit-ies that want the dams. They'd find a way in the law to take the land away from us anyway."

"Somebody must have some say about it," the Swede responded.

"Well, not anybody any of us would know," Stanley re-plied. "They pay good money for the land that's going to be flooded to make the lake. Once they own the land, they can do what they want with it and there ain't no govern-ment body regulatin' dam construction right now."

"That's not true," came the voice of the bearded lum-berjack. "They got to have a license."

"Oh, sure," continued Stanley, "they got to have a li-cense, but all they have to do is send in the papers and they get one. About the only thing they have to prove is that they own the land."

Actually the government was getting more involved in licensing the dams, but the concern was for navigation on waters such as the Mississippi or the Ohio. Since there was no commercial boat traffic on the upper Wisconsin River, there was little control on the building of dams.

The grumbling continued throughout the supper hour, but they had to concede that, for the present time, it was a problem without a solution. Jotham remembered what Old John had said about the dams and he remembered the fight at the feed mill when Frank's logjam hit the millers wing dam. He still wasn't sure the loggers were right. After all, electricity was pretty important too, but he was sure things were going to get a lot worse between the dam owners and the loggers before they got any better.

Jotham waited all week, carrying water for the workers in the lumber camp, helping in the cook's shanty, and doing chores around the Marichetti home, but at last he had another day all to himself. When he arrived at the spot in the woods where he had previously met Old Eagle Feather, he was surprised to find no one there. It hadn't occurred to him that the old Indian wouldn't always be in that same part of the woods. It was a warm morning, with the sun already streaming down through the leaves, creating interesting patches of light on the ground for Jotham to study, so he didn't mind waiting, if that's what he had to do. He had also discovered by now that there would be no use questioning Eagle Feather. The old man would just say that when the time was right he had come. He knew Eagle Feather didn't have a big pocket watch like his father's and he guessed he didn't have a clock in his wigwam like the one in Jotham's house. Indians just seemed to know when it was the right time without the help of such things. There was no use wondering how, it was just one of those things that made the Indian different and, as far as Jotham was concerned, more fascinating.

Jotham sat and marveled at the exhibition nature created around him. He thought perhaps Eagle Feather was right about the way people should think of nature, more as though they were a part of it instead of its enemy. That

sure did sound like it made sense, but then he remembered the winter he had just gone through back in Wausau.
In January there was almost a whole week when school
was closed and people hardly went outside because of the
cold and the snow. It had started to snow on a Saturday
and it was Wednesday of the next week before they could
open the school again. By the time it quit the drifts were
as high as Jotham's shoulders and then, when it finally
did quit snowing, it turned real cold. Uncle Oliver said the
temperature was down to twenty-five below zero and
Jotham knew from past experience that any temperature
below zero was real cold. It was hard to think of nature as
anything other than an enemy that week. It was more like
nature was a wild animal that had to be tamed before
people could live with it.

Today was different, Jotham thought as he watched a
squirrel scamper across the ground under an oak tree and
pick up what looked like an acorn. It was too early for
acorns, Jotham knew, but maybe this one had been hidden under the snow since last summer. The squirrel sat
up on his hind legs and held the nut in both paws. Jotham
thought they should have called a squirrel's front feet
hands, the way they used them. He spoke to the squirrel
as it munched on the newly discovered feast, but the squirrel paid no attention. *I'm nature. You're just a human being.* Jotham imagined the squirrel saying. *I don't have to
pay any attention to you.* It was a silly thought and Jotham
smiled at himself for thinking it.

Jotham had been sitting, listening to the birds and
watching the small animals, for a long time and still seen
nothing of Eagle Feather. He decided to follow the trail
Eagle Feather had followed the last time that led to the
lake. He was learning more about the woods and all the
trails that wild animals had made so he was sure he could
find his way home. Even before he reached the lake he
could see that the forest ended a short distance ahead of
him and that meant he must be close. Eager to get to the
lakeshore and thinking he might find Eagle Feather there,
Jotham started to run. He was right about the lake being
close. He got there in no time at all, but he was wrong
about Eagle Feather. The old Indian was still nowhere to

be seen. Jotham sat down and watched a mother duck swim by with five little ducklings following. He wondered how they could know how to swim so young. He thought Old Eagle Feather must be right about the animals just knowing things in a way people couldn't. Eagle Feather had said it was a gift from the *Gitchi Manitou.* He was going to have to ask the old Indian more about this Manitou thing.

Looking skyward, Jotham could see the osprey circling again. He hoped it would dive into the lake and come up with another fish. It didn't. After a few minutes it glided into the top of a tree that was growing so close to the lake that it was almost in the water. He watched and watched that treetop, but the osprey didn't come out again.

Jotham began to drift off in fantasy, somewhere between being half asleep and half awake. His eyes were still open, most of the time, and he could see the brilliant glitter of the sun reflected from the ripples that were beginning to form on the water. In his imagination the boughs of the trees encircling the place where he sat became the walls of an enchanted cave, a cave like he had read about in the story of Aladdin, and the glistening wave tops were the jewels. In a few minutes it was as though he was really inside the fabled cave. The trees were no longer just trees, but gem trees, and the sky was replaced by the dark recesses of the cavern. Jotham was deep in a dream.

It was midafternoon before Jotham woke up. At first he didn't remember where he was, but when he looked around at the lake and saw the little ducks, farther away than before, but still following their mother, it all came back to him. He wondered why he hadn't found Eagle Feather. He was disappointed and wanted to stay and look for the old Indian, but he was sure it was time to go home. He thought now that he knew his way, maybe next time he could go a little farther and then he'd find Eagle Feather for sure.

Chapter 8

Jotham stumbled and old Maude, the big bay that was pulling the cultivator, lurched to the side putting her big front hoof right on top of a hill of corn.

"Hey there!" Old John yelled to the boy leading the horse, "Ya gotta watch what yer doin'. You can't let your mind go wanderin' off in the woods when yer leadin' a horse through the garden."

"I'm sorry, John. I slipped."

"Ya, well, we take a break now."

When they reached the end of the corn row, Old John led Maude over to a small maple tree and tied her halter rope around the trunk. He came over to the shaded place where his young helper was already sitting. John reached under a bush where his two-quart mason jar of water was tucked to protect it from the sun and offered Jotham a drink. Jotham took two or three big gulps. The water was warm, but it was wet and an afternoon in the sun had made him very thirsty.

"Thanks," he said, handing the jar back to the older man.

"Where was you all day yesterday?" Old John asked, taking a long draft of water for himself. "I didn't see you at the logging camp at all."

"I was out in the woods, over by Lac Vieux Desert."

"You play in the woods all day all by yourself?"

"Sometimes," Jotham responded. "I was by myself yesterday, but lots of times I see Old Eagle Feather, from the Indian village. We talk about the river and the animals and a lot of stuff about the Indians. Do you know him?"

"No, I've heard of him, but I don't know him." John opened the jar again and took another drink. He pulled a big red handkerchief out of his pocket and wiped his lips, then his forehead as he handed the jar to Jotham, who again took a big gulp.

"John?" Jotham asked. "What do you think of the Indians? Are they bad people like some of the workers say they are?"

"Oh, I've seen worse," the old man answered.

"Smiley Bartle says they're bad... and Dominic keeps telling me I shouldn't be going out in the woods and talking to Eagle Feather. He says they'll fill my head with Indian junk and my brain will get mushy." Jotham laughed at the thought. He knew it was his brother's way of teasing him, but he wanted Old John to tell him what he thought about Indians. Jotham talked a lot with Old John, almost as much as with his father, and he knew he could pretty well depend on what the old man said.

"Ya, that sounds like Dominic. Don't listen to Dominic too much. And Smiley Bartle, if I choose between Bartle and the Indian, I'll take the Indian."

"Yeah," Jotham agreed. "But Smiley's okay, I guess..."

"Smiley's okay," the older man cut in, "but Smiley talks too much."

Jotham laughed. He knew that was right. No matter what the subject, Smiley Bartle had a story to tell about it, some unbelievable experience he had when he was out west. Stanley said one day that he didn't think Smiley had ever been west of the Mississippi, but to hear Smiley tell it he had been all over the world.

"Indians never done nothin' to hurt me," Old John continued. "Ya, I hear problems with Indians in Dakota and out west, but not here. I think the Indians here are okay."

Jotham smiled. "Then I guess it's okay for me to keep talking to Old Eagle Feather," he said.

"Good to talk to anybody. People talk more, maybe they fight less," John said. "Now I think we finish the cultivating."

The garden was all cultivated so Old John went back to his work as a sawyer in the logging camp. Jotham hurried through the morning, carrying water to the cook shanty and bringing in armloads of split oak for the cook's fires. By afternoon he had finished his chores. He rushed through the noon meal and told his father he wanted to play in the woods for the afternoon. He went out the same path, but instead of turning toward the lake, as he had before, he continued north. It was a sunny day and Dominic had told him if he got lost he should walk toward the sun. That would bring him to the lake or the river. From either he would know how to get home. As he pressed farther north he heard a distant rapping sound. It was much too slow for the rat-a-tat of a woodpecker. He turned and went toward the sound. The rapping became a loud thumping and soon he could see the source.

A group of Indian boys were all pounding on a big log. An older Indian man was standing to one side, watching, his back to Jotham. They were all talking Ojibway and with no understanding of that language Jotham had no idea what it was all about. It couldn't be Eagle Feather. The old Indian always arrived quietly and alone, but there was more than one Indian here. Maybe they weren't Chippewa. Maybe there were other Indians, those that the men in the logging camp talked about, the ones that weren't friendly like Old Eagle Feather, the ones that scalped white people and kidnapped little boys. Since getting to know the old Chippewa, he had forgotten all about them, even began to believe they didn't really exist, but now the images from all those stories came flooding back.

Those thoughts didn't last long. In a moment the grown-up Indian, who stood watching the boys turned around and Jotham could see the friendly face of Eagle Feather. When the old Indian turned, the boys looked up at the oddly pale child only a short distance away, and for the moment their pounding stopped. Eagle Feather turned back, ignoring Jotham, and immediately the boys returned to their work.

Jotham couldn't understand. He was sure Eagle Feather

had seen him, but there was no typical greeting for his little friend, Ahmeek. Jotham moved closer, but Eagle Feather still made no move to recognize him. Soon it became obvious that the four boys were paying more attention to Jotham than to the task before them and Eagle Feather had no choice but to acknowledge his presence.

"Hello little friend. You come again," Eagle Feather said, "but today I must work with family — show boys how to make *makuk* basket."

Jotham couldn't see any baskets and had no idea what Eagle Feather was talking about, but he didn't ask. That wasn't what impressed him at the moment and brought the happy smile to his face. The only thing he did not like about his summers at Lac Vieux Desert was that there were no other kids his age in the logging camp. He was happy to be with his father and his brothers, but even Dominic was too much older for them to really play together. When they did, it was always the games that Dominic wanted to play and of course that meant Dominic always won. Now there were other children. Even better, they were Indian children. Maybe, since Old Eagle Feather already gave him an Indian name and called him a friend, he could play with the Indian children sometimes.

"I can help," Ahmeek offered. "I'm strong and I help the cook in the camp all the time."

"I know you are strong, Ahmeek," Eagle Feather replied, "but this is work for Indian boys."

This time Ahmeek paused. He waited, much like Eagle Feather so often did, looking very much like he was deep in thought. Finally he spoke. "You gave me an Indian name," he said. "Now I want to work like Indian boys. I want to learn what Indians learn."

"You speak well, little Ahmeek," Eagle Feather said. "You will work with Indian boys." He picked up a club cut from a piece of hardwood. It was about as big around as a baseball bat but a little shorter. He did not speak to the boys nor did he tell Ahmeek what to do. He simply nodded his head and the boys returned to their pounding. Ahmeek watched for a few seconds, then joined in. They pounded and pounded on the log until Ahmeek thought his arms would drop off and he hadn't the slightest idea why they were doing it. It made a lot of noise but seemed to serve no useful purpose whatsoever until he saw a very thin layer of wood — actually it was the thickness of one annular ring — begin to peel away from the rest of the log. Soon a whole section came off and they had a strip of wood about two and one-half inches wide and only one-sixteenth of an inch thick. Eagle Feather cut the strip to an even width and set it aside while the five children continued to pound out another piece. It became obvious that there would be a lot more log pounding before there would be enough strips to make baskets. When they had beaten the log until it would yield no more thin strips, Eagle Feather told them to stop. They could rest a while before starting another log.

The boys began talking again, mostly in Ojibwa. Not being able to understand what they said, Ahmeek decided to move closer to Eagle Feather. The old man just sat quietly and Ahmeek concluded this wasn't going to be a day for storytelling. He decided he would just sit quietly too, but one of the Indian boys came over to him and sat down.

"You pound log good," he said.

The boys had all been speaking Ojibwa. Ahmeek was surprised to hear this one address him in his own language. "You speak English?" he asked.

"A little. I go to government school," the boy answered. "For Indians," he added.

"What's your name?" Ahmeek asked.

"I am Johnny," the boy replied, "Johnny Bearheart."

Ahmeek's jaw dropped and he stifled a little giggle. He was surprised to hear that the boy had a white boy's name, especially in combination with a name like Bearheart. "Johnny?" he said. He didn't mean for it to sound like a question, but it did. He quickly caught himself and added, "Johnny Bearheart, that's a good, strong name."

"The boy Eagle Feather's grandson," Eagle Feather said. It was obvious that he was very proud of the boy.

"And what is your name?" Johnny Bearheart asked.

"Me?" Ahmeek said. "My name is Jo..."

He didn't have a chance to finish. Eagle Feather cut in, "The boy's name Ahmeek."

"Ahmeek?" Johnny Bearheart questioned. He was equally surprised to find a white boy with a name that sounded like he should be an Indian.

Ahmeek shrugged his shoulders and giggled.

"I have white man's name and you have Indian name?" Johnny responded and they both began to laugh.

Johnny Bearheart was shorter than Ahmeek but looked very strong. He had broad shoulders. His hair was black and cut off at the shoulder. He didn't wear a shirt and his body looked very athletic, a lot more muscles, Ahmeek thought, than any of his white friends. *White kids have to spend too much time in school, sitting,* he reasoned. It was obvious that the Indian boy in front of him spent his time running through the woods, working and doing all those things Ahmeek imagined Indian kids did. His small but muscular frame reminded Ahmeek of his brother Gino, but Gino was much older. The Indian boy looked like he might be a year or two younger than Ahmeek.

Eagle Feather explained that some of the Indian women had begun to give their children first names like the white people. Better than the old ways, they said. They decided it was confusing for an Indian child to have to wait to earn a permanent name. When Indians were moved to reservations, the white chiefs wanted to know the names for all of the Indians in the tribe. That meant that children had to have a name and that name was written down in the white man's record books. It could no longer be easily changed, so better to give up the old ways and give the child a name right away. Eagle Feather did not agree with the practice.

"It is better," he said, "young boy get name when he has his dream. If name is given when boy is born, it does not have power. A boy's name should mean something." Eagle Feather told Ahmeek about the custom of fasting to induce a powerful dream and *wanda wasud*, the name giver, choosing a name for a child that the dream suggested. "If Indian Bureau needs name sooner, boy can have two names," he said.

"Bearheart has meaning, doesn't it?" Ahmeek asked.

"Bearheart is Johnny father's name," The old Indian answered. "Bearheart means brave, strong. The boy's father is brave, strong, like the heart of bear." He went on to say that if a boy does not take a name from his dream, mothers will soon follow the white man's practice of giving a name that is just a copy of someone else's name. "The mother of a boy is not *wanda wasud*. If a mother gives the name when child is little, the power of a name is lost."

Ahmeek thought about that and had to agree. Most of the boys he knew were named for somebody else. Some were called Junior, because their name was the same as their father's. Others were named for a grandfather, or an uncle, some only for a family friend, but few had names that were totally original. Even his own Christian name, Jotham, was taken from someone in the Bible, but he hadn't the slightest idea who.

"If boy gets a name that is just a copy," Eagle Feather continued, "pretty soon boy will be just a copy."

For a respectful period of time the children were silent, letting the words of the venerable old man have their effect. The woods remained quiet except for the occasional call of a bird or chuckle of a chipmunk until Eagle Feather decided it was time to continue working.

When they had pounded the logs until Eagle Feather determined they had enough basket strips he signaled them to stop.

"We go to village now, Ahmeek," he said. "We take wood to women and girl children. They make *makuk*."

"Can I come and watch?" Ahmeek asked. "I'd like to see how they make baskets out of these strips of wood."

"No, Ahmeek," Eagle Feather said. "Not good for white boy to come to village."

"Ahmeek should see the baskets," Johnny Bearheart intervened. "He worked hard to help break up wood."

Old Eagle Feather was hesitant. He thought it would be good for white children to learn more about the Indian. Then when they grew to be men and women they might have a greater understanding of the Chippewa and his way of life. They might learn to respect the land and not always try to change things from the way *Gitchi Manitou* had made them. Still, including Ahmeek might not be a good idea. White people were different and he didn't want to cause any trouble. He did not answer right away. He just stood there rubbing his chin. Some of the younger men in the tribe worked in the logging camps and Eagle Feather had heard that Enrico Marichetti was a fair man who had treated them well. The old Indian was also pleased that Ahmeek was interested in Indian ways, but he wanted no trouble with the white loggers. Finally he spoke.

"Your father, he would permit such a thing?"

"Sure," Ahmeek asserted. "Papa would say it was okay. I know he would."

"You will tell him," Eagle Feather instructed.

"Uh huh. I'll tell him as soon as I go home," Ahmeek insisted. "I already told my brother and Old John about you."

"I will permit," Eagle Feather said, "but only to see baskets. After that, Ahmeek must go home and speak with father."

Ahmeek's brief visit to the village of the Lac Vieux Desert Band was full of surprises. He found that the tepee he and his friends in Wausau had built to play in, with long poles for a frame and opened gunnysacks, since they had no animal skins to cover the outside, bore little resemblance to the dome-shaped wigwams that provided shelter in the village. It was not animal skins as he had expected that kept the elements out of Chippewa homes, but birch bark and cedar boughs.

Ahmeek and the boys carried the thin strips of birch to a commons area in the village where the women and children were already waiting. Ahmeek watched as the Indian children selected strips of wood and began to weave them into a small mat, letting each strip extend well beyond the part that was woven together. When the mat was large enough to form the bottom of the basket, the extended part of the wood strip was bent sharply upward. New strips were then inserted to go all the way around the upward extensions to hold them in place and form the sides of the basket.

Weaving the basket was a lot more difficult than Ahmeek expected. After all, he and the other children in his school had woven Easter baskets from colored paper but this sure was different. He tried hard to watch how the baskets were made, but he found too often he watched one particular basketmaker. She was a girl, about Ahmeek's age, a little taller than Ahmeek and, he thought, very pretty. She had long black hair. That was the first thing he noticed. Long hair was the first thing he ever noticed about a girl and it seemed hers was the longest and the blackest he had ever seen. It was parted in the middle of her head and hung down in two long thick braids that reached all the way to her waist. Ahmeek also noticed that her upper arms were long and slender. Her dark skin had a radiance that he had never seen among the white girls he knew and her high cheekbones made her face look strong and self-assured. Every once in a while as she worked on her basket, the Indian girl glanced over at him. Soon he found it hard not to look at her, to see if she was looking at him. He wanted to know who she was, but his thoughts were interrupted by Old Eagle Feather.

"You've seen how we make baskets, Ahmeek. Now it is time for you to go."

Ahmeek didn't want to leave, but he knew Eagle Feather was right. It was a long way from the Indian village to his father's house and he had spent all afternoon in the woods.

"Johnny Bearheart go with you to lake," Eagle Feather continued. "To the place where we caught *wabasso*. You know how to go home from there."

When Ahmeek and Johnny Bearheart were leaving the camp, Ahmeek ask him about the Indian girl who had been watching him.

Johnny smiled. "She is my sister," he said. "Her name is Mourning Dove."

"Mourning Dove," Ahmeek repeated. "That's a very pretty name."

Ahmeek thanked Johnny for taking him back and promised to come to the village again, then hurried down the trail to his home.

Jotham told his father about Eagle Feather, how the old Indian had brought him home when he was lost and about going to the village to watch them make baskets.

"They're really good people, Papa," he said. "They're nothin' like the Indians Smiley Bartle talks about, really."

"Smiley, he talks too much. Eagle Feather's boys worked

for Marty Frederickson last winter. Hard workers, Marty says."

"Then, it's okay if I play with Johnny Bearheart and his friends?" Jotham asked.

"You finish your chores here first," Marichetti answered, "then you see Indian friends if you want. Indians, same as other people, no better no worse."

For Dominic, it provided another excuse to tease Jotham, but Enrico Marichetti was pleased that the boy had found something to do when they were all busy at the camp.

For the rest of the summer, Ahmeek saw a lot more of Johnny Bearheart than he did Eagle Feather. Some days he found the old man in the woods and listened to a story or learned more about the Indians, but most of the time he went to the woods near the village to find Johnny Bearheart. Sometimes Johnny Bearheart was with other Indian children; other times he was playing in the woods by himself.

Johnny Bearheart liked Ahmeek and whenever they were together, showed him how to do things the way the Indians did, things like how to walk through the woods so quietly that even the deer didn't hear you and how to run swiftly between the trees. When the other Indian boys were along, they taught Ahmeek how to play Indian games like *baggataway*. Ahmeek would later learn the white man's name, lacrosse.

Johnny also taught him a few of the simpler Indian crafts like how to make a toy tomtom, from a tin can that had been discarded by the white man. The Indians did not eat canned foods, but they didn't mind improvising with the discarded containers thrown out by the white settlers. Of course the drums that were used to keep time for the pow-wow dances were fine instruments made from a hollowed block of wood with skins stretched over them, but for the children's toy drum the base was a discarded tin can with the top and bottom removed. They wrapped the can with birch bark, then covered the top and bottom with pieces of deer hide. A rawhide strap was laced back and forth between the deer hide drum heads to hold it all in place.

One day when Ahmeek found Johnny Bearheart just outside the Indian village, the younger boy seemed unusually excited.

"Grandfather is going to show me how to make the Chippewa headdress, like the one they wear for the *Pow wow*," he said. " I asked if you could come and watch and he said it would be okay."

Ahmeek was very happy that Eagle Feather and Johnny would include him in such an important activity. Johnny Bearheart had told him about the powwow and how important it was to the Indian. To let him watch his friend, maybe even help a little, was almost like letting him be a part of the clan. The two boys ran every step of the way to the village. They sat down a short distance from Johnny Bearheart's wigwam and waited for Eagle Feather.

While they waited, Ahmeek could see Mourning Dove occasionally glancing out at them from the wigwam entrance. Johnny Bearheart noticed Ahmeek's awkward attempt not to look her way.

"Mourning Dove wants to meet the handsome white boy," he said.

"Ahmeek could feel his face turn red, but he had no chance to stop what was about to happen.

"Mourning Dove," Johnny Bearheart called. "Come here." His sister shyly obeyed. "This is my friend Ahmeek."

"Ahmeek?" Mourning Dove responded. Then she turned away, unable to stifle a small giggle. "Why do they call you Ahmeek?" she asked

Ahmeek told them how Eagle Feather had found him in the woods and how he had given him the new name.

"It isn't my real name," Ahmeek confessed. "But it's a lot better so even back in Wausau some of the kids call me Ahmeek."

Mourning Dove giggled again. "Do they know what it means?" she asked.

"Naw, they don't know any Indian stuff."

Johnny Bearheart slouched down and dropped his head. "Don't seem right," he said. "You're a white boy with an Indian name and I'm an Indian and have to have a white man's name."

"Don't worry," Ahmeek answered, "maybe someday

you'll get an Indian name just like I did. Besides, a few kids call me Ahmeek when we're out playing, but at school or at Aunt Sarah's I have to use my real name. I'd a whole lot rather have a name like Johnny Bearheart than to have to answer to Jotham."

Mourning Dove saw Eagle Feather coming toward them and quickly slipped back into the wigwam.

"You are here Ahmeek," Eagle Feather said in greeting. "It is good that you watch."

Ahmeek remembered the headdress he had made with Dominic and Gino when they played Indian and he was anxious to see how the real Indians made them. His brothers had cut a long strip of burlap, found chicken feathers to insert into the weave of the material, then pinned it around their head. He was soon to find out that was not what Eagle Feather had in mind. The old man picked up a bag and dumped the contents onto the ground next to Johnny Bearheart.

"First we'll make *dewe' igun*," Eagle Feather said.

"Where are the feathers?" Ahmeek asked.

"No feathers," the old Indian answered. "Some Indians make them with feathers, not the Chippewa."

Ahmeek wanted to ask about the feathered Indian headdress he had seen pictured in his school books, but he decided those books were about other Indians and it would be better to just wait for the old man's instructions.

"First we weave moose hair," Eagle Feather showed the children how to tie the cords that would be woven with the moose hair so that it would all stand up when sewn into the headpiece and trimmed. He tied a cord to a small tree for his grandson, then with the other end attached to a stick so Johnny Bearheart could sit on it to keep it taut, he showed them how to weave the moose hair in with a second cord. He said Johnny Bearheart would have to make a long strand to be fashioned into a roach. Ahmeek hadn't expected it to take most of the afternoon just weaving moose hair into a string. He would have lost interest altogether if Old Eagle Feather hadn't brought his own finished headdress to show them. It had a small hole near the front for his own hair to come through and hold it in place. The string was sewn so that all the moose hair stood straight up and it was trimmed like the cropped manes Ahmeek had seen on some of the horses in the camp. He also showed them a porcupine-hair headdress, with some deer hair dyed to a bright red, decorating the center of the roach. It was as majestic as any feathered headdress Ahmeek had ever seen and its memory would remain with him for the whole summer.

"Enough for one day," Eagle Feather said. "You come tomorrow, we finish." Then the old man picked up his bag of materials and walked back across the village to his own wigwam.

Johnny Bearheart worked on his headdress for two more days under the watchful eye of his grandfather. Eagle Feather told them about the many things that could be used to decorate the headdress. In the old days he said that Indians used a variety of materials. Most common were bones, and Eagle Feather had brought some bear claws for Johnny Bearheart to use. He said his grandfather had made a headdress with bright copper bangles pounded from the metallic stones that were found far to the north in the Keweenaw. Ahmeek, while he couldn't make a headdress of his own here at the Indian village, paid close attention. He had determined that he would ask cook to give him some deer hide and moosehair from the animals the hunters brought in and when he had some time, maybe in the evenings back in Wausau, he would make a real Chippewa headdress too.

When the headdress was finished, Ahmeek and Johnny Bearheart played in the woods. Ahmeek only went to the village when he had a specific invitation and Johnny Bearheart rarely went to the logging camp, but if one saw the other nearby he would run out to join him. On a few occasions, if Mourning Dove was not busy with the women in the village, Johnny Bearheart would bring her along. She was a year older than Johnny Bearheart, but that meant she was the same age as Ahmeek and she was delighted to join them when permitted.

During these afternoon play times Ahmeek and the Indian children became close friends. One of them would pretend to be a bear or a deer while the other two would hunt. At first Ahmeek found it impossible to catch Johnny

Bearheart. The Indian boy could scamper through the woods so quietly that even Mourning Dove couldn't hear him. Eventually Ahmeek too learned to slither through the woods so that he could not be seen until he decided he wanted to be seen.

Whenever Jotham was caught up with his chores around the logging camp, he went to the lake or the woods near the village. One of those times he found Eagle Feather and asked about the *Gitchi Manitou*. He didn't get an answer, but instead another fascinating story. Eagle Feather told about the Manitou who chased a stag through the woods only to lose him when he swam out into *Gitchi Gumi*, the great body of water that Jotham knew was Lake Superior. The Manitou was so angered, Eagle Feather said, that he picked up a handful of rocks and threw them into the lake. Those rocks grew and became the islands that the White man has named the Apostle Islands. Ahmeek thought it was an exciting and interesting story, but not very believable and he told Eagle Feather so. Eagle Feather said, "Little Ahmeek, you are very wise for your years." Then he continued, "A story about Manitou is not always true. What it tells is truth." He added, "Manitou made all things."

Chapter 9

Jotham knew what he was going to be, but he wouldn't tell. All of the boys and girls in the school were talking about their costume for the Halloween party that was coming up in just a couple of weeks. Of course whatever costume anyone chose to come in was supposed to be a surprise, but you wouldn't know that to listen to the girls talk. Some of the boys were teasing him. They said they had heard Rebecca Morgan say she was coming as Pocahontas, because she knew Ahmeek would come as an Indian and then they would have to be together at the party. Ahmeek thought that maybe Rebecca had said something like that because a few of the girls asked if he was coming as an Indian.

Rebecca was one of the few students who still called him Ahmeek and she did so only when no one else was around. Over the summer most of the other children, all but his closest friends, had forgotten the name and gone back to Jotham. A few of the boys had a new name for him. They called him "Indian lover," but he refused to let it bother him. He knew that the lumber camp wasn't the only place where you could find people like Smiley Bartle.

Jotham's headdress was almost finished by the time planning for the Halloween party had started. It wasn't as nice as Eagle Feather's, but it was a Chippewa headdress and as good, Jotham thought, as any nine-year-old could make. It wasn't anything like the ones he and his brothers used to make out of burlap and chicken feathers. He had woven the moose hair into strands of cord just like Johnny Bearheart had and wound the whole thing into a roach. Then he trimmed the moose hair so it only stood up in the middle. Then he dipped the white deer hair in some red dye and tied it in the very center of the tuft of moose hair. Aunt Sarah helped him with that part so he wouldn't make a mess. She thought the headdress was a good project for Jotham, so she helped whenever she could. Making his own costume was a kind of work and she believed in the value of learning to work at an early age.

Jotham thought he would like to have a buckskin jacket to go with the headdress, but having none he planned to go shirtless. A year earlier when he took off his shirt on a warm spring day to dive into the swimming hole with the other boys, they teased him about being so skinny. That wouldn't happen now. After a summer of pounding logs to make basket strips and running in the woods with Johnny Bearheart, Jotham looked almost as strong as an Indian brave and almost as brown. Of course Aunt Sarah objected. She found an old brown shirt that already had some big holes in it and removed the sleeves. She cut deep fringes around the shoulders and along the bottom. She used the material from the sleeves to sew fringes on the sides and from a distance it looked almost like buck-skin. Jotham unbuttoned it down to the waist as soon as he was out of the house.

Jotham and Rebecca Morgan, who as the boys had said came as Pocahontas, won the prize for the best costumes and as they had also predicted, Rebecca spent most of her time next to the Indian brave with the handsome head-dress. Rebecca, a year older than Jotham, was just begin-ning to notice boys. Jotham on the other hand, thought girls, Rebecca included, were a little bit silly. They were always talking about their clothes and their hair. When he was younger he had admired Rebecca Morgan's red, curly hair, and he conceded to himself that the girls' brown or golden hair looked pretty enough when it hung down in ringlets the way most of them wore it, but none compared to the beautiful black tresses of Mourning Dove. Jotham remembered watching her when the sun was shining in such a way that it gave her hair a slight blue tint. He thought about his Indian friends often, but that was out in the woods in the summer time. This was Wausau, and having Rebecca beside him gave him a measure of respect among some of the older boys so he neither objected to her interest in him nor shied away. It was a relationship he merely tolerated at first but later would find more to his liking.

The winter of '93-94 was a good year at school for Jotham. As a fourth grader he was still expected to play with the little kids at recess, but even that changed. One day when Amos Barker, one of the older boys, was sick and couldn't come to school the fifth and sixth graders asked Jotham to play softball with them. They wanted to play "sides" and without Amos one team wouldn't have enough players to cover the field. Jotham was happy to get such a chance. He knew he was much stronger than before his summer with Eagle Feather and when it was his turn to bat he swung with all his might at the first pitch. The ball caught a corner of the bat and dribbled slowly toward third base. The pitcher, a seventh-grade boy trotted over to the rolling ball assured of an easy out, but when he picked it up and turned he found Jotham already within a few steps of first base. Johnny Bearheart had taught him how to run like an Indian and by now it was second nature. "*Not like the deer, leaping in the air,*" the Indian boy had said, "*but like the fox close to the ground.*" Jotham could hear all the fourth graders cheering and he wasn't sure, but he thought he might have heard Rebecca Morgan's voice too. In the field Jotham proved to be faster than any of the older boys and no one was able to get a ground ball past him. When his next turn at bat came he didn't swing at the first pitch. He waited until the pitcher threw one clearly over home base. He swung, and his bat hit the ball solidly, sending it just a few feet beyond the fence that marked the end of the playground. From that day on, Jotham was allowed to play with the older boys during recess.

The next week the Northside school was scheduled to play a game of softball with the new school on Wausau's south side. Fourth graders weren't supposed to play so Jotham was only there, along with the other younger kids and the girls, as a spectator. The Northsiders were up first and scored twelve runs in the first inning. It was a substantial lead and it looked like they would surely win over the bigger school to the south. The game was scheduled to go five innings and by the time they got to the last half of the fifth inning the Northside team's lead had been cut to nine runs, twenty-four to fifteen. Then something went wrong. It seemed that every ball the south team hit got past the basemen. Twenty-four to sixteen, twenty-four to seventeen. Soon it was twenty-four to twenty-one and it looked like Jotham's school would almost certainly lose. As Jotham looked on, the next batter hit a ground ball just out of reach of Michael Barry and another two runs crossed home base. Twenty-three to twenty-four with two runners on base and nobody out. There was a big gasp from the crowd when they looked back toward second base. Michael had slipped when diving for the ball and was sitting on the ground, an expression of pain on his face, holding his right ankle. Two of the grownups ran out and helped him off the field, and after a long conference at home plate between Miss Merriweather and the teacher from the south side school, it was agreed that they could substitute a fourth grader for the remainder of the game.

"Let Jotham play," Michael said. "I can't."

Jotham felt very sorry for Michael, but at the same time he was happy for the chance to play in such an important softball game. To the cheers of the whole Northside school he trotted out onto the field. The next batter hit the ball between first and second base and it looked like the game was lost for the Northside, but Jotham scampered to his left and flipped the ball to the first baseman. One out. Another batter for the south side struck out. Two outs. The third batter hit a fly ball that looked like it would drop between second base and the center fielder, but Jotham ran like the fox and caught it. All the kids from the Northside school cheered as the players left the field and started toward the wagon, hitched to a team of Clydesdales, that would take them home. As they walked by Miss Merriweather, they heard old Doc Masterjohn ask how old that boy on second base was.

"You mean Michael?" she asked.

"No, not Michael, the smaller boy that replaced him?"

"Oh!" she said, "That's Jotham Marichetti. He's only in the fourth grade, nine years old."

Doc Masterjohn shook his head. "I've never seen hand, eye coordination like that on a nine-year-old," he said.

Everybody was congratulating Jotham for the way he saved the game, even Michael Barry who skipped along beside him as they went to the wagon.

Jotham was not only good at softball. He won almost all the races, unless they had him race against a seventh or eighth grader. He couldn't beat them, but he was clearly the fastest boy in the other six grades. He also knew about some games that the other kids hadn't played.

Jotham cut some sticks and used some binding twine that one of the boys got from the feed mill — without Mr. Obermeister's permission, Jotham was sure — and fashioned some crude lacrosse rackets. He told the boys that the Indians didn't have twine so they used *wattop* to make their rackets.

"What's *wattop?*" asked one of the boys.

"It's the real small roots from a tree," Jotham answered, "I think it's the spruce tree."

"What's the name of this game?"

"Lacrosse," Jotham said.

"Never heard of it," said another boy.

"It was a famous Indian game," Jotham told the boys. "Eagle Feather, the Indian Chief I told you about, said that the Chippewa once used this game to fool the white man so they could take over an army fort."

He related the story as Eagle Father had told it. The Indians on Mackinac Island, near the place where Lake Superior and Lake Michigan meet fooled the soldiers at Fort Michimillimac by entertaining them with a game of lacrosse.

"Except the Chippewa called it *baggataway*," he said. "When the soldiers started to get excited about the game the Indians kept moving closer and closer to the gates of the fort."

"What happened?"

"Well," Jotham continued, "when they got real close to

the gates they threw their rackets down and pulled out knives that they had hidden in their clothes, and ran inside the fort. The soldiers were so surprised they couldn't stop them and that was one battle the chief said the Indians won."

"You're making that up," one of the boys said. "Either you're makin' it up or your Indian friend is a liar. The Indians didn't win no battles against the army, 'cept for Little Big Horn."

"Okay." Jotham yielded, "Ask Miss Merriweather."

The boy did, but Miss Merriweather said she didn't know the answer and would have to look it up. The next day she came to class and announced that what Jotham had told them was true. The Indians did win a battle at Fort Michimillimac. She said it was during the French and Indian War, so it wasn't the American army, it was the British army that they fooled.

"I told ya," said the boy.

"I didn't say the American army," responded Jotham.

With that Jotham's stature continued to grow, not only in the fourth grade, but in the seventh and eighth as well. Even Miss Merriweather was impressed that Jotham knew so much about American history. After all, American history wasn't taught until the seventh grade.

Chapter 10

Maybe it was because they were on their way home from church; or maybe it was because it was getting close to the Christmas season and everybody was supposed to be a little nicer to everybody else, especially the poor people. It might have been something the pastor said during the service, but Jotham couldn't think of anything. She said it with a friendly voice too, like she was really interested and wasn't mad or anything. It just wasn't what he ever expected to hear from Aunt Sarah.

"Tell me about your Indian friends, Jotham," she said.

Of course she knew about the Indians and the time he spent with them in the summer. Jotham had told her how Eagle Feather taught them to make things when he made his headdress for the Halloween party, but he hadn't said anything about Johnny Bearheart. He had been sure Aunt Sarah wouldn't approve. If she didn't like Gino much because he had been born in Italy and talked like an Italian, Jotham was sure she wouldn't approve of his Indian friends, but here she was asking him to tell her about them.

"I told you about Eagle Feather," Jotham began, "He comes from an Indian village over in Michigan, way up on the north side of the lake."

"Does Enrico... I mean your father let you go to the village?"

"Sure, but I've only been there a few times. I see Eagle Feather in the woods, down near the lumber camp."

"Miss Merriweather says you've learned a lot about the

history of the Indians," Aunt Sarah said. "You must have spent a lot of afternoons in the woods listening to those Indian stories."

"I had to work around the camp a lot last summer, but when I had a day off, I'd go to the woods or to the lake." It seemed to Jotham that Aunt Sarah was asking a lot of questions. Maybe this wasn't going to be such a friendly talk after all. "We didn't just talk all the time. Eagle Feather showed us how to make things."

"Us?" Aunt Sarah smiled, a small knowing smile, but didn't pursue the obvious question, *who was us?* right away. "What kind of things?" she asked.

"Well," Jotham answered, "at first he showed me how to make a rabbit snare."

"Oh, a rabbit snare?"

"Yeah. Eagle Feather had a piece of rawhide string with a loop in it tied to a willow branch, and when the rabbit stepped inside the loop, the branch whipped up and tightened the rawhide around his leg."

"And did it work?"

"Sure," Jotham said. "We caught a rabbit in the first snare he showed me. It was just a baby cottontail though."

"What did you do with it?"

"We let it go." Jotham smiled. He knew Aunt Sarah would like this part. "Old Eagle Feather said we weren't supposed to keep rabbits caged up or anything, that the..." Jotham almost said *Gitchi Manitou*, but thought better of it. "...that nature meant for rabbits to be free to run."

"That's nice," Aunt Sarah said. "I think I'd like this, what was his name? Oh, Eagle Feather."

"Really! Maybe someday..." Whoops. The look on Aunt Sarah's face said maybe she wasn't quite that serious about liking Eagle Feather. "...I mean if you ever came up to the logging camp or anything."

"Well," Aunt Sarah explained, a little unsure how to say it, "that isn't exactly what I meant. I meant I like his ideas, the way he thinks about nature. He sounds like a nice person but you know, Indians and white people, I mean grown-up Indians and white people don't mix."

Okay, maybe he had let his imagination get away from him. After all he hadn't needed to hear what Aunt Sarah was saying to know that was the way people felt, but what bothered Jotham was that he was beginning to worry that the difference between the white man and the Indian was going to affect his own life. He and Johnny Bearheart had become good friends during his summer at Lac Vieux Desert, but he was worried about that friendship lasting when they got older. He was in the fourth grade, and in addition to learning geography, like Gino said he would, he was learning long division, and he had learned to read so well that he couldn't find enough story books. He had already read all of the books for his grade in the library at school and most of the books for the upper grades too. It wasn't a big library, of course, just a few shelves built into a big closet, but folks thought it was big enough for a school that only went to the eighth grade. Even so, it wasn't big enough for Jotham. He liked books about everything. He had even found a book in the library, on the shelf marked seventh grade, that told about the planets and how the solar system worked. When he read it he thought about Old Eagle Feather's stories of the first creation, the making of the physical world, stars, the sun, the moon and the earth with all its mountains and other land features. He found another about chemistry and was fascinated to read how different chemicals acted when you put them together. The problem was he was learning so fast now, faster than the other children in the school, and he was sure much faster than Johnny Bearheart. He remembered what Eagle Feather said, that Indians learned from the stories told by the old ones. Jotham heard those stories too and they didn't say anything about chemistry or mathematics. Johnny Bearheart went to the Indian school, but they didn't teach them the same stuff his school taught white kids. The problem was that Jotham and the Indian children could play and make things together and listen to old Eagle Feather's stories now, but what would happen when the kind of things Jotham learned to make and the stories he liked to hear or read got to be so different from the things Johnny Bearheart liked. Then they might not want to do things together anymore and that would be a problem because he was one of the best friends Jotham ever had.

"Jotham?" Aunt Sarah's voice broke into his thoughts.

"Yes, Aunt Sarah?"

"Jotham, what did you mean when you said, *us?*" Her voice was soft and overly gentle. Not the kind of soft reassuring voice like when Miss Merriweather talked about the Indians. It was the kind of soft, Jotham thought, that says you better be careful, that you're moving into dangerous territory.

"What did you mean when you said *us?*"

"Huh?" Jotham didn't remember when he said us and really didn't know what Aunt Sarah was asking about.

"When you said Eagle Feather showed you how to make things. You didn't say *showed me,* you said *showed us.* Who was *us?*"

Well, that was it. No more keeping a secret, Jotham thought. He didn't know how far this might go. If grownups talked about him, and ever since the softball game, grownups did talk about him, and then if they talked to their kids, pretty soon everybody might be asking about Mourning Dove and Johnny Bearheart. He had no choice but to tell Aunt Sarah.

"Oh that," he began, trying to make it sound as insignificant as he could. "I played with Eagle Feather's grandkids some days."

"Oh?" That's all she said, but Jotham knew that the way she said it meant she wanted him to tell her more.

"Yeah. He showed us how to make the headdress and how to make Indian baskets."

"How old were Eagle Feather's grandchildren?"

"Well, the boy was eight, I think. You know how we made the baskets?" he continued in a vain attempt to change the subject, "You have to start by pounding on this pole until it breaks up into thin strips of wood, thin enough to weave. It takes a lot of pounding and your arms can get pretty sore."

"I'm sure it does," Aunt Sarah cut in. "What about the other grandchildren?"

"Huh?"

"You said grandkids," Aunt Sarah said. "And you told me about the boy. Were there others?"

"There was a girl too," Jotham answered. "She was a little older, but I didn't see her so much."

"What were the children's names?"

That was it. The last barrier between his summer life as Ahmeek the Indian boy and Jotham Marichetti, that school kid in Wausau the rest of the year, was about to be broken down.

"The girl's name is Mourning Dove..."

"Mourning Dove," Aunt Sarah broke in. "That's a pretty name."

"...and the boy is called Johnny."

"Just Johnny?" Aunt Sarah asked. "That doesn't sound like an Indian name."

"Johnny Bearheart," Jotham added. He explained what Eagle Feather had told him about the younger Indian women wanting to give their children permanent names when they were born like the white women do, instead of following the old ways of waiting for the boy's dream to provide a name. They continued to talk as they walked along the narrow road that led from the Methodist church to their home. Jotham said that he liked Johnny Bearheart and that he wished he could go to his school instead of Indian school. He mentioned the things he had been thinking about and his concern that he was growing up so much different from the Indian boy that he wasn't sure they could still be friends when they got older. Aunt Sarah was sympathetic. She said she knew it would be difficult for Jotham to lose his friend, but people are always losing friends and making new ones.

"God made all kinds of people," Aunt Sarah said. "It sounds to me like your friends at the lake are nice people, even if they are Indian boys and girls, but they're different. They're still savages and they have no need for our kind of schooling."

"They're not savages," Jotham protested. "I've read about savages. The ones in the west and some in other countries. The Chippewa in Michigan would never take a person's scalp or kill them for no good reason or steal children. When Old Eagle Feather found me in the woods that first time, I was kind of lost and he took me home."

"Kind of lost?"

"Well, I mean I could have found my way back to the house if I tried, but Eagle Feather took me there faster. All the savages I've read about were mean. Eagle Feather was never mean."

"I guess I didn't really mean savages," Aunt Sarah said. "What I meant is that the Indians are not Christian and they're not civilized, that's all. People who aren't civilized have no need for school. Instead of book learning, they have to learn to hunt and gather berries and wild rice..."

"But they could learn reading and writing too," Jotham cut in.

Aunt Sarah laughed. "Whatever would they do with it?"

"I don't know," Jotham admitted. "The same things we do with it, I suppose. Maybe if they learned to read, they could read the Bible, then maybe they could become Christian and be civilized."

"Oh, Jotham. You have such grand ideas. You're probably right but that would take a lot longer than you and I are going to live. They're a long way from being civilized and for now I think we just have to accept that. They're different. Even if they did go to school it certainly couldn't be the same school as the white children."

"Why not?" Jotham protested.

"It just wouldn't work that's all." Aunt Sarah was adamant. "There are too many differences. The white men and women around here wouldn't allow it and neither would the Indians I imagine."

"Yeah," Jotham conceded. "I suppose you're right. I heard one of the guys at the camp say the only good Indian is a dead Indian."

Aunt Sarah's face took on a look of shock that Jotham thought was real. "Jotham," she said, "don't ever think anything like that. I know the Indians are different, and I know we can't live together with them like we do with other people, but I never understood how people could hate them so much."

"Then you think Indians are okay?" Jotham asked.

"Yes, I do, Jotham. But you've got to remember they are different from us. They are savages of a sort, and you won't be able to be good friends with them all you life."

"That's what I was worried about," Jotham confessed.

"Well you shouldn't worry about it dear," Aunt Sarah said. "I've heard what a lot of people say about the Indians, some of your young friends here in town even, and I'm glad you don't talk like that."

Jotham smiled and Aunt Sarah continued.

"We couldn't have them living right here in Wausau with the white people, but that doesn't mean we have to hate them. I think it's nice of you to be tolerant of the Indians and I'm glad you have them to play with when you're gone in the summer. What were there names again?"

"Mourning Dove and Johnny Bearheart."

"Yes, Mourning Dove and Johnny. Mourning Dove is such a pretty name isn't it? Is she a pretty girl, I mean for an Indian?"

Jotham could tell by the way Aunt Sarah asked that it was time to be cautious again. "Yeah," he said, "I guess so, I mean for an Indian girl."

Aunt Sarah smiled. She was sure the message had gotten through. Jotham on the other hand wasn't sure what the message was. He was pleased that Aunt Sarah said it was okay for him to have Indian friends, at least for now. He didn't know what she meant by tolerant. He'd have to remember to look that up in the big dictionary at school. He thought it sounded like white people somehow thought they were better than Indians. Jotham didn't know if that was quite right. Sure, they were better at the kind of learning you get in school, but Indians had their own kind of learning and nobody at his school could beat Johnny Bearheart or Mourning Dove at that. He still worried about their relationship in the future, but for now he was happy to know nobody was going to try make him quit being their friend.

Chapter 11

Jotham continued to live and to learn with one foot in each culture, summers with Eagle Feather and Johnny Bearheart, winters with Aunt Sarah and school in Wausau. With the Chippewas he learned to make baskets and tom toms. Johnny Bearheart showed him how to make a bow and a supply of arrows. They mastered the red man's method of tanning hides and fashioning a variety of useful items from them: pouches, belts, moccasins and drum heads. One summer project provided a handsome pair of snowshoes, which Jotham thought were probably very practical for Johnny Bearheart and Eagle Feather when winter came to Upper Michigan. He would like to have become more proficient on them himself, but he found them to be of little use in Wausau where a team of horses pulled a snow plow over the roads after each snowfall. He learned to make twine from the bark of the basswood tree and to make fish nets from nettle-stalk fibers. They made mats from bulrushes and bags from the inner bark of the cedar. Each summer he would find Johnny Bearheart and each summer he would learn more stories and new Indian crafts.

Eagle Feather told them about medicines that could be derived from plants: jewelweed to cure poison ivy and cedar wax to stop bleeding. He told them about *Midewiwin*, the Grand Medicine Society, and how it required years of training to become a medicine man or woman. Not only did they have to learn the curative properties of plants to care for the body but also the ceremonies to tend to needs of the spirit.

Ahmeek discovered more about the history of the tribe and the legends, most of them extrapolations of a vague truth, the remnants in story form of a distant past. He heard the same stories over and over, about the sky woman, *Nakomis*, who, when her daughter *Winonah* died, raised her grandchildren, *Mudjeekawis* the wanderer and *Nanabush* the messenger.

He also learned of dance, the war dance, the victory dance, the deer dance, the snowshoe dance and the significance of the various festivals. He discovered that the powwow was not just a show, but a spiritual celebration.

As Ahmeek became older his appreciation of the Indians and their way of life continued to grow. In his visits to their village, he discovered that much of what his school books taught him about Indians was not true of the people he knew. The books dwelt primarily with the plains Indians, the Sioux and the Blackfoot. Little was said about the Algonquin, of which the Chippewa were a part. They lived in a wigwam, not a tepee and they wore very few feathers, not the big feathered headdress of the Dakota. He noticed the division of labor in the Indian village and was surprised to see that the tasks he would have considered to be the hardest, often man's work in a white society, were done by the women of the tribe.

During his summers with Eagle Feather and Johnny Bearheart, Ahmeek had become familiar with the Indian language as well as with their culture. When he visited the village, or when he was with his friends in the woods near Lac Vieux Desert, he assumed the character of Ahmeek the white Indian boy. In Wausau and back at the logging camp he retained his faithfulness to the mores of whites and became Jotham, the boy who knew so much about the Chippewa. Learning the language helped him learn to understand the people. He began to see difference between the thought patterns of the white man and the Indian. It seemed perfectly logical that people who believed they had little control over their world should speak a language that emphasized nouns rather than verbs. In the world of the red man nature was the molding force. People, like birds, animals, forests and even the waters, were only a molded part.

Two different worlds, but Ahmeek was happy in both. He enjoyed learning in school and was very attached to his friends there. That timid little tyke who had no talent for getting along with other children was all but forgotten. Instead his schoolmates knew a boy who was both Jotham and Ahmeek, who combined superior intelligence in the classroom with an almost uncanny athletic prowess on the playground, was the hero of younger children and the envy of older ones.

Now that he was twelve years old, one of those attachments, his relationship with Rebecca Morgan, was undergoing a mystifying transformation. Sometimes the transformation was almost too confusing. Why had she been so upset the day he helped Jeannie MacGregor with her arithmetic problems? She said she didn't believe Jeannie was having trouble with her arithmetic at all; she just wanted to be near Ahmeek. He had gotten used to Rebecca's desire to be physically close, even touching so much of the time. A year ago he wasn't quite ready for that and slithered away when she leaned her head into his or reached for his hand, but one year had changed things and Ahmeek too found the sensation of a touching relationship pleasant.

When the summer of his twelfth year came Ahmeek discovered some of those same changes occurring in his relationship with Mourning Dove. Because Ahmeek rarely saw Mourning Dove when he went to the village and they were together only when she came into the woods, Johnny Bearheart was always present. This was beginning to irritate Mourning Dove. Johnny Bearheart wanted to play warrior or run races the way they did when they first started to play together. Ahmeek, still a young boy himself and a close friend of Johnny Bearheart, agreed to what the younger boy wanted. Besides wanting to be diplomatic, he was always bursting with excess energy. He didn't know where it came from, but he looked forward to the opportunity to burn some of it off dashing through the woods with Johnny.

Mourning Dove would rather spend an afternoon sitting and talking and she made no secret of the fact that she preferred that Johnny Bearheart go back to the village and find someone else to play with so she and Ahmeek could be alone. He wouldn't go of course, but at least he would run off into the woods for half an hour or so before returning with some discovery and another suggested game the three of them could play.

Mourning Dove found the stories Ahmeek told about his school and the things he did in the winter in Wausau fascinating and she found the handsome dark-skinned face he was rapidly acquiring irresistible. After a few weeks in the sun each summer, Ahmeek's ethnic heritage would manifest itself in his skin color and, were it not for his lower cheek bones, he could have easily passed for one of the Indians.

It was a warm, early August day. A few white billowy clouds were reflected in the lake which hadn't a ripple on it except for the occasional explosion of a big pike breaking the surface in quest of a butterfly. The afternoon air was so still that no wind could be heard whispering through the pine trees and most of the birds, whose songs had filled the morning air were now silent. Only the faint undertone of crickets tuning up for the evening along with the booming croak of a bull frog in the meadow that bordered the headwaters of the river could be heard. The white boy and the Indian girl sat by themselves, looking out over the lake. Johnny Bearheart had been sent off on an errand contrived by Mourning Dove.

"Oh! Look," she said, pointing to a mother duck and a bevy of ducklings swimming along behind her. As she said it she cuddled closer clutching his upper arm and pulling it firmly against her youthful breast. Ahmeek found the proximity disturbing, but he did not pull away. He had noticed changes that were gradually transforming Mourning Dove from the pretty girl he had known to a lovely young woman, but he had tried not to let his observations become too obvious. The two of them sat silently for a long time watching the mother duck and her brood swim around a log protruding from the shore. One of the ducks tried to crawl up onto its mother's back. Mourning Dove giggled and again Ahmeek was aware of her body huddled tightly against his. This time he felt no discomfort. She looked up and smiled. He returned the smile as he reached over with his free hand and gently held hers.

"They're pretty when they're young," Jotham heard Smiley Bartle say as he entered the cook's shanty, "but they turn ugly afore you know it."

"That's a lot of crap and you know it, Smiley," Stanley shot back.

"Is that so, well let me tell ya something Polack, I knew a squaw man when I was out west. He said he regretted the day he ever married her. She was Oglala Sioux. Prettiest little thing on the plains, he said. He gave the chief twenty beaver skins for her, but he said it wasn't five years afore she got to lookin' like any other squaw. Had a passel of young'ns. He said that was the worst part. Them papooses ain't like regular kids, ya know. Wild right from the start, he said."

"Smiley's right," chimed in Ben Wigghers. "If ya can't get along without women, well then, ya better take a few days off and head over to Hurley. Payin' is a lot better'n gettin' tangled up with savages."

Somehow Jotham knew that was where the discussion was going. Whenever the men in the logging camp started to talk about women, somebody would bring up Hurley. That small settlement on the Michigan border about fifty miles to the west was already developing its reputation as a wide-open town and would retain it for the better part of the next century. Hurley had a plethora of gambling and prostitution throughout the heyday of the northern Wisconsin lumbering era. It was rhetorically teamed with another town located in north central Wisconsin, not quite as earthy as Hurley, but chosen probably only for the sake of alliteration, Hayward. Any other village in the area that wanted to make a reference to its rough-and-tumble past would call up the cliché, Hayward, Hurley and Hell, their town of course having at an earlier time been the latter.

"Sure, you can go to Hurley if you want to," Stanley said, "but you got a better chance of keepin' your scalp at the Chippewa village."

"I don't know," Frank chimed in with a thick French accent, addressing his bunkmate, "It's your wampum you'll lose in Hurley, but you're damn well likely to lose your scalp if some of those braves catch you in the hanky-panky with their village women."

"You listen to him, Polack," Ben Wigghers added. "If the Frenchman doesn't know about hanky-panky then I guess I don't know who does." Wigghers broke into a hearty laugh and was quickly joined by all the men at the table.

Of course Jotham was well aware of what they were talking about. Living with Aunt Sarah and Uncle Oliver, rather than at the logging camp, he had maintained his innocence but not his naiveté. By this time, with summers in the camp, he had heard it all or at least thought he had. No one there had made it a practice to shield Jotham. His father was too busy, and Dominic, who usually had been left in charge of his little brother, was too engrossed in expanding his own knowledge. Jotham could still remember a time when he was about six years old and some of the men in the camp, recently returned from a weekend of revelry, were providing some enlightenment for Gino and Dominic. The two older boys had become an appreciative audience for the lumberjacks and the more they relished the tales being recounted the more ribald they became. Finally one of the men took notice of Jotham standing wide-eyed and jaw-dropped along side his brothers and cautioned the others that "little ears" were listening.

"That's okay," Dominic had said, not wanting to miss any of the details of the conversation himself. "Jotham knows all about that stuff." From that time on he learned a lot from the lumbermen, but none of it really meant very much... until now.

"Well," Stanley broke in, sounding serious again, "as I see it the Indians are just about like anybody else, no better, no worse." He turned toward Smiley Bartle as he continued, "and, Mr. Western Cowboy, that goes for the women as well as the men."

"Yeah, Polack," Bartle shot back, with a good-natured smile, "then why don't you marry up with one of 'em? If yer thinkin' they'd make such a good wife."

"Same reason I never married a white woman, 'cause I wouldn't bring a woman into this kind of life, havin' to put up with the likes of you."

Another round of laughter rose from the table. Stanley smiled, acknowledging the point the crowd had just awarded him in the game, then he continued. "You know the only thing I want to do is cut timber. I like working in the camps. I like workin' outside. You know I got some education. I can read and write and figure some, but I took a job inside once and I couldn't wait to get out of it. I don't like farmin' and if I went to a ranch I'd have to put up with a whole bunch of Smiley Bartles, so I wouldn't do that." Again some laughter answered Stanley's comment. "I like workin' in the woods, but it's no life for a woman."

"Maybe not a white woman," Smiley Bartle answered, "but an Indian woman ain't nothin' but a squaw."

It was not an accepted practice for young people to get into these conversations in the cook's shanty. Even Gino, who was almost a grownup said very little, especially when Smiley Bartle got started, but Jotham couldn't take any more. "There's nothing wrong with a squaw," he said. "Squaw is just the Indian word for a wife or an older woman."

"Shut up, Jotham," Dominic cautioned, his voice just above a whisper.

"Oh, who's that talkin'?" Smiley asked mockingly.

"That's Jotham," Stanley answered, "and he knows what he's talking about. He knows the Indian language well enough to talk to them."

"The language isn't all he knows," added Ben Wigghers with a grin. "He's got his own little Indian girl he plays in the woods with."

Dominic jabbed his brother in the ribs with his elbow. "See what I toldja," he said.

"Ya better watch it Jotham," Smiley Bartle warned, his yellow teeth exposed in a mocking smile. "She's a pretty little thing now, but afore you know it she'll turn ugly on ya, jest like that."

It was the last time Ahmeek would see Mourning Dove and Johnny Bearheart before he went back to Wausau to begin eighth grade. It would be his last year in grade school. He should have been in seventh grade that fall of 1897, but in the middle of his sixth-grade year, the teacher had decided he was so far ahead of the other students in his class that she would move him up to the seventh grade. This was a common practice in the schools of Ahmeek's time. It was already getting crisp in the early morning hours and, though it would warm up later in the day, it was obvious that autumn was well on its way. As he followed the narrow path that led from the Marichetti house to the lake, he could see a glimpse of red on the leaves of many of the maple trees. Smiley Bartle said that meant it was going to be a hard winter, but Ahmeek didn't believe much of what Smiley Bartle said. He wasn't really an Indian, but he knew the wisdom of some of their beliefs and he knew it was the animals, not the plants that were given the gift of knowing the future. He thought about the teasing the men had given him in the cook's shanty. He didn't mind the teasing so much. It was what was behind the teasing that bothered him. It was the loggers' way of saying the same thing Aunt Sarah had said on the way home from church that day. *White boys don't belong with Indian girls.* It might not be true, but it was a thought that Ahmeek found depressing.

Ahmeek saw Mourning Dove coming down the path toward the lake, Johnny Bearheart beside her. She stopped at the top of the hill and looked out toward the water. The sun pressed down on her hair giving it that blue tint Ahmeek had always admired. She stood straight, tall and confident, beautiful. Seeing Mourning Dove in this light, in this setting, made Ahmeek more sure than ever that Smiley Bartle didn't know what he was talking about. Mourning Dove could never turn ugly.

She turned toward him and her lips parted, just slightly, in a coquettish smile. She moved quickly, yet gracefully, as she descended the hill to the place where Ahmeek was waiting. Johnny Bearheart followed. As usual, Johnny Bearheart suggested the game. On this particular day, this last day before going away again for the winter, Ahmeek was the one who would rather sit and talk, but the excess energy caged up in the young Indian boy would not permit that. Johnny had never been one for talking, he was a child of action, an attribute that was to be his trademark in later life. The game Johnny suggested imitated the life of the Indian, the young brave stalking his prey. Johnny usually wanted to be the young brave, but this time because it was his last day, Ahmeek would play that role. Johnny and Mourning Dove would be the deer. Ahmeek would have to bury his face and give the Indian children a chance to find a hiding place or to slip off into the woods, then try to find them. Of course Ahmeek knew this game well. The kids back home called it hide-and-seek, but Johnny Bearheart had added the role play to make the game more interesting.

Ahmeek would rather have been the animal being hunted instead of the hunter, but in Johnny Bearheart's game, being chosen as the hunter was an honor. The trouble was that the two Indian children knew the woods so much better and it might take him forever to find them. He might not find them at all. Ahmeek thought it was a silly game for the two twelve-years-olds, but to his surprise, Mourning Dove agreed to play with no objection. He had to admit that he still enjoyed these games too, but not today. It was his last day at Lac Vieux Desert and he didn't want to spend it sneaking through the woods all by himself.

He was looking at an old stump that he thought one of the Indian children might have chosen as a hiding place. It was tucked in among some big pine trees and was hollowed out on one side, probably from a forest fire that went through the woods many years earlier. If one of them was there, they hadn't seen him yet. He crouched down low to creep past a heavy clump of alders that formed a chamber surrounded by dense, leafy undergrowth. He felt something grasp his wrist and before he could set his feet he was yanked into the cluster of brush, Mourning Dove leaning over him, stifling a giggle and holding her hand in front of her mouth, palm forward. "Shhh," she said in case the gesture wasn't clear enough. Ahmeek could see in her smiling eyes that this was a trick she was playing on Johnny Bearheart. The Indian boy would stay securely hidden for a long time.

Ahmeek lifted himself to a kneeling position, facing Mourning Dove. She reached out and took his hands. She glanced from side to side, a sly smile crept across her face as she squeezed her fellow conspirator's hands and pulled him closer to her. No sound came from their lips as they sat looking at each other for a long time. Words could not have said so much, especially since her English was as limited as his Ojibwa. When it seemed that everything had been said that could be said, Mourning Dove quietly slid over beside him. He put his arm around her and she pressed her cheek against his. At that moment, Ahmeek wished he didn't have to go back to Wausau. It felt good to be resting here cuddling close to Mourning Dove but he knew he could not be so close to Mourning Dove for long. She was a pretty Indian girl, but she was just his friend's sister. As much as he admired Mourning Dove, he could never feel the same way about her as he did Rebecca Morgan.

Chapter 12

"Now what the hell do you want to do a thing like that for?" Jotham had heard Stanley Rodzaczk say. "Yer father needs you to help here at the camp." He had been talking to his older brother Gino.

"My Papa doesn't need me as much as my country does," Gino had responded.

"It's no use, you try to stop him," the older Marichetti had said. "When I hear what you tell me from the paper, I wish I'm young enough to go myself."

That brief conversation had taken place in April, during Jotham's annual spring visit to the logging camp. Gino had been adamant. Ever since news about the sinking of the battleship Maine down in Havana had appeared in the newspapers, he talked of nothing but going off to fight the Spaniards. By June, when Jotham returned to Lac Vieux Desert, the oldest Marichetti son was with Colonel Roosevelt, but no one knew where. Sooner or later he would be in Cuba, they thought, but for now he was probably training somewhere, Papa said. Gino had waited until war had been declared, but that was only a few weeks after Jotham had returned to Aunt Sarah's. Jotham missed his older brother, but mixed with those feelings was a deep sense of pride. He was proud of Gino, fighting for a cause he believed in. The fact that he was part of a cavalry contingent called the Rough Riders also made a big impression on the younger Marichetti.

Gino had said he was going to see other lands and do exciting things and, by golly, he was doing it, Jotham remembered. Maybe not as a sailor, like he had said, but he was doing it.

Jotham had arrived for another summer at the logging camp, but he wasn't really sure it would be just for the summer. After the eighth grade most boys in his class were going to work on their father's farms or at some store in town. Jotham knew that he could work at Lac Vieux Desert, but a new high school had been built in Wausau. He had always wanted to go to high school. He would be the first Marichetti to go, but with Gino gone, he thought his father might need him at the logging camp.

He was also anxious to see his friend Johnny Bearheart, but that would have to wait. With his older brother off to Cuba, there was going to be lot more work for him. The camp had changed little over the years, but this year it seemed to have just gotten up and moved. The work area moved constantly as loggers cut one grove of trees, then moved on to the next, but this spring the bunkhouse and cook's shanty had been torn down and rebuilt closer to the new cutting.

Jotham also saw a big change in the use of the river. A railroad spur had been put into Eagle River and all of the pulp wood for the Wausau and Rothschild paper mills was now shipped out by train. The new dam at Grandfather Falls left a spillway that was almost dried up by midsummer, so floating a big logjam down the Wisconsin as far as Wausau was no longer possible. Most of the big pine used for lumber had already been cut and the Marichetti camp had switched primarily to cutting hardwood for paper pulp.

Shipping so much timber by train meant hauling it with horses to the railhead and that meant hiring more skinners. Old John had said that was the job Jotham was going to learn; Papa Marichetti wasn't so sure. He had heard from Aunt Sarah how well Jotham was doing in school and he wanted a better life for his youngest child. Enrico Marichetti had never intended to be a logger. He had heard about the exciting life on the western frontier of the United States, and when he immigrated, he was intent on being a cowboy. He got as far west as the Dakotas, but there he found the life of a cowboy wasn't quite what the stories said it was. Most of his day had been spent, not in the saddle, but in the corral mending fences. The ranchers still let their cattle wander the open range, and that meant a spring roundup, but the movement of the railroad across the plains had eliminated long cattle drives and the young Italian found that a cowboy's life had lost its appeal.

Jotham started thinking about high school back in the sixth grade when he had heard that to be an engineer on the trains you had to have a high school education. As he got older, he gave up his dream of becoming a railroad engineer, but he still wanted to go to high school. For one thing the new school would have a football team, and as the fastest kid in one of the two grade schools in Wausau, he was sure he would be on it. Besides, he didn't want to leave his friends in Wausau. In 1898 there were no laws requiring a child to finish school and many didn't even finish the eighth grade, but among those friends who would go on to high school was Rebecca Morgan. Because the teacher had moved Jotham ahead one year, he and Rebecca were scheduled to graduate from grade school together. Jotham had decided, if Aunt Sarah could persuade his father to send him to high school, that's what he really wanted to do.

Jotham rode the saddle pony along the trail that lead from the logging camp to Land-O'-Lakes. With the extension of the railroad, the Milwaukee daily newspaper now reached northern Wisconsin and the general store at Land-O-'Lakes had a supply brought in from Eagle River. It was a morning paper, but it was always midafternoon before it got to the general store. One of Jotham's chores was to saddle Jenny every day and go to town for a paper. He used to go to Eagle River for the paper, but that was just the Sunday edition for Stanley. Stanley shared the news with the rest of the camp, most of whom couldn't read.

This summer, with Gino off with Teddy Roosevelt's Rough Riders, it was Jotham's father who wanted a daily paper to get the war news. When the elder Marichetti came home from work, Jotham's first job was to read the paper to him. His father had never learned to read nor write in English and had always depended on one of his sons if something had to be read. Jotham admired Papa for being a successful businessman with such a handicap. Of course he knew that his father's unusual ability with numbers made up for his lack of reading skills. Enrico Marichetti also had a gift for making friends, was a great storyteller and as Old John would say, "a good talker". He was never intimidated, had a reputation for being honest, and was as much at home talking to the president of a paper company as with other loggers. For the past fifteen years, since giving up the life of a cowboy, Enrico Marichetti had been a success, dealing directly with the lumber and paper mills. Many of the small jobbers sold their pulp or saw logs through him. When he handled such transactions he received a commission on the sale. There had been tough times during the past fifteen years, including a period of sluggish economy back in the '80's, but once the Fourdrinier paper-making machine had been brought into the area, the timber industry flourished.

It was only a three-mile ride to Land-O'-Lakes. The trail followed the river. Jotham was always amazed at how fast the creek coming out of Lac Vieux Desert became a full-sized river just a few miles down stream. Of course it was nowhere near the size it became by the time it got to Wausau, but there were no dams north of Eagle River to make it as wide as a small lake and flowing so slowly it didn't seem to be running at all.

Dominic and his father were waiting when Jotham rounded the last bend in the trail that lead to the Marichetti house. At his father's suggestion, Dominic took Jenny to the barn and removed the saddle so Jotham could get right to reading the paper. That the news would be several days old by the time it found its way to Land-O'-Lakes made little difference. The 1890's was not an era of instant information and old news or not, it was still news.

Jotham read how General Henry Lawton had defeated the Spanish at El Caney. Another story told about American successes in the Philippines, a wrap up of events that had happened in that remote part of the world more than a month earlier. Commodore George Dewey had destroyed the entire Spanish fleet protecting the harbor at Manila and American forces had taken over the island capital. A more recent article said that Commodore Winfield Schley had successfully established a blockade around Santiago Harbor and since May 28th the Spanish fleet in Cuba had been rendered ineffective.

"Maybe the war ends before Gino get there." The older Marichetti sighed hopefully.

"Yeah," Jotham agreed, "and if it does Gino is going to be real disappointed." Jotham didn't say so, but he sounded like he too would be disappointed if Gino had to come home without having seen action.

"You don't know war, my young son," his father said. "What else does the paper say?"

There was another story about a conflict between a logging company and a wing dam operator. This one was fought out in court, however, with the dam operator being ordered to remove his dam. New federal laws required that dam construction be cleared with the U.S. Coast Guard. Although the dam had been there when that law was passed, the judge ruled that his dam interfered with river navigation. Since the lower Wisconsin was navigable water, once a dam was lost due to natural causes, it could not be rebuilt without a federal permit. Papa Marichetti laughed at that, a judge deciding that a logjam was a natural cause. It seemed that things were finally going in favor of the loggers, but it no longer made a difference to the Marichetti camp. With the new dam at Grandfather Falls, none of their logs could be floated down river as far as the wing dams anyway.

Jotham scanned the paper looking for other articles that would interest his father. His eyes caught an ominous headline: *WATER CONTROL DAM PROJECT IN AREA FUTURE.* He started to read the article.

The demand for hydroelectric power has been so great along the Wisconsin River that the power companies are finding it hard to keep up during the dry months of August and September. A power company engineer has come up with a solution to the problem. A series of small dams will be built over the next five to ten years for the purpose of water storage. While these dams will be very small and can provide no electricity production themselves, they will hold water in a series of lakes and ponds above the hydro dams to be released when natural rainfall is too low for the power dams to operate efficiently.

The article went on to discuss the controversy between the logging interests, who wanted to continue to use the river for log transportation, and the power companies, but pointed out that most of the waterways being considered were not large enough for a cost effective logjam anyway and that, because these dams were not to be built on navigable waters, they could be constructed without the permission of the U.S. Coast Guard.

Marichetti listened with concerned interest, but when Jotham finished reading the article his reaction was not rage, but resignation. He knew the days of big timber and logjams would not last much longer. That was not the case in the bunkhouse where Stanley Rodzaczk, the undisputed gazetteer of the logging camp read the same article aloud to his coworkers.

"Damn it, Frank," Stanley yelled. "We don't have enough big timber left to put a logjam together. It's all pulp wood now. When was the last time you rode a logjam to Wausau anyway?"

"Two years ago," Frank replied, "but that don't make no difference. How 'bout Marty Frederickson and the other guys on the east side? They still got pine and they still need to float logs to the mill."

"Frank's right," Swede cut in, "Those guys can't make it on pulp wood."

"You bet," Frank said. "You dam this river and she's all over for them."

"Well it don't say they're gonna dam this river," Stanley said. "They're just talkin' about the little creeks that run into the Wisconsin they want to dam."

"Ya," Swede responded, "That's all they dam, but if they dam the water from those creeks, where's the water come from to carry a log. Be just this little trickle out of Lac Vieux Desert all the way to Eagle River."

"It don't make no difference anyway," Stanley said. "By the time they build one of those little dams, the big timber here will be all gone."

"It'll be gone all right," Frank agreed, "and I'll be gone with it, but before I go, I'm gonna find those dam builders and pound some sense into 'em. Mark my words."

Chapter 13

A whole week had gone by before Jotham had a chance to go out into the woods to see if he could find his Indian friends. Of course he no longer believed that Old Eagle Feather had any special powers to find him so he went directly to the Lac Vieux Desert village. He was happy to see the old Indian, and Johnny Bearheart looked as strong as ever and just a little bit older than last year. After an exchange of warm greetings with Old Eagle Feather and his grandson and a tactful interval of silence, Ahmeek asked where Mourning Dove was.

"Mourning Dove stay with women," the old man replied. "Must not play in woods with brother and white boy."

"Why not?" Ahmeek asked, innocently.

"Mourning Dove is no longer a child. Now she's a woman of thirteen summers. When a young man and young woman are no longer children, an Indian woman must stay with an Indian man and a white man with a white woman. It is time for Mourning Dove to be a woman and to find a young brave in village to marry, to raise many papooses, great-grandchildren for Eagle Feather."

There was a note of finality in Eagle Feather's voice and Ahmeek knew he should not pursue the topic further. Assured that his message had been understood, Eagle Feather continued, "We are happy to see you again, Ahmeek. You too have grown." The old man turned and went into his wigwam.

"It is the Indian way," Johnny Bearheart said, after the

old man was out of sight. "We cannot change it."

"I know."

"Good, let's go hunt *wabasso*."

Ahmeek and Johnny Bearheart did hunt rabbit, not only on that day but on many other days. Ahmeek quickly transferred the skills, learned with the toy bows that he and Johnny had made as small boys, to his new hunting bow and soon he was surprisingly accurate. Johnny showed him how to hunt with bow and arrow. They hunted together often bagging many rabbits and squirrels and on one occasion a small deer. The young Indian boy even taught him how to use the bow and arrow to catch fish.

Johnny Bearheart held the arrowhead right next to the water's surface and let go of the bowstring. Then he quickly reached in and lifted the six-pound walleye from the water. The fish flopped wildly, trying to shake the arrow that pierced its body just left of the dorsal fin.

"You see, Ahmeek," Johnny Bearheart said, "hold the arrow close to the waters."

Ahmeek tried several times, but all he found was his empty arrow floating back to the surface. "It's no use Johnny," Ahmeek said. "I can't seem to hit any of them."

"You aim too high," Johnny Bearheart said. "Fish is not where you see him in the water. You must shoot below what you see. Then you will get him."

Ahmeek tried and much to his surprise the arrow disappeared under water and surfaced again several feet away with another big walleye.

"Wow!" Ahmeek exclaimed. "I thought I was shooting way below him."

"The water plays tricks on your white man's eyes, my friend," Johnny Bearheart teased.

"Don't let the white skin fool you," Ahmeek answered. "I have Indian eyes, like the eagle's."

Some times Johnny Bearheart and Ahmeek just sat by the lake or river and talked. Ahmeek had known his Indian friend a long time, but until now, he thought, he hadn't really known him at all. When they were children they had no time for talk. He had known nothing of the young Indian's past life or his dreams for the future. It hadn't occurred to him that Indian children had such dreams.

Johnny Bearheart was the product of Eagle Feather's teaching. He loved the land and could not understand the white man's desire to change it. Yet, he had learned about the white man's world in the government school and wanted some of the advantages of that world too. He was fascinated when Ahmeek told him about electricity coming to Wausau and thought an electric light in the wigwam would make an Indian boy's life a lot better. He wanted someday to leave the Indian village so he could see all the things he had read about in the white man's cities.

He asked Ahmeek about riding on the trains. He was sure the train trips Ahmeek had taken to get to Lac Vieux Desert were a lot of fun. Ahmeek made the train sound so fast, and Johnny Bearheart liked speed. He ran fast through the woods and paddled his canoe fast over the lake. He could imagine riding behind a steam engine with the wind whistling through his long black hair. He had read in his school books how the Indians in the west rode fast ponies and he wished the Chippewa had ponies to ride.

Ahmeek wanted his friendship with Johnny Bearheart to last forever. The Indian boy was his link to a way of life he had learned to love almost as much as his own. Deep down in his heart he knew that it would change. Old Eagle Feather was right. He had heard the men in the camp talk about the way they felt about Indians. He had heard the people in town, even people with good intentions, like Aunt Sarah, believed there should be no social discourse between the Indians and whites. They looked at Indians, Ahmeek thought, like they were something less than human. What had Aunt Sarah called them back when he first became friends with Johnny Bearheart? Savages, she had said, uncivilized. They had their own civilization, he thought. It wasn't the same as the white man's civilization, but if white people could learn to understand them the way he had, how they lived and what they believed, they certainly wouldn't call them savages.

He thought about the history book he had read in school and what it had said about Indians. It was full of stories about the Indian wars out west. Practically nothing was ever said about the Algonquin, the so-called "Woodland Indians." He could find nothing about the beliefs and legends of any of these native people, the stories Old Eagle Feather had told him. *That book wasn't the history of the Indians,* he thought. It was fiction, reports of the people's impressions, pioneers, who had gone to the frontier, afraid of the unknown and armed only with ignorance. Their heads only held the stories of those who had gone before them and been attacked by people whose lands they were about to invade, stories embellished so much that they had only a grain of truth remaining. To make the heroes appear more brave, the villains had to be made more brutal, and that brutality became the settlers' image of the Indian.

Jotham shared his concern with his brother Dominic. Dominic didn't tease him any more, the way he used to. With Gino gone, Jotham was the only brother Dominic could talk with and besides, now that Jotham was a teenager, they could have serious discussions. One night after they had all gone to bed, Jotham told his brother what had happened at the village. Of course he had long ago told him about Old Eagle Feather and his grandchildren.

"You know, Dominic," Jotham said, "with all the progress made in the world people should have learned to get along together. After all, this is 1898."

"People from civilized countries can't even get along," Dominic answered. "Haven't ya ever read the Bible? I used to go to Sunday school and I remember most of the Old Testament was just one war after another."

"Yeah, if the whole country can be at war against Spain, how can I expect anyone to understand a white boy and a couple of Indian kids being friends? After all, no one thinks of the Spaniards as uncivilized savages."

Jotham became silent again, thinking. No matter how long he thought about it he couldn't escape the conclusion that Old Eagle Feather was right. Perhaps someday things would be different, but for now, the world just wasn't ready.

"Jotham?" Dominic's voice interrupted his thoughts.

"Yeah?"

"What about your girlfriend in Wausau?"

"Rebecca," Jotham answered. "What about her?"

"Well, Pa says you're going to go to high school and if you go to high school Rebecca and all the kids down there will be your real friends, won't they?" Before Jotham could answer Dominic continued. "I mean Rebecca, and the kids in your school. They're your real friends, aren't they?"

"Well, yeah. I guess so," Jotham admitted.

Though he said it, Jotham didn't know himself what he meant. He and Rebecca Morgan had grown closer and closer during the school year. All the other kids at the school in Wausau knew that Rebecca was Jotham's girl and none of the other boys would dare try to change that. Though it took a long time, he had gotten used to the idea of Rebecca as his girlfriend and when he was in Wausau he never thought about how his Indian friends fit into the picture.

He had spent so many summers with the Indians, and so many winters in Wausau that it was like two totally different worlds, almost as though he were two totally different people, Jotham and Ahmeek. The teacher and Aunt Sarah still called him Jotham and expected him to behave as they thought a Jotham should. None of the Indians ever called him Jotham. At their village that Jotham person had ceased to exist. Only Rebecca knew the whole person. Like other children, she used his real name in school or when grownups were around, but when they were alone or with their closest friends, she called him Ahmeek.

Jotham was afraid this could be the longest and saddest summer he ever spent at Lac Vieux Desert. He would learn that he was wrong about it being long. It would go fast, but even he couldn't anticipate how right he was about it being sad.

Chapter 14

Ahmeek still saw Johnny Bearheart, but he saw Old Eagle Feather a lot less. That pattern had started to develop more than a year earlier when the children began to show signs of greater independence. The old man had apparently told them all the stories that he had to tell. Ahmeek had less time to spend in the woods now that he was older and had a lot more chores to do. Johnny Bearheart came to the logging camp frequently. He helped Jotham with his chores so they would have more time to hunt or practice with the bow and arrow. Over the years, though the Indians and the white loggers had not become friends, they had learned to tolerate each other's presence and on some occasions, when they had interests in common, to communicate.

Jotham spent almost as much time with Dominic as he did with Johnny Bearheart. He went hunting with his brother, much like he did with the Indian boy, but not with bow and arrow. Dominic carried their father's Winchester 73. Jotham carried a .44-caliber Colt revolver, the only other firearm his father owned. Dominic was an expert with both weapons and a good teacher for Jotham. Not satisfied with just teaching his brother how to shoot, he also taught him how to use a gun safely.

"There's just one rule," he said, "and if you never break it I can guarantee you won't have an accident with a gun. Never, never point a gun at anything you don't want to shoot."

Of course no matter how important that rule was,

Dominic knew it would be broken; so he also taught Jotham all the other things he should know to use a gun safely.

"Don't chamber a bullet until you get to where you're gonna hunt," he said, "and then be real careful how you lower the hammer so the gun don't go off accidentally."

Jotham knew how important that was. One of the loggers in the camp didn't pay attention to that rule when he leaned his gun against a fence so he could climb over it. When he inadvertently bumped the fence, the twelve-gauge shotgun had fallen, discharged, and sent a load of BB shot into his calf. The damage was so severe that the doctors had to amputate his leg just below the knee. For the rest of his life he walked on a wooden peg where his left leg used to be. That was Peg Leg Blake, but even with a wooden leg his dad said he was as good a sawyer as anybody he'd ever worked with.

Dominic knew a lot more about shooting than just safety rules. He hunted frequently and kept the camp in meat much of the winter. He could shoot a tin can with the Winchester, whip the lever back to chamber another shell and shoot it again before it stopped rolling, then repeat the process until he had emptied all seven bullets from the magazine. When Jotham ran to pick up the can he would always find seven holes. Then Dominic would toss another can and do the same thing with the Colt .44, except there'd be six holes because the Colt only held six bullets. No matter how hard Jotham tried he always had to wait until the can lay still on the ground before he fired the second shot. He had the consolation, however, of knowing that Dominic couldn't hit the broad side of a barn with a bow and arrow and Jotham could hit just about anything Dominic set up within a hundred and fifty feet.

"Jeez, Jotham," Dominic said, "Ya spend so much time with those Indians I think yer gettin' to be one of `em yerself."

"Think we can go hunting this winter?" Jotham asked.

"Maybe at Christmas time," Dominic responded, "but there ain't much to hunt then except a few snowshoe rabbits. By then the deer are all yarded up so far back in the swamps it'd take all day just to get to 'em and the bear are hidden away sleepin' all winter."

"I thought maybe I'd stay here this winter and we could go hunting before the deer start to herd. Dad says he's going to let me learn to be a skinner."

"Yeah, he'll let ya learn to be a skinner, Jotham, but not for winter work. You know him and yer Aunt Sarah want you to keep goin' to school, maybe even college. He figures you can learn to drive the teams that pull the scoot next summer when we get the pulp wood out."

Jotham didn't know whether to be disappointed or pleased. There wasn't any school in the summertime and he'd have to work in the logging camp. Being a skinner was what he wanted. It was what his father had said he would do, but what impressed him about it wasn't the two and four horse teams that skidded the pulp wood out over the bare ground, but the big six- and eight-horse teams that he had seen bring saw logs out over the ice-covered logging roads in the winter. Of course, with the depletion of the big pine, the winter work was mostly hauling pulp wood too.

As much as he might like to stay in the lumber camp with Dominic and his father, he also missed his friends in Wausau and was excited about having a chance to continue his education. There seemed to be so much to learn and he wanted to learn it all. He wanted to learn to shoot like Dominic, to drive the horses like Old John and to run a train or be a banker or a judge or one of those other jobs that the people in town did, maybe even a surveyor like his uncle Oliver.

He also knew he wanted to see Rebecca Morgan again. That wouldn't have seemed important a couple of years ago but now he was almost fourteen years old and girls were becoming very important to him. In fact, that was the one thing he hated about the logging camp this summer. There just weren't any girls around. He spent a lot of time thinking about girls in general and about Rebecca Morgan in particular. He and Dominic talked about girls, but Dominic had a different way of looking at things. Whenever Dominic went to Eagle River, the girls all swarmed around him, but it seemed to Jotham that his brother paid no attention to them. Dominic had dark wavy hair and a perpetual smile. He wasn't tall, but stocky. He never did seem to go through that awkward stage that Jotham was just beginning to experience, a feeling of being all arms and legs. Jotham was already taller than Dominic, but not nearly as broad-shouldered. Jotham was at his best in school, and though he liked his visits to the logging camp, if he was really honest with himself, he knew that he wanted to go back to school come fall.

Enrico Marichetti was gone for the two days before the big Fourth of July celebration, a double celebration at the Lac Vieux Desert logging camp. It was also on the fourth of July that they celebrated Jotham's birthday. His birthday was actually on July fifth, but celebrating two days in a row seemed like it would be a little too much, so the tradition of Jotham's birthday party and Independence Day fireworks on the same day had been well-established. In the summer of '98 the festivities were much more elaborate, more food, more fireworks, more of everything. That was because, in addition to reaching fourteen years, Jotham had just graduated from the eighth grade, an accomplishment worthy of note in those days. There was also a surge of patriotism resulting from the war with Spain that was constantly fed by the newspapers Jotham brought back from the general store in Land-O'-Lakes.

Jotham's father brought the fireworks when he came back from Wausau. He had gone to meet with officials of the railroad and arranged to buy timber stumpage. The railroads were expanding as rapidly as the power companies and they had bought up large tracts of land where plans were underway for trunk lines. Ten years earlier loggers had to deal with the state and federal governments to buy timber stumpage, but ownership had shifted to private corporations and most of those corporations were railroads.

After a scrumptious meal of venison supplied by Dominic, and fresh fruits and vegetables — the likes of which the men in the logging camp rarely saw including two of Jotham's favorites, oranges and bananas — the cook brought out a birthday cake for both Jotham and the nation. It was decorated with a picture of the American flag, a new one with forty-five stars for all forty-five states including Utah, which had just entered the union two years earlier. It was the biggest birthday cake Jotham had ever seen. The fourteen candles on it didn't even look like they were close together and that disappointed him because he thought it made fourteen seem a lot younger than it was. After Jotham's second big piece of cake they all sang happy birthday and then Swede got up and gave a toast to the wonderful country where he and his friends had immigrated. Stanley followed with a special toast to the young Marichetti boy, Gino, who, serving that country with Teddy Roosevelt and the Rough Riders, was someplace in Cuba. Stanley's toast brought a big cheer from the whole camp and Jotham couldn't hold back the tear of pride for his brother that ran down his cheek. Oddly nobody mentioned it, though it must have been obvious. That was because many of the others, including some of the toughest lumberjacks, were feeling just a little extra moisture in their eyes too.

Outside, Stanley and Frank set off skyrockets and Roman candles. They were given the job because Jotham's father was sure Stanley Rodzaczk was the only person who could read the directions well enough to do it safely. The Frenchman could help because he would take directions from Stanley, even if he wouldn't listen to anyone else. The Roman candles didn't go very high into the air, but Jotham and Dominic watched with awe as the skyrockets went up and up before exploding in a cluster of multicolored stars. Jotham wondered if the Indians could see the skyrockets and, if they could, what Old Eagle Feather and his people thought of them. The fireworks they had on other Fourth of July holidays hadn't been so elaborate and the big skyrockets that went so high up were a new addition. In years past they'd mostly had some firecrackers for Gino and Dominic to set off during the day and just a few Roman candles at night.

The next morning was Sunday. It was a good thing because everybody was up so late the night before that nobody felt like going to work. Jotham had his job though. He went to the shed and got the saddle out for Jenny. The pony was in the same corral that Old John had built the year they got her. His father bought Jenny just before the Fourth of July the first year Jotham was old enough to start riding into town for newspapers. That was three years ago, on his eleventh birthday. After last night he thought, maybe he should have named her Skyrocket.

Jotham couldn't hear a single sound coming from the direction of the camp when he rode by. He slapped the reins lightly on Jenny's neck and she broke into a trot. It was a good ride to Land-O'-Lakes and he wanted to get back before it got too late. The men in the camp, especially Stanley, would be wanting their Sunday paper.

By the time he returned the loggers had completed the morning routine of cleaning their area of the bunkhouse, having made their beds and eaten breakfast in the cook's shanty. Other items like checking equipment to be sure it was ready for the day's work were not a part of the Sunday routine, but a thorough check would be made before retiring that night. Most of the men sat outside to enjoy the fresh summer air and engage in a favorite activity. Frank was whittling. Swede was sitting on the wooden rack that held the grindstone, sharpening his axe. Stanley was sitting, waiting for the paper. He was patient, just enjoying his surroundings. Jotham looked over at Swede. He thought the wood frame that supported the grindstone might collapse under the huge man's weight. The whole thing, stone and all, which must have weighed at least one-hundred pounds, shifted from side to side as his heavy foot went up and down on the pedal board. The board was attached by an iron rod to a small crank on the side of the stone wheel, which was about two feet in diameter but looked much smaller under Swede's broadax.

Jotham walked over to Stanley, handed him the Sunday paper and found a comfortable place to sit down. Stanley read the front page of the paper intently. Then he scanned other pages, reading some articles, skipping others before handing sections over to Jotham. He anxiously waited, wanting to get the news, but recognizing that it was Stanley's paper and he had priority. After the lumberjack was through with the paper, Jotham would gather the several sections together again and take them to read to his father, who wanted all the news about the war.

While Jotham waited, he read some of the back sections. This is where he found many of the items that were of greatest interest to him. He saw that Robert La Follette — "Fighting Bob" the newspapers called him — had said he would run for governor of Wisconsin in the next election. The appellation "Fighting Bob" had been conferred by reporters in response to LaFollette's successes in fighting the political machine in Wisconsin for the past eight years. There was another story about an airplane with a motor, but no pilot, flown by Pierpont Langley, the director of the Smithsonian Museum. The article said the craft had been powered by a steam engine. Jotham didn't imagine there was much practical value in that. He was impressed by the big steam engines that pulled the train load of logs out of Eagle River, but to try to make one fly didn't make a lot of sense. He had, however, read a lot of things about the Smithsonian Museum in Washington and hoped he would be able to go there someday. An item that interested him was another story about Clarence Darrow winning the right to strike for labor unions. Jotham wasn't sure about this right to strike business, particularly after the riots at the Pullman strike in Chicago, but he was fascinated by the lawyer himself. He had read other stories about Darrow, especially his defense of the underdog. He thought that if he wasn't going to stay in the logging camp with his father and Dominic, if he was going to go back to Wausau for four more years to finish high school, then he might as well plan on going to college too and maybe someday he could become a lawyer.

There wasn't a lot of news about the war in the paper this particular Sunday, but what there was caused a stir in the logging camp. Teddy Roosevelt's Rough Riders, it said, had taken San Juan Hill in Cuba. That had happened on July first. It took more than a day for that news to travel to Miami, the dispatcher having to wait for a naval ship that was making the trip for supplies, but once in Miami it was transmitted by telegraph to Associated Press Headquarters on the East Coast and then relayed to all the subscribing newspapers across the country. The attempt by Pascual Cervera to run Schley's blockade of Santiago Harbor on Friday, which resulted in the loss of the whole Spanish fleet, would be several days yet getting to the news-rooms of Associated Press. There was also a short item about Colonel "Blackjack" Pershing's successful campaigns in the Philippines, but that was about it for the war news.

Stanley put down the comics and picked up a cross-word puzzle. He reached into his pocket and retrieved a stub of pencil, inspected it and seeing that the lead was broken, dug deeper into his pocket for his knife. Before he could find it Jotham handed him his own jackknife.

"Okay if I take the funnies?" Jotham asked.

"Sure, go ahead. I'm through with them." Stanley started to sharpen the pencil. He paid no attention to the thump-thump, of the axe hitting a tree a few yards behind them. After he rubbed his fingers over the pencil point to see that it was sharp enough, he handed the knife back to Jotham and reached for his crossword. Inches before his fingers touched it the axe came sliding along the ground and whipped the paper away from his outstretched hand.

"What the hell?"

Stanley jumped up to see where the axe came from just as Frank stepped out from the other side of the tree. Pay-ing no attention to Jotham and Stanley, he started to pick up his axe.

"Frank, what the hell are you doing?" Stanley asked with a pretense of anger in his voice. Stanley and Frank were bunkmates and though Stanley knew that he was the only lumberjack who could get away with reprimanding the Frenchman, he also knew a serious complaint would do no good.

"Sorry. I guess I missed the tree," Frank admitted. "I was just practicing my axe throwing and I missed with that last throw. I didn't see you guys sittin' there."

"Jeez, no brains at all," Stanley answered, a sing-song lilt in his voice suggesting he had said the same thing many times before under similar circumstances.

"Watch your tongue, *monsieur*, or we send you back to mother Russia!"

Jotham sat back a little and laughed. He had watched this scene played for his benefit a number of times before and by now he knew the routine by heart.

"Russia?" Stanley yelled.

"Yeah, Russia. With a name like Rodzaczk, what else could you be?"

"Ya damn Frenchman, you know I come from Poland."

"Poland? If you were a Polack your name wouldn't be Rodzaczk, it would be Rodzaski."

"I'll Rodzaski you, ya French lunatic, you throw that axe at me again." Stanley reached down and picked up the axe.

"Well, make up your mind." Frank continued "Which is it, a Polack Rodzaski or a Russian Rodzaczk? I told ya I was throwin' at the tree."

The Frenchman reached for the axe, but Stanley pulled back and held it out of his reach.

"Come on, give me my axe, ya Russki."

Stanley tossed the axe toward the tree Frank had been throwing it at. Moments later both men were on the ground wrestling. Of course Frank could have whipped Stanley in less than a minute if he'd wanted to fight, to box, but this was a friendly scuffle and he played by rules that would make it an even match. After a respectable time the Frenchman allowed himself to be pinned to the ground and the match ended with both contestants and Jotham laughing heartily.

"What's in the news?" Frank asked.

"Teddy Roosevelt's Rough Riders beat the Spaniards at some hill in Cuba," Jotham answered proudly.

"San Juan Hill," Stanley added.

"Gino's with the Rough Riders, hey?" the Frenchman responded. "He'll be a fighter, he will."

"He is a fighter," Jotham said. He picked up the newspaper. "I gotta take these and read the news to my pa."

The next week was a week of hard work. The corn had become too big to cultivate but other parts of the garden had to be tended. The potatoes needed to be hilled, a job Jotham thought was one of the hardest of all his chores. He also continued to carry wood to the cook's shanty and by Wednesday Jotham felt like the week should be over. Tired as he was, he had to accept the fact that it had only reached the midpoint. Wednesday wasn't a day off, but he looked forward to it because on Wednesdays he rode to Land-O'-Lakes to get the mail. He went in twice a week, Wednesday and Saturday, and since he knew how to read better than anyone else in the camp it was his job to sort the few letters that came in and be sure that each one got to the person whose name was on the envelope. He had saddled Jenny and made a quick trip, coming home at a fast trot because there was a letter in the bag addressed to his papa. Since Enrico Marichetti didn't read a word of English, Jotham wondered why he would be getting a letter, especially a letter from Colonel Roosevelt. He hurried as fast as he could, delivering all the mail to the men in the camp. When he dropped the last letter on the lumberjack's bunk, he rushed home to bring the letter from Colonel Roosevelt to his father. As he ran he let his imagination run wild. He thought maybe Gino had done something special. Maybe he was a war hero and the colonel was writing to tell his pa about it. He dashed into the house and called to the elder Marichetti. Then he opened the envelope, unfolded the letter and began to read.

"I regret to inform you that your son Gino Marichetti..." Jotham started to choke as he continued to read. He felt a big lump in his throat and a tear rolled down his cheek. Colonel Roosevelt went on to say that Gino had died a hero, bravely charging the Spaniards at San Juan Hill and that his father should be proud of him and the sacrifice he made. Enrico Marichetti sat heavily in his chair as he listened. Death of a loved one was not a new experience for him but he dropped his head and began to weep.

Chapter 15

Jotham stood atop the *scoot* load of logs and guided the four-horse team along the crooked trail that led to the landing. The pulp sticks would be hauled by wagon from there to the rail spur, then loaded onto gondolas for the trip to the mill. Unlike saw logs, pulp for the paper mills was hardwood, usually poplar, and too heavy for log booms. In addition, dam development on the central part of the Wisconsin prevented floating a logjam that far. The trails back into the slashing areas were too rough and twisted for the wagons. In the winter, when the scoot slid over the snowpack, a skinner could sit on the logs and have an easy ride, but this was not winter. Jotham worked in the camp only in the summer time and the bumps and rocks along the snowless trail made sitting impossible. Instead he stood on the bouncing and often shifting load, trying to absorb the jostling with his knees.

Jotham enjoyed working in the woods. Being a skinner was hard work, but that just toughened him up for football in the fall. When his father and Old John told him about skidding logs, he'd only thought about driving the big four-horse teams. He hadn't known that he would also have to load heavy hardwood bolts, sometimes by himself, onto the scoot, then unload them onto the high piles that stretched across the landing area. In addition to exercise, he enjoyed the mental relaxation. He felt that he was best able to think when he was doing something physical. This was his third summer skidding wood; winters still devoted to school. As he drove around a sharp bend he thought back on those three years. A lot had happened. For one thing they had managed to move into a new century without the world coming to an end as some oracles had predicted. "Fighting Bob" La Follette had become Governor, the first Governor of Wisconsin to have been born in the state. The Spanish-American war had ended almost as quickly as it had started, but not soon enough for Gino. He had read that of over five thousand soldiers from Wisconsin who fought in that war only one-hundred thirty-four had died. His eyes became moist. Gino never had a chance to achieve his dream of traveling the whole world. He had gotten only as far as Cuba.

Maybe it was the sharp curve in the trail, maybe it was the sun shining through the treetops, or maybe it was the tear that had blurred his vision, but just then one runner of the scoot struck a low stump. Jotham was able to retain his balance as the load shifted wildly. Then it righted itself, but not before one of the logs slipped off the front stake. The forward end of the log, a big one, over a foot in diameter, dug into the soft earth. The stake at the back of the dray held fast and upended the log so that it swept across the top of the load, caught Jotham in the buttocks and hurled him some fifteen feet ahead and to the right side of the trail. The horses, feeling the resistance from the stump, stopped just about the same time Jotham hit the ground beside them and rolled several feet down the track. He lay in a pile of soft brush, stunned. After a minute or two he tried to move. Much to his surprise, nothing seemed to hurt. He thought surely he would have a broken leg or at least a sprained ankle. He appeared to have no such injuries. With a sigh of relief he thought, *Just knocked the wind out of me,* and he put his head back and closed his eyes. He had barely caught his breath again when he heard footsteps running toward him.

"You okay?"

Jotham opened his eyes. "Yeah," he said, "I guess." Then it occurred to him how ridiculous he must have looked, flying though the air like that, and he started to laugh.

Johnny Bearheart joined in his laughter. "Ahmeek! You are the beaver. You look like you're trying to be the eagle."

"Johnny! What are you doing here?" Jotham rarely saw

Johnny Bearheart any more. His work at the camp left him much too tired to hunt with his old friend and both boys had grown apart as they had grown up.

"I come to look for you."

"Well, you found me. But I wish I'd been standing on my feet. What happened anyway?" He looked back and saw the big log lying beside the trail. "Damn, that's a big one! I had to get Smiley Bartle to help me load it."

"I'll help you." Johnny extended his hand and pulled his old friend to his feet. Then they walked over to the log and lifted it back onto the load.

"Why were you looking for me?" Jotham asked.

"I came to tell you about the feast," Johnny Bearheart replied, "to ask you to come."

"Feast?"

"Yes. A young brave in the village, Jimmy Little Wind, killed a big doe and brought it to Yellow Wing, mother of Mourning Dove. There will be a feast..." Johnny Bearheart stopped.

Neither man spoke. Jotham knew the Chippewa custom. When a young man found the woman he wanted, he would first serenade her with the courting flute. To let the girl's family know he intended to marry her, he would kill an animal and offer it to them, to assure them he would be a good provider for their daughter. If the family invited him to stay for a feast, it meant that permission for him to marry the young maiden was given.

Johnny Bearheart broke the silence. "She is granddaughter of Eagle Feather. He sent me to tell you and to ask you to come."

"It has been a long time since I've been to the village," Jotham said.

"He is an old man," the Indian boy continued. "He sees you like his own son, or grandson. For his happiness, for Mourning Dove's happiness, you will come to the feast?"

Jotham smiled, an understanding smile. "I will come. When is the feast?"

That settled, the young men sat beside the trail to renew their friendship. They reminisced about the times they played together as children and about the lessons learned under the skillful tutorship of Old Eagle Feather.

Johnny confided that at first he was fooled by his sister's errands, but he soon realized they were just a ruse to allow her and Jotham to be alone. He regretted that their ways had separated, but said he could not live the life of the white man. Jotham admitted that he was becoming more and more a part of the white man's world, but that he would never forget what he had learned with Johnny Bearheart and Eagle Feather. At the end of the visit, Johnny Bearheart slid silently into the woods and Jotham mounted his load of logs, started the horses and returned to the camp.

"Well, Jotham. So you are going to be a lawyer?" Stanley of course knew what Jotham's plans were. Everyone in the camp knew that Jotham had one year of high school left and then he planned to study law. The question was just a matter of formality, sort of a ritual that would set the agenda for cook-shanty conversation.

"I guess so," Jotham replied. "The coach at high school says if I have a good football season he might be able to get me into a college where they would give me some sort of job so I could play football for them. Maybe even the University of Wisconsin in Madison."

"Jotham, I used to think you were growin' up bad 'cause you were bein' too much of an Indian," Smiley Bartle chimed in, "but now I got to admit I was wrong."

"Thanks Smiley."

"Ya, bein' a Indian ain't half bad as bein' a lawyer."

That brought a laugh from everyone including Jotham. He was used to the friendly jibes that characterized cook-shanty talk.

"What ever happened to that little squaw you used to go out to see?" Smiley asked.

"She grew up so it was time to quit seeing her."

"Well, you was smart to quit. You remembered what I told you."

"Na, it wasn't that," Jotham added. "Some of the tribe saw you one day and decided that an Indian girl ought to find a better class of folks to hang around with than a lumberjack."

Another round of laughter and the score was even.

Jotham usually enjoyed this mealtime banter. It made him feel like he was part of the lumberjack clan instead of a summer visitor. On this occasion, however, he was just playing the game. He didn't tell them Mourning Dove was getting married. He knew that would bring comments from Smiley Bartle that he couldn't take as a friendly joke.

"Well, you better hurry up and get that schoolin' so you can come back here and get an injunction or somethin' to stop those power people from blockin' up the rivers."

"Injunction hell," Frank broke in. "The Polack reads too much. The only way we'll stop 'em is a good fight. Just let me and Swede go and talk some sense into them."

"I agree with the Frenchman," Smiley Bartle said. "Those dam people own the law. They got the judges on their side. The only way you're going to keep the rivers open is if all the loggers band together and don't let 'em come in."

Pretty soon everybody was talking at once, most agreeing that some kind of fight was the only way to save the waterways. Jotham wanted to say something that might bring them back to their senses, but he knew that things had gone too far for anyone to listen to a high school kid. Then he saw his father stand up and heard his baritone voice booming out over the din.

"Hey, shut up you mouth and listen a little. You all talkin' crazy. You want to talk with your fists, huh Frank? You'll just end up spendin' more time in jail. I'm talkin' to the electric company people over by Tomahawk. They said the dams up north here are gonna have a sluice. Only one log at a time, but the loggers still cuttin' pine can float their logs past."

"One log at a time and it takes forever," Frank yelled.

"How else you gonna do it?" Marichetti answered. "Ya gotta cut the boom to get past the rapids anyway. You work for me, you don't fight the dam owners."

"Awright," Frank conceded, "but the independent jobbers won't agree to that. They keep buildin' dams farther upriver and they'll have a small war on their hands. Mark my word."

There was a bit of grumbling and mumbling but soon the lumbermen went on to discussing other subjects.

Jotham knew that the trouble was far from over. The newspaper reported that one of the independent loggers had
been arrested for shooting a dam operator, but no one was
sure it had anything to do with the dam. Rumors were
floating around that the logger caught the dam operator
with his wife. The trial was still a few weeks off.

Jotham arrived at the tribal village just a little late, hoping to stay in the background as much as possible, but
Johnny Bearheart spotted him immediately and took him
by the arm. Johnny led Jotham through the crowd and
introduced him to Jimmy Little Wind. Jimmy Little Wind
was a handsome brave who looked very capable of providing for Mourning Dove. He was tall for a Chippewa, but
the high cheek bones and shoulder-length black hair
marked him as a member of the tribe. He greeted Jotham
warmly, a demeanor that made Jotham feel strangely un-
comfortable.

After greeting other members of the tribe who remembered him from his childhood visits, Jotham took his place
beside Johnny Bearheart and Old Eagle Feather. As he ate
the venison and wild rice, his eyes momentarily caught
those of Mourning Dove. She immediately looked down.
Neither she nor Jotham allowed themselves to smile.
Jotham knew that would not be permitted. If he had smiled
at her it might not have been taken as anything improper,
but if she returned a smile it would be interpreted as flirt-
ing, a behavior that was a serious taboo for a married
woman in the Ojibwa culture. No matter how much her
new husband may have understood, he would be expected
to punish her and she would be shunned by other members of the tribe. Jotham knew this was the way of the
Chippewa, but that did not make the situation any less
distressing. He wanted to greet her, to say the kind of
things he would have had it been a white girl's wedding,
but he could only look and hope that she understood.

Mourning Dove was married to Jimmy Little Wind. To
Jotham it was symbolic of the separation of the races.
Everyone understood that separation more than he, for of
all those present, only he had breached the barrier that
stood between the *Anishnabeg* and the white man. How

firm that barrier was became even more apparent in the weeks that followed.

Jotham's friendship with Johnny Bearheart continued. He no longer had time to visit the Indian village as often, but Johnny Bearheart came to the camp frequently to help him finish work a little earlier so they could spend the evening hunting or fishing. Unlike the Plains Indians, the Chippewa did not use horses in their day-to-day life. They engaged in little agriculture and, while a few had adopted the white man's riding habits, most preferred to travel through the woods on foot or over the water in a canoe. Sometimes Jotham gave Johnny Bearheart the reins and the young Indian mastered driving the team as quickly as he did everything else he tried. Impressed with his ability to drive and willingness to work, Enrico Marichetti hired the Indian boy to help his son and to take over the job when Jotham returned to school. A few of the loggers grumbled about having an Indian in camp, especially sharing the table with him in the cook's shanty, but soon even Smiley Bartle learned to control his tongue when Johnny Bearheart and Jotham were around.

Two of the fastest horses were hitched to the wagon and Johnny Bearheart sat on the plank across the front holding the reins. He waited patiently for Jotham to come out with his two travel bags. It was time for Jotham to return to Wausau for his final year of high school. If Johnny Bearheart was to skid logs come fall, he needed cold weather gear so he was going to drive Jotham to Eagle River. They planned to stop at the general store before train time and buy the things the Indian youth needed.

Johnny Bearheart talked constantly as they rode. He had never been to a town as big as Eagle River and the only store he had seen was the little general store in Land-O'-Lakes. Also, he had never had money before and was anxious to see what he could buy with his first month's pay. He quickly tied the horses and followed Jotham inside. He had never seen so many things: food, clothing of all kinds, tools and hardware items. Jotham helped him pick out good sturdy work clothes and select a size that would fit. Boots, socks and a heavy jacket were the most important. The storekeeper scowled as he watched Johnny Bearheart try on a pair of boots.

Having found a complete outfit of work clothes with time to spare before Jotham's train was scheduled to leave, they walked through the store looking at other items while the storekeeper continued to keep a sharp eye on them.

"Wow!" Johnny Bearheart exclaimed. He had picked up a hunting knife with a bright pearl handle and a smooth, sharp blade. The hilt and butt plate were nickel-plated and he thought owning such a knife would make him the envy of the village. He slid the instrument back into its leather sheath, then to see how it looked, slipped it under his belt.

"What are you doin', you thief," the storekeeper yelled as he hurried across the store.

Johnny Bearheart was startled and, had it not been for Jotham's reassuring hand on his shoulder, would have darted out the door.

"Wait," Jotham cautioned. "It's okay."

"You heard me," the storekeeper shouted. "What are you doin' with that knife?"

"I only want to see how it looks," Johnny Bearheart answered.

"Sure, you want to see how it looks 'til you walk out the door with it," the storekeeper continued. "I know when one of you Indians is tryin' to steal something from me."

"Just a minute," Jotham cut in. "You've got no right to say that."

"You don't understand, son. You can't be too careful with his kind. I don't know what a good-lookin' young man like you is doin', hangin' around with one of these thievin' Indians anyway."

"I do not steal," Johnny Bearheart said. "If I want it, I will pay for it. I have money."

"Money," the storekeeper pretended a laugh, "where would you get money... unless you stole that too. Indians!" he spat out the word. "There ain't an honest one among you. Now get out of here, both of you, before I call the sheriff."

"Call the sheriff if you want to," Jotham answered, "but

he needs these clothes and the boots. We've got money to pay for 'em and the knife too if he wants it."

Johnny Bearheart took the bundle of clothing out of Jotham's arms and threw them on the floor in front of the horrified storekeeper. "No, my friend," he said through clenched teeth. "I do not need the clothes. If this is the way white men treat Indians, I do not want a job in the white man's world." He took the knife out of its sheath and threw it down, driving the point into the floor between the storekeeper's feet. Then he let the sheath fall on the pile of clothing. "I don't need the white man's knife either," he said and walked confidently out of the shop.

Jotham looked at the storekeeper. His face was pale and his hands were shaking. "Don't even think of getting the sheriff," he said. "You had no right to call him a thief." He turned and ran out to catch Johnny Bearheart. Jotham's bags were sitting on the boardwalk and Johnny Bearheart was already in the wagon.

"Go back to my father, Johnny," Jotham said. "You can still drive the horses and he will get you the clothes and boots you need. We are not like this storekeeper."

"No, Ahmeek," Johnny Bearheart answered. "It is not just the this man. I know what Smiley Bartle and some of others say when they think I can not hear them. We will always be friends. Come to the village when you return."

Before Jotham could answer, Johnny Bearheart cracked the reins and the team started at a trot back toward Lac Vieux Desert. He put the team in the Marichetti barn, removed the harnesses and rubbed the horses down with a blanket. No one saw him leave the camp.

Chapter 16

Jotham's college years passed quickly. He was given a job in the athletic department at the University of Wisconsin that provided him with tuition and living expenses for four years. Of course to keep the job he was also required to be on the football team. American style football had been played in colleges for about twenty years, but the governing organization that would regulate athletic policy was not yet in place when Jotham started college. Providing jobs for players was a common practice and there were even rumors of schools that hired non-students for their football teams. Jotham was given his job and the spot on the team because of his passing ability. Eastern universities, where rules of the game were controlled, were talking about legalizing the forward pass and the Wisconsin coach wanted Jotham on his team when that rule change was adopted. Otherwise his football career was less than spectacular. He played quarterback on the varsity team, but never became a regular starter. He was faster than any of his teammates, but much too small for the rough-and-tumble game that characterized football at the turn of the century. It was his ability to be a team leader and to call the plays that allowed him to play at all. He could pass the ball as well as any quarterback in the country in practice, but on the playing field only short passes behind the scrimmage line to other backs were allowed. The forward pass would not be legalized until two years after his graduation. The game in which Jotham found himself was based on brute strength, size and roughness. Even among the bigger players, injuries were more common than touchdowns and the only reason Jotham stayed with the game at all was to keep his job in the athletic department.

Jotham was no football hero. His job on the field was to call the plays that made heroes of his teammates. The closest thing to a moment of glory for him came late in the season of his junior year against Iowa. It was fourth quarter with the score tied. The quarterback called his own number. He barely got the snap from center when the Iowa line came crashing in on him. As they carried him from the field, the coach turned toward Jotham.

"Marichetti," he yelled. Jotham's heart skipped a beat. "Get in there and show 'em what you can do."

Jotham huddled with his team and called the play. It was a play Pop Warner had created called the lateral option. It called for Jotham to take the ball in a single wing to the right formation and start an end run. If the tacklers came at him, as he knew they would, he was to lateral the ball to the wingback, who should be a few feet behind him on the right. He started his sweep to the right, but found his wingback already lying on the ground, victim of an Iowa lineman. Upfield it looked like the whole Iowa team was gathering like a herd of wild animals in front of him. He turned and retreated to the other side, then cut sharply upfield past the Iowa line. He saw the Iowa backfield waiting for him but he darted past the first would-be tackler like he was one of the trees he and Johnny Bearheart dodged around running through the woods. He ran straight for the last man in front of him, then at the last second crossed his feet the way the Indian youth had taught him to run the trails and crossed the goal line untouched. Wisconsin won the game.

"That was a great run," the coach commented when the game was over. "I knew you could pass, but I thought you were too small for a running back."

"I am too small," Jotham answered. "That's what made me run. If those big guys from Iowa caught up with me you'd have had two injured quarterbacks."

"Where'd you ever learn to run like that?" the coach asked.

"From a friend of mine up north," Jotham answered. "You should have him for a wingback, coach. He's about my size but a lot faster, tougher too."

"Really, what's his name? Maybe we could get him on the team."

"Johnny Bearheart," Jotham answered, "Chippewa."

"No wonder you could run like that. Your Indian friend graduate from high school?"

"Just grade school, Coach," Jotham said, "but it sure would be great if he could play football here. He deserves a chance a lot more than I do."

"Maybe," the coach said, "but they'd never let him come here anyway, not an Indian. His only chance would be with Pop Warner's team at Carlisle. That's a big Indian school in Pennsylvania."

Jotham didn't think it was right that Indian's didn't have a chance for an education like he did, but he was thankful to have his job at the University. The Marichetti logging business was doing well, but not well enough to provide for college. He put all the money from his summer work in the bank. He knew there would be no time for football and no job for his law school education.

Not taking football too seriously left Jotham with more time for his studies. It was no surprise when he graduated *magna cum laude* in the class of 1906 and was immediately accepted into law school.

Rebecca Morgan had been out of school for two years by the time Jotham finished college. She completed teacher's training at the new Normal School in Stevens Point and by 1906 was in her second year of teaching at the State Graded School in Eagle River. Jotham's summer work not only gave him a chance to save for law school, but also more time with Rebecca. He made the long train trip from Madison to Eagle River each Christmas and Easter and always spent at least one day with her before going out to the Marichetti camp. During the long months between he took time out from his studies to write Rebecca weekly.

Jotham also wrote regularly to Stanley Rodzaczk who kept him posted on the goings-on at the camp. He would have written to his father, but Enrico Marichetti could read

no English. His brother Dominic had only the barest education and little reading ability of his own. Stanley could
be counted on share information with them and he knew
more about the power dam controversy than anyone.

The conflict between the loggers and the dam operators was getting hotter and Jotham searched for a legal
solution that might prevent an all-out fight and possible
bloodshed. By the end of his second year of law school he
was sure that time was running out.

When Jotham arrrived for his final summer of work camp
everybody was anxious to talk to the law student. Most of
the loggers just greeted him, then drifted away. He was
the same old Jotham; still he was an educated man now
and they didn't know exactly how to talk to an educated
man. When they had any previous brush with a person as
schooled as Jotham, he was likely to have been sitting
behind a very high desk ordering them to spend a few days
in jail to sober up.

Stanley was an exception. He wanted to hear all about
the goings-on in Madison and he wanted to tell Jotham
about problems at the camp. Both knew this would probably be his last summer. When he finished law school the
next spring he would be a lawyer, not a skinner; and Stanley
hoped he could find some way to bring peace to the Upper Wisconsin River Valley.

"It's not so much the guys in this outfit," Stanley said.
"Yer dad has them pretty much under control, but it's those
independents over on the east side of the lake."

"What seems to be stirring them up?" Jotham asked.

"Oh, it's Bob La Follette and his new law that sets up
that Wisconsin Valley... Whatchamacallit."

"The Wisconsin Valley Improvement Company," Jotham
offered.

"That's it. There talking about putting in more dams."

"Yeah, but they're not a power company. They just want
to dam some of the small streams and creeks to control
the spring runoff."

"Well some of those streams and creeks come right up
here to the state line."

"Damn!"

"Not damn, but dams," Stanley continued. "A lot of them and the loggers are getting fed up."

"Hell! When I heard they agreed to put in a sluiceway to get saw logs past the dams, I thought all this nonsense of fighting with the power company would be over."

"That's just the big power dams," Stanley responded, "not these little dams they're puttin' in. If they're buildin' 'em to control the spring runoff they ain't gonna have no sluiceway. The only time these creeks have enough water to float a log is during the spring runoff and if they hold the water in the creeks back, the Wisconsin won't have much water either. Some of the jobbers on the east end of the lake are threatenin' to organize a gang of scrappers to fight soon as they start buildin'.'"

"That doesn't make sense, Stanley. The Wisconsin Valley Improvement Company won't build all those little dams overnight. They've planned something like twenty-six dams up north, but that's over the next thirty years. By the time most of those dams are built there won't be any more pine in this area and it won't make any difference."

"Yeah, I told the guys that's what I read in the paper, but Marty Frederickson says he heard they're plannin' to start one right here on Lac Vieux Desert this summer."

"Where'd he hear that?"

"I don't know, but it makes sense doesn't it? This is the biggest headwater lake on any of the Wisconsin tributaries. If I was makin' a thirty-year plan, this is where I'd start."

Jotham hadn't heard of plans to build a dam across the headwaters of the Wisconsin at Lac Vieux Desert and he didn't believe it was part of the state's plan, but he knew if the independent loggers thought it was, there'd be no telling what they might do. If they wanted to get a bunch of lumberjacks together for a fight, some workers in his father's camp would join in, though Enrico Marichetti had convinced most of his men that power dam construction was helping the logging industry more than hurting it. The northern highlands pine was running out fast and it was hydroelectric power that made the paper mills so hungry for hardwood. Electricity ran the machines that produced the paper. It also ran the presses that made the demand for paper so high. Marichetti told the loggers that most of them wouldn't have jobs if it weren't for the power that made those mills run. It was also true that hydroelectric power was no longer just for streetcars and paper mills. Even some of the smaller cities were getting electric lights and folks were predicting that electricty would even be in the farm houses before long.

Jotham tried to convince the loggers that the Wisconsin Valley Improvement Company wasn't created just for the electric companies. Its main purpose, he said, was to prevent the farms in the southern part of the state from flooding every spring. The loggers were hard to convince. They had been fighting with the power companies so long that it was like a family feud. None of the arguments made a difference. The people that built dams across rivers would continue to be the enemy. Even if they agreed with Jotham, it wouldn't alter the fact that lumberjacks liked a good fight. Many of them had friends in the smaller camps and if battle lines were drawn, loyalty would outweigh common sense.

First, Jotham had to find out if there was any truth to what Stanley said about a Lac Vieux Desert dam. He worked most of that night on a letter to one of his law professors in Madison. The next day he saddled Jenny and started the long ride to Eagle River. He could have mailed the letter in Land-O'-Lakes, but the mail train came as far north as Eagle River now and a letter would go out faster from there. In addition, he wanted an excuse to stop and see Rebecca. Of course he would look for an excuse to ride into Eagle River to see Rebecca under any circumstance, but this time he felt a need to talk about the Lac Vieux Desert problem with someone other than loggers. He had been talking with loggers for almost a week and they were all of one mind. Anything that had to do with dams was wrong. He needed a fresh outlook, a chance to discuss the problem with someone more objectivity.

Jotham flipped Jenny's reins around a post and hurried up the outside stairway that led to Rebecca's room above the general store. He reached out to knock on the door, but it opened before his knuckles touched it. Rebecca had heard Jenny's hooves on the gravel road and was watch-

ing from the window when Jotham pulled up. She ushered him in and closed the door quietly behind him as she
had many times before to make sure no one else was aware
of his visits. The stairway was dark and it was unlikely
that anyone saw Jotham enter, but a woman schoolteacher
in 1908 was not to have male visitors. Of course Rebecca
tried to be discreet, but her concern was limited. She didn't
expect to be a school teacher for long after Jotham finished law school. Women schoolteachers in Rebecca's time
were also expected to remain single and that was not a
part of her plan.

Rebecca threw her arms around Jotham and kissed him.
That, too, was a regular part of their meeting. He returned
the kiss, but this time Rebecca sensed that Jotham was
tense. It was obvious that his mind was not on her. He
held her a long time without saying anything. It felt good
just to have her close to him, to feel the warmth of her
body against his, the reassurance that everything was all
right. Rebecca waited patiently; then sensing the moment,
she was first to release the embrace.

"Ahmeek, is there something wrong?"

"I'm sorry Becky. I guess I'm a little tired. It's been a
long, hard week."

He told her about his talk with Stanley and then about
going from one camp to another trying to allay the lumberjacks' fears and calm their anger. He said that he came
to Eagle River to send a letter and find out what the Improvement Company's plans were.

"I was hoping this would wait until I could pass my legal exams," Jotham said, "so I could do something to prevent a fight. But it isn't going to wait, Becky. I think this
whole thing will come to a head this summer."

"If there is a fight, your dad won't be a part of it, will
he?"

"No he won't, but a lot of the men who work for him
will. Dad can't talk any sense into them either."

"You've got to convince them that they're wrong,"
Rebecca answered. "Electricity is... well electricity is going to make everybody's life easier in the future."

"I don't know. I don't know if they're wrong. Sure there
are a lot of things you can do with electricity and it's mak-

ing life a lot better for folks in the cities..."

"Not just the cities," she interrupted, "but the small towns too. I was reading an article in the *Milwaukee Journal* that told about all the things electricity will do for us. It told about all kinds of things Thomas Edison has been working on. He invented the electric light bulb, you know and the article said you could turn night into day if you wanted to..."

She continued to speak but Jotham couldn't hear her anymore. He thought about turning night into day and it seemed to be interfering with the most elemental aspects of creation. He knew he was in Rebecca's room but her voice was drowned out by the voice of Old Eagle Feather. *Nature*, he had said, *you cannot change nature.*

"But it isn't natural to turn night into day," he broke in at last. "Can you imagine never seeing another star? Can you imagine a world where Mr. Edison's Gramophone replaced the sounds of the birds in the morning or the chirping of crickets at night? Electricity can do amazing things, but dams across rivers, lights all over a city, those things all go against nature. I don't know how long people can go against nature. I don't know how much the good Lord will allow!"

"Now you sound like your Aunt Sarah," Rebecca replied with a slight chuckle.

"No." Jotham joined her laughter. "But I sound like someone else I know that I always thought was a lot smarter than Aunt Sarah."

"Oh, who?"

"Just someone. I told you about him a long, long time ago. His name is Eagle Feather."

Jotham didn't find a solution to the Lac Vieux Desert dilemma talking to Rebecca Morgan, but he did manage to relax and even get the problem off his mind. The conversation became lighter and the rest of the evening passed quickly as evenings with Rebecca always did. It was well after midnight when Jotham slipped quietly out of Rebecca's place and went to get a room at the hotel. It was much too late to start the long ride back to the logging camp.

Chapter 17

The hammering was so loud Jotham thought it would break down the door to the cook's shanty. When Dominic scurried to the door and answered it they were greeted by the unshaven face of Marty Frederickson. Marty looked like all the city folk imagined a logger should look. He had a heavy black beard that framed his large, round face. Equally round was his oversized body. His muscles bulged under his red checkered shirt. His black pants were tucked into his fourteen-inch leather boots which were laced with rawhide. Behind him were half a dozen more independent loggers who worked the woods on the southeast side of the lake. Jotham didn't know all of them, but he recognized Michael Thomas McMannus and Kalle Kuukinnen. McMannus had a reputation equal to Frank's except, lacking the Frenchman's mean streak, he was known as a top-notch drinker, but was a little less adept as a fighter. In contrast to Frederickson's bulk, McMannus, while broad-shouldered, was otherwise trim, with the triangular frame of a prizefighter. Kalle was only a few years older than Jotham. Kalle had started logging in the Marichetti camp when he was fourteen because he wanted to "work outdoors where you could see the sun shine". He had walked all the way down from the Gogebic range where his father and brothers worked underground in the iron mines. He was a big strong Finlander, even at fourteen, and would have stayed with Marichetti had he not had to return home when his brother was killed in a mining accident. When he came back to Lac Vieux Desert, a few years later, the Frederickson camp was just opening, so he signed on with Marty.

"What's all the ruckus about, Marty?" Jotham's father asked. "You don't have to beat my door down. We let you in."

"Ya gotta help us, Marichetti," Fredcrickson said. "They got a whole bunch of men comin' in to dam up the river at Lac Vieux Desert. Some of the boys got in a little scrape with them last night over at the Blue Goose Saloon. Said they were here to build a dam on the Wisconsin."

"That's got to be at the outlet from the lake," McMannus chimed in. "Ain't no place else they'd be a puttin' one up this far."

"What happened to you, Michael?" Stanley asked. "That shiner looks like you mixed it up with somebody."

"Yer damn right, ya Polack, but it took three of 'em to be doin' it to me. If I'd had you and the Frenchman there we'd a whipped 'em good, I'm tellin' ya."

Marichetti tried again to convince them that benefits of a dam might outweigh the problems. Why, in the cook shanties alone there were dozens of jobs where electricity could help. He told McMannus it wasn't just electric lights. They could get electric grinders to sharpen the saws and axes. That would save a lot of time overdoing it by hand with a grindstone and a file. The dams provided electricity and electricity could make their life a lot easier, but the east side loggers wouldn't listen.

"Easy for you to say, Enrico," Kalle Kuukinnen said, "but most of your operation is on the west end of the lake. What about us on the east side? All the 'lectricity in the world ain't gonna help us get our logs all the way over to the spur. We need the lake and we need the river runnin' out of it."

"The lake will still be there, Kalle," Stanley broke in, "and that gets yer logs almost as close as where we are."

"But if we floated them across the lake an' then hauled 'em to the spur, we'd have to have a crew on both ends," Marty answered, "Costs a lot of time and money to handle all the timber twice."

"'Sides that, they dam the river, the lakes gonna be changin' too," McMannus added. "No tellin' where the shore line will be and we can't be affordin' no steam barge to push the logs out over deeper water."

"They're not plannin' on a big power dam, guys," Stanley responded. "They're plannin' to put in just an itty-bitty dam to keep the water from the spring runoff. Just a few hundred gallons here and there to keep feedin' the dams down south when they go dry in July and August."

"Sure. Ya talk about all the things electricity'll do for us," Frederickson answered, "but this dam ain't even gonna give us that. All they want to do is hold water back for somebody else's electricity."

"It's not just electricity," Jotham said. "You won't sell many saw logs if the farmers downstate lose their crops to floods." He might as well not have said it. The indirect relationship between farmer's crops and selling saw logs was more than the loggers could comprehend.

Things were happening too fast. It would be at least a week before Jotham could expect an answer from his law professor and already the loggers were talking about arming themselves for a fight. Jotham had read about the battles that were fought in Kansas and Oklahoma between the cattlemen and the dirt farmers — range wars, they were called. A lot of people had been killed and a lot more thrown in jail. He wondered why, in such a big country with so much land, people had to fight over it. It seemed to him there was enough for the farmers to plow their fields and put up their fences and still have plenty left over for cattle. Now here he was in peaceful Wisconsin and he was seeing the same thing happen, except here it wasn't land they were fighting over; it was water.

Wisconsin wasn't a territory. It was a state, and in a state there were laws to prevent things like this. He had spent two years studying law, but the law didn't seem to apply to this situation. If the power companies changed the path of the river, landowners could sue them, but there was no plan to change the path of the river. The dam would just control the amount of water flowing through it. Riparian rights covered the landowners along the lakeshore if the lake was expanded enough to flood their property, but the loggers weren't landowners. Most of the land they logged was owned by the state or by the railroads and they only bought the timber stumpage. Of course flooding the land would destroy a lot of timber too, but the loggers had no legal recourse for that.

Jotham was so deep in thought that he didn't really hear what was being said in the conversation still going on around him until Stanley mentioned his name.

"Jotham's written to some of the law school people in Madison to see what they're up to and see what we can do. There ain't much else we can do 'til we know what the law has to say about it."

"The law won't do us no good after the dam is built," Frederickson answered.

"True, Marty, true," Michael Thomas McMannus said, "but he's right you know. Nothin' we do now will do us any good if they got the law on their side."

"We can at least get 'em to put in a sluiceway," Marichetti added.

"Hell, Enrico," Frederickson answered, "a sluice won't do any good on that little river. The whole damn outlet to the lake ain't nothin' but a sluiceway when its runnin' free."

"What have you found out from the law people?" Kuukinnen directed the question to Jotham,

"Nothing yet, Kalle. I just sent the letter off the other day when I heard the state's planning to build dams up this far."

"Ya mean they're plannin' to build more of 'em?" Marty asked.

"Twenty-six, but that's over the next thirty years," Jotham answered. "I'm trying to find out which rivers are involved. If they plan to build one of them at the headwaters of the Wisconsin, maybe we can get them to change the project."

"Afore ya know it, they'll dam every trickle of water in the county."

"The papers said twenty-six dams, Marty. By the time they've finished all twenty-six most of the big timber on the lake will be gone anyway. What's left will be hardwood and by then the railroads will have spur lines all over to haul that out."

"Yeah," Frederickson replied, "we bin hearin' about those spur lines for years now, but they're mighty slow in comin'."

"They'll come," Stanley interjected. "The paper mills are eatin' up the popple as fast as we can cut it and you know you can't float popple even if you got a river."

"Maybe so, Polack, but it ain't the twenty-sixth dam I'm worried about. It the first two or three and it looks like the dam on this lake is gonna be one of 'em."

"Well if we could just hold 'em off for a few days..." Jotham started. but was cut off by Smiley Bartle.

"How about your Injun friends? Maybe they could help us." Smiley had been quiet until then, but Jotham suspected sooner or later he would be the one to bring the Indians into the picture.

"They're no part of it," Jotham shot back, "not yet anyway."

Jotham thought there might be some way Eagle Feather and his tribe could be part of a long-range solution, but he didn't want them involved in the present crisis. He thought he ought to search his law books, then talk to the old Indian to find some real common sense that might apply. Neither Jotham nor his father wanted to admit it, but the short term solution was obvious. Just as it was obvious, it was also dangerous. They would have to stand their ground against the construction workers. That didn't necessarily mean a fight, a river war comparable to the range wars in the west, but it did mean taking up positions at the river headwaters and preventing, for as long as possible, the construction men from doing their job. The Marichetti camp reluctantly agreed with Marty and his men. They decided to post guards and when workers came to start building the dam, all the loggers from all the camps, over two hundred men, would take their rifles and form a human barrier across the work site. No one was to fire a shot, but they were sure the construction crews would not try to cross a line of lumberjacks. Of course the Wisconsin Valley Improvement Company people could bring in the law, but that would take time. The workers would have to contact their supervisors, who in turn would get hold of the sheriff. By the time the sheriff could get a posse together large enough to stand against the loggers, they hoped to find some way to get the law on their side.

When Marichetti called for a volunteer from his camp

to stand guard, the first hand to go up was that of Smiley Bartle. Jotham took a deep breath, but then relaxed when he saw that his father ignored Smiley and waited for another volunteer. *The one thing we don't want,* Jotham thought, *is a loud-mouthed braggart who fancies himself a cowboy standing guard.* As for Jotham, he would be off to the county seat at Eagle River tomorrow to see Judge Moran and try to get an injunction that would prevent the dam from being built.

Chapter 18

Jotham sat alone on an old pine stump atop the ridge overlooking Lac Vieux Desert. The sun was creeping down below the tall pines that towered over the Marichetti house. The lumberjack who had been standing guard during the day had gone back to camp. They knew the construction company would not move equipment into the area after dark.

An osprey swooped down over the lake. It reminded Jotham of those first days he spent on the lakeshore with Old Eagle Feather, when they had seen an osprey dive into the lake and come up with a fish. He closed his eyes and tried to imagine Mourning Dove and Johnny Bearheart sitting cross-legged on the ground beside him. Jotham sat quietly with his eyes shut and after a few minutes the voice of the old Indian came slipping out of his memory as though riding on the gentle breeze that followed the evening calm. *Each animal had to ask the Gitchi Manitou for its special gift, the eagle's keen sight, the bear's strength, the vulture's patience, the dog's love for his chief.* Jotham remembered how Eagle Feather looked right in his eye when he talked about the beaver. That look made the words that followed more than legend, a statement of faith, the principles by which he must live. The voice became stronger, more distinct, almost as if it were coming not from his imagination, but from Old Eagle Feather himself; *Gitchi Manitou gave to beaver the gift of peace.*

Jotham's eyes popped open. He almost expected to see the old Indian standing beside him, but Eagle Feather was not there. Neither were Johnny Bearheart and Mourning Dove. Jotham was alone. He felt alone, alone with a problem he could not pass on to his Papa, Aunt Sarah, Eagle Feather or anybody else. Without realizing why, he began to speak aloud. He did not pray, for he was never quite able to understand prayer the way Aunt Sarah did, nor was he cursing or crying out. He felt the muscles in his chest and neck strain as the words came out:

"God, *Gitchi Manitou,* whoever and whatever you are, tell me how to be the beaver. How can I bring peace to this conflict?"

Jotham stopped and listened, though he did not expect to hear an answer. Of course he was not disappointed. Even the voice of Eagle Feather was gone now and all he could hear was the rustling of leaves. He waited patiently while the evening sun slipped behind a bank of clouds coming in from the west. Then he waited a little longer, hoping for a vision or at least some semblance of an idea.

By the time he got up to walk home it was dark. That did not bother Jotham. The trail was familiar. He had said many times he could walk it with his eyes closed and once, when he was about ten years old, he had tried, only to find himself hopelessly tangled in a cluster of hazel brush. He felt a strange relaxed feeling, totally different from the anxiety he felt when he had walked out to the lake just an hour before. He hadn't heard any clear answers from Eagle Feather, nor from the *Gitchi Manitou* for that matter, but he now knew one thing that had escaped his earlier considerations. He *was* the beaver – and he must do what beavers do. He must use the gift that was his. Somehow he had to keep peace at Lac Vieux Desert. Anything other than a peaceful solution was ruled out.

Jotham left the camp shortly after daybreak the next morning. He was not there to witness the events that followed, but he would hear them told and retold in the cook's shanty for months. The morning went smoothly, for the young Kalle Kuukinnen, who was assigned the duty of watching for construction activity. He sat under a tree watching a big pike swirl in the shallow bay and munched some beef jerky the cook had given him for lunch. Suddenly he heard the sound of horse hooves and the squeal of wagon wheels along the tote road to the east. Kalle spun around to see not only horses and wagons, but a whole load of tumble buckets.

That's not logging gear, he thought. *Those buckets are for movin' dirt.* It was clear that these were the workers they had been waiting for and with equipment like that it would take no more than a few weeks to build a dike across the whole southwest corner of the lake. Kalle jumped on his horse and streaked across the flat to the nearest logging camp. From there, riders were sent in all directions to alert other lumberjacks. Within ten minutes the first loggers began to line the lakeshore next to the river armed with rifles and axes. Marty Frederickson fired a shot from his .44-Winchester into the air and the caravan of earthmoving equipment came to a halt. By then the wagons were no more than two hundred yards from the line of lumberjacks.

"Stay where you are," Marty called. "Don't come any closer."

The foreman from the construction crew held up his hand to signal for teamsters to stay back. He could see a dozen or so lumberjacks on the north ridge by the river, but wasn't aware of the one hundred-plus more that were slowly filtering in from more distant camps. With his men safely stopped behind him, he started to walk toward the loggers. He had only taken a few steps when he heard the sharp crack of Marty's rifle and saw the bullet kick up a cloud of dust about fifteen yards ahead of him. Marty was careful to place the shot to the foreman's left, where there would be no chance of a ricochet hitting any of the workers.

"Hold it," the foreman shouted. "None of my men carry guns. I just want to come up and talk to you."

"Okay, come on up," Marty yelled in response, "but make sure nobody else moves, ya hear?"

"Nobody will." The foreman took a few measured steps. When there was no reaction from the loggers, he quickened his pace. It took a few minutes before he had crossed the considerable stretch of ground that remained between him and the loggers' line of defense. When he was apace with Marty he opened his mouth to speak, but

Frederickson cut him off.

"I thought you said your men don't carry guns," he said. "I just saw a carbine come out of a saddlebag. There's another one over there." Marty pointed toward the line of construction workers along the road.

"Well ya, they got rifles, some of them, but I mean they ain't armed for no fight. Most of 'em don't have any gun at all, just those that like to hunt and watch for bear and stuff like that."

"Well, ya better tell 'em not to try to use them."

"They won't. What the hell's going on here anyway?"

"Maybe you oughta tell me. This is a loggin' operation. We cut down trees and we float 'em down the river — and you guys don't look like lumberjacks to me."

"Well, we ain't lumberjacks," the foreman answered with a bewildered expression. "We were sent her to build a dam, or at least a dike. The dam buildin' crew comes in later after we have the shoreline ready for 'em."

"Well," Marty answered, "that's all very interestin', but we don't really need a dam here, do we, boys?"

A chorus of no's went up from the assembled crowd of lumberjacks, which had been growing steadily as they talked. By now every camp was represented and there were more than a hundred armed men on the ridge.

"Look, Mister..."

"Frederickson," Marty cut in.

"Look Frederickson..."

"Mr. Frederickson," Marty interrupted again.

The foreman took a deep breath and paused for a long time, then continued.

"Mr. Frederickson. We ain't lookin' for a fight. We just want to do our job. The state sent us here to..."

"The state?"

"Yes, the state of Wisconsin. The Wisconsin Valley Improvement Company. They're a part of the state government and they say we're supposed to prepare this site for a new dam."

As he finished Enrico Marichetti joined them.

"What'sa goin' on here, Marty?" Marichetti asked.

"This fella says the state of Wisconsin sent him and his men here to build a dam."

"To prepare the dikes," the foreman corrected, "the dam buildin' comes later. Who are you?"

"Enrico Marichetti. Now I know you got your job to do, but there's gonna be no dam here, not right now anyway."

"But you can't stop us."

"Well, you see, my boy, he's a lawyer. He's gone to town — to Eagle River now — to see if this dam buildin' is all legal, Okay?"

"Well, of course it's legal." The foreman raised his voice in frustration. "The state ordered it and we're gonna do it."

Marty Frederickson looked first to the right, then to the left, drawing attention to the line of lumberjacks. "I don't think you want to do that."

"I'll get the sheriff."

"You gotta do it, go ahead," Marty said. "As long as ya don't bring those tumble buckets any closer."

The foreman turned and went back to the construction crew. Marty and Enrico watched along with the other lumberjacks as he stopped to talk to a group of workers. A few minutes later they saw the chuck wagon pull off the road into a small clearing. It was obvious that the construction party would make camp for the night. They also heard the hoof beat of a horse and rider heading off toward Eagle River and they knew it wouldn't be too long before the sheriff would be on the scene.

"Well," Frank said, "that buys us a few days, maybe a week at the most, while the sheriff rounds up a posse to chase us off."

"That's okay," Stanley said. "By then maybe Jotham can get a court order or something to stop this dam buildin' legally."

"Meantime we gotta see that they don't start diggin'," Marty Frederickson said. "We'll keep a crew here to make sure they stay down in the hollow. The rest can get back to working the timber."

Marichetti and Frederickson picked twenty men to stay at the lake and make sure the construction workers didn't move their equipment onto the ridge. The rest were sent back to their camps to work. It could be days before anything happened and they wanted to lose as little logging time as possible.

Sleep was a rare commodity for the next few days. Frank
and Stanley sat up late into the night playing cards and
talking. Stanley said that ultimately Marichetti would have
to pull out and leave the fight to the small jobbers. After
all, the Marichetti camp was close to the spur and it made
little difference to them whether the dam went in or not.
Frank didn't see it that way. He felt that, as lumberjacks,
they had an obligation to be loyal to the camps on the
east side of the lake that needed the river to float logs.

"Ya know, Stanley," Frank admitted, "I miss the logjams."

"Frank," Stanley responded, "You don't give a damn
about the logjams or damming the river for that matter.
You just miss chasing women and the boozing you did
when ya took a bunch of logs into town."

"Ya. I suppose that's it," he chuckled. "Now that we
ship all the timber out from the rail spur, I hardly ever get
to town anymore."

Stanley's prediction was very close. It was the third
day after the initial confrontation when word came to all
the camps that the construction line was starting to move.
The Marichetti crew wasted no time getting to the lake.
Enrico asked Stanley and Frank to stay with him as they
approached the construction site. He wanted the Frenchman for protection and he wanted Stanley's cool head and
calculating mind. As one of the few men in the camp that
could read, Stanley had the respect of the other men and
might be able to stave off bloodshed even when Marichetti
himself could not.

Marichetti didn't stop to talk to the men at the lake.
Instead he called for Marty Frederickson to follow and
hurried down the hill to meet the construction crew. By
the time they reached the first wagon there were less than
a hundred yards separating them from the loggers waiting
on the ridge.

"What you doin'?" Marichetti called to the foreman. "You
wanna get those men killed?"

"We got the sheriff," the foreman answered. "He's on
his way out with a posse now. Said he'd be here in less

than an hour."

"Then you wait an hour," Marty barked it like an order. "Those men on the hill don't know the sheriff's on his way and even if they did, I'm not sure we could keep their fingers off the trigger."

"We've waited for three days now," the foreman responded. "Those lumberjacks ain't gonna shoot nobody. That's just a bluff."

The foreman was waving his arm about as he talked and pushing his forefinger into Marty Frederickson's chest. From the ridge where the loggers stood with their rifles it looked like he was beginning to force his way past the two camp bosses. Stanley was about to give Frank his best guess about what the three men down below were saying when he heard the voice of Smiley Bartle behind him.

"I got that sucker in my sights," Smiley said. "He start to push his way up here and he's dead."

Stanley turned in time to see Smiley pull back the hammer on his Marlin 1894. His right hand shot out like a kicking mule and slapped the barrel skyward. The .44-caliber bullet was spent in the clouds, but the thunderous muzzle blast froze everyone on both sides in their tracks.

"Now what did you do a thing like that for?" Smiley asked.

"You dumb cowboy," Stanley scolded, "you start a war and you gonna get half these people killed."

"I weren't gonna shoot nobody. I was aimin' over his head just to give 'em a scare if he needed it."

"You said you had him in your sights."

"Well I didn't," Smiley whined like a hurt puppy. "That was just talk."

"Who's shootin' up here?" Enrico Marichetti was still puffing from the run up to the ridge.

"It was a accident," Smiley Bartle answered. "Damn Polack hit my gun and it went off."

"That right Rodzaczk?"

"Yeah, I guess so. I thought he was aimin' at somebody so I batted his gun up in the air."

"Put the guns away," Marichetti ordered. "Nobody shoots, nobody gets hurt."

"They're gonna stay put," Frederickson added. "The

sheriff's on his way up here. When he get's here we're gonna move out."

"Move out!" Frank objected. "Hell, we can handle the few men the sheriff'll have with him."

"Maybe we can, Frank, but we won't."

"We got no legal right," Marichetti added. "We work in this great country, we obey its laws."

"Sacre bleu..." Frank muttered as he walked off toward the trail that led back to the logging camp.

Stanley looked at Marichetti and shrugged his shoulders. "There he goes again," he said. "He's been lookin' for an excuse to take off. We won't see him for at least a week now."

Marichetti and his crew returned to the camp and went about the business of cutting timber. Marty Frederickson and the other big operators pulled their men back too. The only ones remaining were some of the small jobbers who thought they couldn't survive without the waterway. They tried to disrupt the construction, felling trees in the way of construction workers, and in general harassing them as much as they could, but without Marichetti and Frederickson it had little effect. Over the next week the logging camp was full of talk about the few minor fights that broke out at the dam site, a logger getting beaten up by the construction worker or a dam builder getting beaten up by a logger, but nothing more serious.

Jotham's visit with Judge Moran accomplished nothing. The judge said he couldn't grant an injunction because there was no evidence that building the dam would result in pecuniary loss to the logging interests. The claim that operating cost would go up might be valid, but it was an unsupported claim. Riparian rights, even if they were an issue, dealt with compensation after the fact and couldn't serve as a basis for an injunction. He agreed with Jotham that those laws probably wouldn't apply anyway, because most loggers did not own the land where they cut timber.

Dominic and his father had gone to bed, but Jotham was still sitting by the kerosene lamp pouring over his law books. A light rain was falling on the roof. Jotham liked to sleep when it was raining. The sound of rain on the roof helped him relax, but tonight he could not sleep nor was relaxation possible. There was still time if he could find something in the law that would help. Work was progressing rapidly on the dike, but that was just the first step. The dam itself would be built from concrete, not earth and that would take several weeks. If there was some way to get a court order to stop construction before the dam actually went in, it might not be too late for most of the loggers. *Loggers,* he thought, *am I really doing this for the loggers? I don't have to do anything for the loggers. I have to do it for the river.* He thought about the river the way it was when he was young. Then it had been surrounded by alders and, a little farther back, a big grove of pines. The alders were still there, but now the grove of pines had become part of some city. They were churches and stores and homes and hotels. Only their smallest offspring remained along the shores of the northernmost reaches of the Wisconsin. Again he was haunted by his childhood talks with Eagle Feather. *Eagle Feather...* an idea struck, but before it could take full form, his thoughts were interrupted by an awful ruckus, a hammering on the door. Jotham hurried to answer it.

"Let me in, damn it. That crazy Frenchman is going to kill me!"

Jotham looked out at Stanley, drenched as a result of his run all the way from the bunkhouse.

"Stanley, what's the matter?" Jotham asked.

Before Stanley could answer Jotham's father and Dominic came running into the room.

"What's the matter, you damn Polack?"

"Ah, it's... it's Frank." Rodzaczk stammered. "He's back from his drunk. He's back that is, but he ain't sobered up yet. He's mad 'cause me and the Swede won't stand up and let him throw axes around us."

"What?"

"He want's to throw axes around us like he saw in a circus once. Ya gotta do something about that lunatic before he kills somebody."

Marichetti put on a rain coat and followed Stanley out. Dominic sat down with Jotham.

"Golly, it's nice to have Frank back," he said. "I was scared he was gone for good this time and the camp would be kinda dull without him."

Jotham didn't answer, but his smile said he agreed. His thoughts went back to that day when Frank was practicing and missed the tree behind him and Stanley.

"I wouldn't want to be in the Polack's shoes," Jotham said. "Frank's not too good with axe throwing, at least not when he's sober."

"Well," Dominic answered, "maybe he's better when he's drunk."

They all knew Marichetti could settle Frank down if he had to, but by the time he and Stanley got to the bunkhouse, Frank was sound asleep.

Chapter 19

Just before Stanley came crashing in, Jotham thought he might have an idea to save the river and, of a little less concern, save the logging interests on Lac Vieux Desert. The next day he tried to retrieve that thought and turn it into a plan of action, but whatever it was, Stanley's problem with Frank had blotted it out of his mind. Once the loggers retreated from their position it seemed that preventing a fight was no longer a major issue, but he expected tempers to flare again once actual dam construction started. Jotham tried hard to remember, something to do with Eagle Feather. Yes, Eagle Feather and the Indians. If there was no law that would protect the river for people like his father and the other loggers, perhaps there was something in the law about the rights of the Indians. He couldn't get an injunction from a local judge, but maybe the Indians could petition the Bureau of Indian Affairs for federal intervention. Jotham knew that agency did not have a good record as protector of Indian rights. In addition, since the Dawes Act allocated lands to specific individuals, not the whole band, it was unlikely they would act on behalf of a tribe, but he had nothing else left to try. The northwest side of the lake was home to the Chippewa. Most of the village was on high ground, but the southern part of those Indian lands would most likely flood when the dam increased the lake level. Even if their lands didn't flood, they were dependent on the lake for walleyed pike and wild rice, the two biggest staples in their diet. Any major change in water level would make it more difficult for them to harvest their food.

Jotham had to contact Johnny Bearheart and ask him

to arrange a meeting so Jotham could talk to the elders. It had to be done soon, as there was little time left to lodge a petition with the federal government. The construction crews had been working for just one week and already they had completed the dike on the south side of the proposed dam site. That one was short because the shoreline dropped from a high ridge. The north dike would rise out of low swampland and they would need to move a lot more dirt to complete the earthen portion of a dam on that side. He estimated that would take no more than two weeks and he knew that the wheels of government turned very slowly.

It seemed to Jotham that he had been waiting for hours. Actually he had come to the village at midmorning and waited until just past the noon hour. He didn't know how much longer it would be, but his knowledge of the culture told him that neither sun nor clock would determine when the council should begin. That would be determined by Eagle Feather's sixth sense, something beyond the understanding of white the man, that told the old man when to call the elders together. Johnny Bearheart sat with Jotham. Every once in a while he would look at Jotham and smile, a smile that said; *I know what you are thinking, but be patient.*

He saw Eagle Feather twice, walking about, checking on this or that. Each time the old man went by, Jotham thought the council was about to begin, but each time he was disappointed. As they were waiting, watching for any sign that the delay would soon be over, a young brave came walking toward them. Jotham did not recognize Jimmy Little Wind until he was already standing in front of them.

"You are Ahmeek." Jimmy Little Wind said in such a way that it was obviously intended as a greeting.

"And you are Jimmy Little Wind," Jotham answered, happy that he remembered the name in time.

"Mourning Dove has told me much about you. About the white boy who played with Indians when you were children."

"That is true," Jotham responded, not sure where this conversation was leading and a little bit apprehensive that

Mourning Dove might have said something Jimmy Little Wind would have found offensive.

"She says I should not be fooled by your white skin. That inside, you are very much an Indian."

"Ahmeek knows the way of the Ojibwa," Johnny Bearheart offered. "He is like one of us. He is my blood brother."

"How is Mourning Dove?" Jotham asked, overcoming his apprehension.

"She is a good woman, and a good wife, Ahmeek, already she has given me two sons."

"I am happy for you, Jimmy Little Wind. I wish you and Mourning Dove many happy seasons." Jotham said.

"And I wish you many happy seasons, Ahmeek." With that, Jimmy Little Wind walked across the ceremonial grounds and stood talking with a group of young braves.

Jotham looked after him as he went. He really did feel happy for Mourning Dove and Jimmy Little Wind, but he was at the same time unhappy that he was still an outsider and could never be seen talking with Mourning Dove again. He turned his head back just in time to see Old Eagle Feather raise his hand in gesture to the drummers. The beating signaled that it was time for the council to begin. Jotham was ushered to a seat in the circle of elders. He remained quiet until all had arrived and were seated. When the drums stopped, Eagle Feather explained to the others why they had been called to council. Jotham wished he remembered his Ojibwa better. He could understand the native tongue of the *anishnabeg* well enough when he was younger and spent a lot of time with Johnny Bearheart. Being separated from his Indian friends and concentrating on the language of the law, much of that Latin, made him slow to follow the words of Eagle Feather. He hoped the old man would switch to English when it became Jotham's turn to present his case. Fortunately, all of the elders knew enough English that he would not have to try to speak Ojibwa. He also knew he could not count on Eagle Feather to help him clarify the issue. A chief of the Ojibwa did not enter into debate. He was a leader, and as such was expected to listen to the debate of others, then render a decision. Jotham had never before been admitted to the council, but he knew from the lessons he had learned with the Indian children and what they had said about life in the tribe, that was the way of the Ojibwa. Eagle Feather did not speak long. It was not he who had a petition to bring before the council. Jotham was not sure he was ready when he heard the old man call him by his adopted Indian name.

"Ahmeek," Eagle Feather said. "The council will hear you now."

Jotham told them about the plans to put a dam at the Lac Vieux Desert outlet. Members of the tribe had seen the work on the dikes, but did not know what was being done. None of the early construction work interfered with the river or altered the lake. He told them of the state's plan to build a series of dams in the north to keep the water in the springtime from flooding farmland in the south. He told them that the loggers had tried to stop construction but had failed. He said that only the Indians had a chance to stop the dam builders. He wanted them to sign their names to a document that would ask the Bureau of Indian Affairs to take action against the Wisconsin Valley Improvement Company and prevent them from placing a dam on their lake. The elders listened intently and patiently. When he was finished one of them asked a question.

"The dam. It is like the dam built by the beaver? It will make the lake bigger?"

"Yes," Jotham answered, "but it will hold water from the river."

"*Maskinozha,*" someone muttered. Then another and another until several elders at once were saying something about *Maskinozha,* the pike. At first Jotham didn't understand, but then he realized they were making a logical if faulty assumption: bigger lake, bigger fish, or perhaps more fish. He tried to make them understand that he believed a bigger lake could just as easily mean less fish, but this was not so logical to the tribal elders.

"We must keep the lake as it is," Jotham said. "If we change the lake, we will change the fish's home. If the lake is deeper the rice will not grow. The *manomin,* we must save the *manomin.*"

At this, some of the elders began to laugh. Wild rice grew in the water so they could not see how it could be flooded. Eagle Feather held up his hand indicating that Jotham should let the elders discuss the problem. Jotham tried again to follow what was being said, but most of the time found himself hopelessly lost in a sea of unfamiliar Ojibwa words. He recognized words like *wawashkaesh* and *wabasso,* the deer and the rabbit. He heard other references to fish and to the woods. After a while everyone became quiet, the elders sensing that Eagle Feather had heard enough and would soon speak for them. The Chief sat silently in thought for what seemed an eternity. Then at last he spoke.

"The elders say this is white man's fight. The elders say what white man has done to forest is worse for Indian than what he does to lake."

"But what about the rice?" Jotham protested. "Your people need the rice."

Again there was a brief murmur among the elders and again Eagle Feather listened, then spoke for them.

"The rice will stay. Rice has powerful Manitou. White man's dam cannot hurt rice."

"Grandfather Eagle Feather," Jotham pleaded. "Do you understand what they will do to the river?"

"We know, my young friend," Eagle Feather answered, "but you too must understand. After the great wars, we took the land white man gives us. It not good land, only land the white man did not want. In the springtime it floods. We know the floods. In the winter it is so cold we must build big fires just to live. In the summer it is too cold for corn to grow so we have learned to eat rice. How can white man's dam make it worse? The elders say it is the forest we must get back. The lake will take care of the lake. I too love the river, but we cannot sign your paper."

That was it. The council was over. The last chance Jotham had to use the law for the preservation of peace was gone. As he left the circle he was met by Johnny Bearheart.

"I am sorry, Ahmeek," Johnny said. "I know how you feel. It is not right that they should dam the lake, but the elders feel that the Indian has fought enough. They would rather let the white man fight the white man. I cannot change what the elders think."

Jotham thanked Johnny Bearheart and started to leave the village. As he rounded the last turn on a path that would put him on the trail back to the logging camp, he caught a glimpse of Mourning Dove. The early afternoon sun made her long hair look blue, the way he remembered it when they were children. Their eyes met briefly, but before Jotham could open his mouth to speak, she turned quickly away and slipped into her wigwam. Jotham smiled, not a happy smile, but a knowing smile. That was how things were supposed to be. He walked slowly away from the village and back to the Marichetti camp.

Chapter 20

Work on the Lac Vieux Desert dam was progressing rapidly, but Ahmeek saw little evidence of it from the lumber camp. Over the years they had moved around the southwest corner of the lake far enough that by the summer of 1908 they were closer to the rail spur than to the river. For the last two years they had transported their timber overland so for the Marichetti's it was business as usual. He might have forgotten that a dam was being built were it not for the nightly conversations in the cook's shanty.

"I heard the Johnson brothers pulled out today," Stanley said.

"Ya," Swede answered. "They got the river blocked off now, puttin' cement down. Pretty soon all the camps close down, you bet."

"Well, we won't close as long as the timber holds out," Marichetti said. "We got only three miles o' road to the rail line and maybe they still bring the spur out to the lake."

"It'll be a cold day when a spur comes in here," Frank said, "but three miles ain't a long haul, especially in winter when the ice is on the road."

"And they still got the river below the dam for saw logs."

"River," Frank hissed. "Your river just be a trickle when that dam she's finished."

Whatever happened to the river, Jotham knew there would be few logging camps left. Already some of the smaller jobbers had quit. Now the Johnson brothers were gone too. McMannus and Frederickson were big enough and close enough to survive, but time was running out for others on the east shore. Marty Frederickson, whose timber stumpage was right next to the dam on the south side of the river said he saw the forms and they could expect concrete to be poured in a matter of days. A few of the lumberjacks had threatened to start a fight, to drive the workers off the land. Two men were arrested by the county sheriff. They had tried to dig a trench through the dike, a futile effort at best. A whole crew working with shovels for a week couldn't do enough damage to slow down a construction crew with horses and tumble buckets. Jotham felt bad about the small loggers being forced out, but he had done all he could. His attempt to get the Indian village to file an objection had been his last hope. Jotham took little comfort in the fact that no major fight had started. He knew the lumberjacks' temperament and was sure they couldn't be counted on to remain peaceful for long.

The dam was being built and the land along the river where he had first met Eagle Feather would never be the same. It was like a part of his childhood, a very important part, was being ripped away. He decided to go out to see the dam for himself. He wanted one last hour in those familiar surroundings to think. Perhaps there was something he missed, some result of damming the river that had escaped him, anything that might provide a legal reason to stop construction.

The next afternoon Jotham brought the horses in early, removed the harnesses, fed them, then headed out to the dam site. It was a bright July day and sunset would come late, about eight-thirty. Jotham had always liked July. It was really the only month when he could be sure of summer weather this far north. By July the cold spring rains that lasted into June were over and the fish and wildlife became more active. When he was little, of course, it was the month when they celebrated his birthday. He hadn't been to the construction site since they started work and he had wondered how they could build a concrete dam in the water. When he pushed aside the last cedar bough that blocked his view he was very surprised. The earthen dike that he thought would lead up to the dam actually went all the way across. The river was completely blocked off and the forms for the concrete dam stood on dry ground in the old riverbed. Thirty yards north there was a breach in the dike to let the water through. Jotham looked at the structure for several minutes before he began to understand what they were doing. Once the concrete hardened, he concluded, they would tear out the south dike, the one that blocked the old river channel, and rebuild the north dike where the river now flowed. All the water would then run over the new dam where they could control the lake level with the thick planks that ran across the top of the obstruction.

It was all very interesting and Jotham marveled at the design, yet he had some serious reservations about the effect. In the springtime, when they were saving water from the runoff for later use, the lake would rise more than a foot. He thought that might flood a lot of good timberland along the west shore, between the dam and the Indian village. The village itself was on high enough ground not to be flooded. That was not true of the wild rice beds on the Michigan side of the lake, however. The council of elders in the village was sure there would be no problem with the rice, but Jotham was very concerned that they might be wrong. How much water could wild rice beds take? Would the plants die out if the water was too deep? And what would happen when the water level dropped back down? He didn't know the answers to these questions, and he was afraid the Indians didn't either. They also didn't seem to worry about the fish. Lac Vieux Desert had been a ready source of walleye in the village for generations and while they might be right about more walleye in a bigger lake, there would also be more water and more places for them to hide. Other potential problems for which he had no answers.

Jotham also wondered about the river. The development company said it would no longer flood downstream in the spring or almost dry up as it had in some very dry summers. The white man in Jotham thought that sounded very good, positive, but the Indian in him said it was wrong. It was against nature. For centuries, birds, fish and animals had learned to thrive on fluctuating water levels. Fish, he thought, needed the high water in the spring because that was when they went upstream to spawn. Perhaps there were other creatures of nature in need of the dry riverbed. Would the berries that fed the birds in early summer be there without water flowing freely in the spring? And what about the fall flowers that grew in the valley only when the land was arid? What was nature's way? There were birds, trees, and flowers that flourished when it was wet and there were those that flourished only when it was dry. Didn't we then need both the wet and the dry season for all the plants and animals to live as they had for hundreds and thousands of seasons? Old Eagle Feather's words kept coming back to him. *Where there is woods they want to make field. Where there is meadow they put trees. They put dam on river to make lake. They dig ditch by lake to make river. Never leave alone. Better they learn to live with the world the way Gitchi Manitou made it.*

Jotham smiled. He enjoyed remembering the words the old Indian had used to explain nature. He closed his eyes and tried to imagine those days when he was a young boy, growing up half-Indian, half-white. As he sat deep in thought, he heard a voice. It was not Old Eagle Feather. It sounded more like the voice of Johnny Bearheart.

"You have come to see the white man's dam?"

The voice seemed so real, Jotham thought it might be *ninbawadjige,* the dream experience, but then he opened his eyes and saw the young Indian standing before him.

"Johnny Bearheart," he said, startled. "What are you doing here?"

"The same as you, my blood brother." Johnny Bearheart answered. "I came to see what the white man does to the river."

Johnny Bearheart surveyed the area, looking first at the dam, then at the lake and finally a long look at the river downstream. Neither he nor Jotham spoke for several minutes. It was the Indian way. Johnny Bearheart was the grandson of a chief. He would some day be a chief himself and Jotham knew he must allow Johnny time to take in the scene before him and draw his own conclusions from it. Finally the young brave spoke.

"I do not like what I see," he said. "I do not like the white man's dam and I think I do not like the white man's ways."

"I am a white man, Johnny."

"No, Ahmeek. You are not the same as the dam build-ers. You are not all white, just as I am not all Indian. Do you not remember when we opened our skin, placed our arms together and let our blood mingle? Even if only a few drops, even if only one drop of blood flowed from your body to mine and from mine to yours, my brother, you are some Indian just as I am some white."

Jotham knew there was no real exchange of blood in that boyhood ritual, but he also knew that did not dimin-ish its significance.

"It is not good, what white man does, Ahmeek. The river has been here since the turtle rose out of the flood, since the beginning."

"I know."

"I am sorry the elders would not sign your papers," Johnny went on. "They do not want the dam, but they do not want the men who cut down the trees either. For them it is worse to lose the forest than to lose the lake. From the lake they get the walleye, but from the forest they get much more. The deer, the rabbit, wood for fires that keep us warm through the cold winters and *zinzibakwud,* the sugar of the maple, the special food *Gitchi Manitou* gave to the Ojibwa. The lake is important, but the forest is more important and they are the leaders of a peaceful tribe. They do not want to join in this white man's fight."

"Johnny Bearheart, my brother. I understand why they do not want to be a part of this fight. Tell them they must not be a part of it. If there is a fight the Ojibwa must sit back and watch. No matter what happens, the Indian must not be a part of it. Soon I fear white man will fight against white man at Lac Vieux Desert, but the Indian must not join in."

Chapter 21

"Hey, Polack," Frank called out from his bunk. It was late Saturday afternoon and the lumberjacks were resting up from the morning's work. During summer months the lumberjacks worked a five-and-one-half-day week and took Saturday afternoon off. Summer hours were long, with breakfast call at daylight and the day's work lasting until six or seven at night, so an extra half-day of rest on the weekend was essential. Stanley was sitting by the window where there was enough light for him to file his saw. Frank had spent the afternoon whittling a wooden chain from a piece of hard maple, then gone to his bunk for a well-deserved nap.

"Whaddya want, Frank?"

"This damn dam business, it's been gettin' to me.   I gotta get outta here."

"So?"

"So Kalle Kuukinnen's takin' a wagon into town to get supplies for Marty. I think you and me should go in and have a few drinks and talk this thing over."

"Sounds good to me," Stanley answered. "I need a new pair of boots anyway. Good chance for me to get some."

Stanley and Frank jumped down from the wagon box and thanked Kalle Kuukinnen for the ride to town. Kalle snapped the reins around the rail fence between the road and the general store. Once inside the three men separated, each looking for needed supplies. Stanley bought his boots, also a pair of doeskin work gloves, a new saw file, a couple bags of Bull Durham and a pack of cigarette papers. After the purchase, they crossed the road and strolled past a half dozen rigs already lined up in front of the Blue Goose Saloon. Frank bolted through the door and headed straight for the bar. Stanley hesitated, then satisfied that most of the patrons were loggers or farmers, not construction workers, he dropped his bag in the corner and joined Frank. Frank had a glass of Old Crow waiting when he settled down on a stool beside him. Stanley took a big gulp, then after a long breath, finished the glass. Frank was one step ahead, signaling the saloon owner for a refill.

"You fellas gettin' off to a quick start tonight," the owner quipped, then, not realizing he was touching a dangerous sore spot, added, "Due for a big one now that the dam's finished, eh Frank?"

"I been due for a big one since they started," Frank answered. "Been up to me, there wouldn't be no dam finished."

"Well, I guess you can't stop progress."

"You call that progress?" Stanley asked. "Ya, maybe for you here in Eagle River. You get some pretty lights in your place, but it ain't progress for us."

"I was just jokin', Stanley. The dam ain't doin' me no good either. Two months ago this place was filled up by this time every Saturday night. Now so many of you guys have pulled out, I had to let my barkeep go last week. We ain't so far away we don't feel the pinch, believe me."

A dozen or so other lumberjacks joined the lament, all relating sad tales of how the dam was ruining the good times they'd had in Vilas County. Now that the river was so low, logging companies were moving on. They went to other forests, of course, but none of them, they said, were a match for the forests along the Wisconsin-Michigan border.

"Hell," Stanley said. "Last summer you guys said the timber was running out all over the country, and you," he pointed to a stocky logger sitting on a corner stool, "you said timber in the Lac Vieux Desert stand wasn't near as good as where you came from."

"Well," the lumberjack answered, "I was wrong about that."

"Ya never heard me say anything like that," another chimed in.

The one thing they all agreed on was that they should have done something to stop the dam. Of course no one seemed to know what.

"We shoulda blown the thing outta the water," came a voice from a corner table.

"Hell," Stanley broke in. "Yer all fulla *I shoulda's*. I shoulda said this or I shoulda done that. Easy to say now. None of you did those *shoulda's* then 'cause ya knew they'd land ya in jail." He got up and took his drink over to a table away from the crowd. After a few minutes Frank joined him. The grumbling at the bar continued.

"Listen to 'em, Frank. They all got great ideas now that it's too late to do anything."

"They're right, Stanley. We shoulda done somethin'."

"What?"

"I dunno, but somethin's better'n nothin'." Frank was beginning to slur his words and it was obvious neither man was thinking quite as clearly as when they had come in.

"Well, maybe so, but it's too late now."

"Who says it's too late?"

"I says. The dam's built and it'd take dynamite to tear it down."

"Well maybe we can't tear it down, but we oughta do somethin' to get even."

"Get even?"

"Yeah, get even. Maybe I go see those dam owners. Give me two minutes, man to man; they change their mind about buildin' all the dams."

"How you gonna see the dam owners?" Stanley scoffed. "You couldn't get close to the mansions they live in, and even if you could; they're way down in Wausau, not here in Eagle River."

"Then let's go to Wausau."

"Use yer head, Frank. It won't do us any good to go to Wausau."

"Why not?"

"Well..."

"Well, why not."

"'Cuz."

"'Cuz what?"

"Damn it Frank, cuz it would take us two days to get there and we'd be sober by then!"

Both men broke into a laugh. It relieved the tension, but not for long.

"Well," Frank continued, "anyway, we oughta do something to get even."

"Well, there ain't a hell of a lot we can do. They got all the power and were just a bunch of dumb lumberjacks..."

"Power!" Frank interrupted. "That's it. Power."

"What're you talkin' about?"

"Power. You said they got the power."

"Yeah."

"We cut off their power."

"Huh?" Stanley looked at Frank, confused.

"They call them power dams. We get even by cuttin' off their power. "

"They're hydroelectric dams and it ain't that easy to cut the power."

"No, I don't suppose," Frank admitted, "but you can do it. You been readin' all that stuff about 'em in the Sunday papers."

The idea was totally irrational, but the combination of self pity and Old Crow made it somehow appealing. Stanley remembered that the nearest hydroelectric dam was one that had recently been erected about fifteen miles west of Eagle River. He told Frank about it.

"How we gonna get there?" Frank asked.

"I dunno. Walk, I guess."

Frank broke into an inebriated laugh. "Walk!" he exclaimed, "Are you in any shape to walk?"

"Hell, then we'll crawl."

"That'd take all night. I got a better idea."

Frank got up and walked unsteadily toward the door. Stanley staggered along behind him. Out on the street the two men supported each other as Frank stumbled his way to a team of horses hitched to the rail a short distance from the saloon. He untied the reins while Stanley crawled up onto the wagon. Then as the horses started to walk away, Stanley pulled Frank up, laughing uproariously as he sprawled onto the wagon bed. Frank got to his knees, moved slowly forward and finally got control of the team. They had no thought of being surreptitious and both yelled wildly at the horses as they turned and headed out of town. The men in the saloon heard the noise, but they reached the street just in time to see the wagon stirring up a cloud of dust as it departed.

"Hey, that's my team," one of the saloon patrons yelled.

"Come back, you horse thieves," another voice called out, but that only brought laughter from the wagon.

"He-yah," Frank yelled as he whipped the loose end of the reins at the horses. The team picked up its pace to a gallop, the wagon skidding on two wheels when it rounded the turn at the end of the street. The rig's owner along with a number of the men who had been in the saloon boarded another wagon and soon were in hot pursuit.

"It's that damn Frenchman," the driver of the second wagon called out. "He never comes to town there ain't some kind of trouble."

"Well, there's six of us on this wagon. He ain't gonna be no trouble for the six of us."

"Don't be so sure," the driver responded. "From what I hear that's just about how many it'll take."

Frank kept the horses at full gait until they got to the trail that led to the dam. With only two of them on board they were lighter than the wagon following and got far enough ahead to stop the team and run into the woods. The fresh air and the adrenaline pumping through their veins during the harrowing ride sobered them up, at least enough that they could stay on their feet and know they should keep quiet. They hid in the woods near the trail until they were sure the team owner, satisfied at getting his rig back, was not following. Actually, Frank's reputation persuaded him to go back and get the sheriff rather than face the Frenchman himself.

A half-hour later Frank and Stanley reached the dam. The two night operators proved no trouble for Frank. Stanley just watched. One of the operators was a burly fellow who looked like he might put up quite a fight. Frank danced in, jabbing his left fist three times on the man's jaw. When he raised his hands to protect his face, Frank caught him with a hard right to the mid-section. By the time the burly one could throw a punch the ex-boxer had danced back out of reach. A wild, desperation swing from the operator found Frank darting in close with an upper-cut that put the big man on the floor. His partner hardly joined the fight. Seeing the big man knocked down, he took but one step before the Frenchman's lightning fists dropped him for a short nap.

The dam looked like the one that had been pictured in the Sunday paper and it took Stanley only a short time to find the switches that shut off the power to the lines.

"That's it?" Frank asked. "Just a little lever like that? Hell they'll get the power back on in no time if all they gotta do is push that little lever."

"That's what cuts the power, Frank."

"Well, that ain't enough. Maybe I find a sledge ham-mer."

"No you don't, Frank. You hit the wrong thing and that electricity'll kill us both."

"What?"

"That's right," Stanley continued, "It's just like bein' hit by lightning. I read about a guy that grabbed the wrong wire and poof, just like that, he's dead as a mackerel."

"Well, pushin' that little lever's not enough. We gotta do more than that."

"Okay, Frank, okay. We'll do a little more." Stanley's reading had given him a fair idea of how the hydroelectric dams worked and, though he'd never been inside a power house, he knew what to look for and generally what it looked like. Water had to enter the dam through penstocks in order to turn the dynamos. To control the flow and to make periodic maintenance possible, there were giant gate valves that closed the penstocks for each of the three gen-erators just before water entered the turbine. Stanley found the valves and closed them. One by one they could hear the three giant dynamos come to a stop.

At first all seemed silent, at least in contrast to the loud whirring sound of the turbines. That, however, was only an illusion and, after a moment they became aware of the men from the saloon returning with the sheriff. Frank would have stayed for a good fight had Stanley not shown better judgment. With some difficulty he convinced Frank there were too many men, even for the likes of him, and they had better be out of the power house before they were found. The voices grew louder as Frank continued the argument, so loud Stanley was sure they were about to open the door. He grabbed Frank by the arm and with a good tug propelled him toward the exit. In Frank's condition, inertia was a more powerful force than intent and the two of them slipped quietly off into the woods moments before the posse entered. They started to walk back toward Lake Vieux Desert and, when far enough away to be sure they wouldn't be discovered, settled in for the night. Once settled under a big pine tree that leaned rakishly over the trail along the river, Frank reached into his pocket and pulled out his half-pint bottle of Old Crow and offered the second sip to Stanley.

"Damn it, Frank," Stanley quipped. "You gotta give up this drinkin' and fightin' all the time. Yer gonna get us killed."

"Worse than that," Frank said. "In jail." He continued with a quiet whimper in his voice, "Ya know, Stanley, they don't let a man have any whiskey in jail."

"Then that's where you belong, you crazy Frenchman. Yer a menace to the community when you get to drinkin'."

"Me?" Frank feigned a shocked expression. "It was you that shut off the power."

They laughed for a long time, then kept talking on into the night, drinking frequently and reliving the night's adventure. They continued until the bottle was dry and they both fell asleep, an old owl hooting in the tree above them, and a posse combing the woods several miles away.

Chapter 22

Jotham whistled as he slipped into the bunkhouse Sunday morning with Stanley's paper. He had stopped going for the paper each Sunday when he started regular work in the camp, but it seemed like weeks since he had talked to the old logger and he wanted to surprise him by delivering the news again. He missed those Sunday morning visits and the simple philosophy Stanley always voiced. When he reached Stanley's bunk he was surprised to find it empty. The bed had obviously not been slept in. He knew Frank had gone into town the day before and didn't expect to see him, but Stanley? Sure, Stanley would occasionally go out with the other loggers on a Saturday night, but he was always up and ready for his paper come Sunday morning. Jotham was more confused than worried. Stanley knew how to take care of himself, but where he was that Sunday morning was a mystery.

The mystery was quickly solved when the Vilas County sheriff rode in to the camp along with Dan Brooks, the manager of the power company. The owner of the rig Frank and Stanley had commandeered the night before was with them. Sheriff Michaels was small, but tough. Jotham's idea of a sheriff was Sheriff Norton, back in Wausau when he was in grade school. As a grownup he realized that Norton had been more politician than lawman. Buck Michaels, who was now dismounting the Mustang that he had shipped all the way from Montana, was all lawman. He wore a pair of Colt 45 revolvers and a beaver hat that looked more suited to the western plains than the timber country of Northern Wisconsin. Jotham's father met him at the door.

"We're lookin' for two of yer men that caused quite a ruckus in town last night," the Sheriff said.

"Who are they?" Marichetti asked. "And what'd they do?"

"One of them was the logger they all called the Frenchman," Michaels explained. "Everybody knows him. He's got quite a reputation as a scrapper. The other guy nobody seems to know, 'cept that the scrapper called him Polack. Folks don't remember seeing him in town much."

"They weren't back yet when I looked in the bunkhouse this morning," Jotham told him. Then he asked, "What kind of trouble they get into?"

"They stole my rig," the wagon owner said.

"Your rig?" Jotham asked.

"Yeah, my wagon and a damn good team of Morgans,"

"We get it back for you," Marichetti responded. "Okay? Come in. We talk about it."

"We got the rig back already," the sheriff said as he took a chair and sat at the table opposite Marichetti. "I'm afraid that's not all there is to it. After they took the wagon, they went up to the dam, the one out west of town, and the Frenchman beat up the two fellas that were workin' there. Then they shut the dam down."

Enrico Marichetti put his hand on his forehead and heaved a sigh.

"Shut the dam down?" Jotham asked.

"Yeah, shut her right down." the power company manager answered. "Closed the penstocks and shut off all the power."

"Who is he?" Jotham asked the sheriff.

"This is Dan Brooks," Michaels responded. "He's the manager of the power company. The two men Frank knocked out work for him."

"Are they hurt bad?" Marichetti asked.

"Nah," the sheriff answered. "Just banged up a bit. They'll be good as new in a day or two."

"Then it's no big problem, eh? They'll be okay. You turn on the dam and I tell Stanley and Frenchman to stay outta town; maybe we all forget."

"I'm afraid I can't let it go at that this time, Enrico," Sheriff Michaels answered. "Ever since they put the dam on Lac Vieux Desert, I've been spendin' too damn much of my time dealin' with trouble in the camps. I'm afraid somebody's gonna have to go to jail for this one."

Jotham turned to Brooks. "You know, we can keep these guys from going back into town for a while. You don't press charges, the sheriff will have to let them go. You charge 'em and we're going to have to have a trial and that'll cost the county and the power company a lot of money for nothing."

"A trial?" the sheriff yelled. "What the hell do you mean a trial? We've never had to hold a trial to throw a couple of lumberjacks in jail for a few days coolin' off before."

"Well," Jotham continued, "that's 'cause they never insisted on their legal rights. Their right to a trial."

"You listen to my boy," Marichetti added proudly. "He's gonna be a lawyer."

"Well, he ain't no lawyer yet," the sheriff replied.

"No," Jotham said, "I can't practice law yet, but I can advise them."

Dan Brooks thought about that for a minute. "It doesn't make any difference. My boss down in Wausau isn't going to want to let this drop. The power company doesn't care about costs. Sheriff, you arrest those two as soon as you can find 'em."

"Are you sure?" Jotham pleaded.

"I've already filed the complaint. This kind of prank costs a lot. I don't care about the assault charges, but vandalizing company property is another matter. The big wigs in my company won't want to let that go unpunished."

"If you don't care about the fight," Marichetti asked, "then why you don't just start dam back up again and we forget it?"

"It's not that easy, Mr. Marichetti" Brooks said. "You see, a dam that produces that much power has three dynamos, that's the machine that makes the electricity. They can't just be restarted. The dam produces what we call sixty-cycle alternating current and the three units would have to be synchronized."

"What you mean, 'synchronize?'" Marichetti asked. "I don't understand."

"Well, they all have run together," Brooks said. "Ya ever work a team of horses that try to take turns pulling? They just seesaw back and forth on the doubletree and the load goes nowhere. They've gotta pull together. It's the same with the dynamos. All three of them have to work together and run at the same speed, otherwise one dynamo cancels out the power from the other two. It could take a week or more to get all three generators synchronized. We've restored some power to the town with one generator," he added, "but until we get all three running again, it's not just the power company but the lumber mill and every other company that needs hydroelectric power that's going to lose money."

Enrico Marichetti wanted to provide some protection for two of his best loggers, but what little he could understand of Brook's explanation sounded serious. He reluctantly agreed to turn Frank and Stanley over to the sheriff as soon as they returned.

The summer sun filtered through the trees. The tall pines along the Wisconsin formed a giant parasol that prevented the rays from waking Stanley Rodzaczk. It was almost noon before a break in the canopy left his right eye vulnerable. Even then he resisted until a fly persistently found his nose a perfect resting place. He swatted two or three times, half-asleep, then his eyes popped open. He looked at the long, lean body of the Frenchman lying against a Norway pine, his head tilted at a rakish angle. A few minutes later he realized where he was, but even then he had no recollection of what had happened the night before. He remembered being in the saloon and not much after that, but if he was waking up in the woods at midday he knew he had reason for concern.

"Frank! Frank! Wake up, dammit. What the heck we doin' out here in the woods?"

Frank groaned and rolled off the tree trunk, his shoulders dropping just about enough to bring him to consciousness.

"What, Stanley?"

"Where the hell are we?"

Frank looked around. "Looks like the Wisconsin. Yep. I recognize that bog over there. She's about... straight west of Eagle River."

"You recognize that bog. Who you tryin' to kid? You don't know where we are any more than I do."

"Sure I do. You never took the jams to Wausau. I know this river like the back of my hand."

"Well, what we doin' here?"

Frank tilted his head back and forth like he was trying to start an old watch. "I don't remember for sure. Was I in a fight?"

"Well, how would I know?"

"I guess I was. My knuckles smart."

"You always get in a fight when ya get drunk. Course you were in a fight. Now if you really know where you are, do you know how to get us outta here and back to the camp?"

"I only know from runnin' the river. I don't know the roads, but if this is the Wisconsin all we gotta do is follow it upstream. You can figure out which way that is can'tcha?"

"Well, I know that," Stanley answered. "I just thought if you'd been here before you'd know a shorter way out. Jeez, I'm hungry."

"You better plan to stay that way for a while. I don't think we can go back to town."

"Why not?"

"It's not a good idea, Stanley. We did somthin' bad last night. I don't know what, but there's gonna be trouble for us in town. I'm sure of that."

"Jeez, I don't know why I ever go to town with you, you French maniac. Get up and let's see if we can find our way home."

Frank stretched and stumbled to his feet. A few minutes of tossing his head around and he was completely conscious and ready to travel. They headed north following the deer trails that bordered the river. It was going to be a long walk. It would have been about a half-day by road, but they would have to follow the winding course of the river all the way. If they didn't want to spend a few days in the county jail, maybe even worse, they had to stay out of sight, at least until they could find out what happened and what they had done.

Jotham kept Jenny at a steady trot as he rode to Eagle River. His father's instructions had been specific. Find Frank and Stanley and tell them not to come back. Tell them to head up to Michigan for a couple of months. The elder Marichetti reasoned that if they didn't come back he wouldn't have broken his promise. He figured after a month or two, when the dam was back to normal operation, the company would forget about pressing charges. Jotham had hoped to find Frank and Stanley wandering northward along the road, but when he got to the familiar sign for the Blue Goose Saloon and still saw no sign of them, he knew it was going to be a long search.

Jotham told himself this wasn't the logical place to start. If they had come back to the saloon, Sheriff Michaels would already have them in jail. It was a big country and Frank and Stanley could be anywhere. If he was going to ask if anyone had seen them, the only person he could ask was Rebecca.

"No," Rebecca answered. "I haven't seen them, but I certainly have heard they were here."

Eagle River was a small town. Jotham was sure that everyone had heard what happened. "I've gotta find them, Becky. I think they might be in really big trouble this time."

"Jotham," Rebecca pleaded. "If they're in trouble, that's their problem. You're going to be a famous lawyer someday, like Clarence Darrow. You can't afford to waste your time trying to get people like Frank out of scrapes."

"If it was just Frank they could lock him up and throw away the key. He's been in jail so many times already it looks like home to him, but Stanley never gets into trouble by himself. He's worth helping."

It was too late in the day to go looking for the missing lumberjacks. Rebecca fixed supper for the two of them, nothing complicated, just some canned vegetables and a pot roast that had been simmering most of the afternoon. Jotham could start looking for Stanley and Frank in the morning. Jotham put his arm around Rebecca's shoulders as they sat on her couch and pulled her close to him, but he couldn't get the loggers off his mind. He hardly noticed how the light from the kerosene lamp highlighted her red hair and gave a glint of green to her eyes. It had been a summer of problems, but once the construction crews pulled out there would be no one left to fight. The loggers thought the power companies were the real enemy and they were untouchable, thus hostilities gave way to mere frustration and even that had started to wane, but now Stanley and Frank, with one rash, drunken act, had revived it all..

They talked for an hour or so. Both Jotham and Rebecca knew that they would be married as soon as he passed the bar and started a law practice. On some of those evenings when they had been together, they had talked a lot about that, even done some planning. She would continue to teach until he passed his law exams, then they would move to the city and settle down.

He had planned to go to the hotel, but it had been a long hard day and soon he was asleep on Rebecca's shoulder. She gently lay his head on a pillow and covered him with a blanket. Jotham slipped quietly out of Rebecca's place early the next morning.

Chapter 23

Jotham knew when he left Rebecca's early Monday morning that he would have little chance of finding Stanley and Frank. Half the town, including the sheriff, was looking for them too, but for totally different reasons. If Sheriff Buck Michaels and a good part of the gentry of Eagle River couldn't find them, there was no reason to assume his luck would be any better.

Rather than waste time in town, Jotham decided to ride out to the dam. He knew they would be a long way from there by now, but he might see some sign, something that would tell him which way they had gone.

The dam was much quieter than Jotham expected. Only the sound of water rushing over the spillway and the weak whine of one generator, that tried valiantly to provide electricity while its two partners stood still, broke the silence. He followed the trail along the flowage. About a mile upstream he came upon the grove of pines. There, glistening in the morning sun, was the empty Old Crow bottle. It was a sure sign Frank and Stanley had spent at least part of the night there. Jotham was heartened by the discovery, but more than an hour of searching produced no further sign of the two men. The only response to his many calls was the chuckle of the squirrel or the caw of the crow. They could have taken any of a dozen or so routes to... to where? He had to admit that he had no idea. Finally, accepting defeat, he turned the horse toward the town road that would take him home. He'd have to tell his father that he had failed.

Jotham's mind drifted as he followed that familiar trail from Eagle River to Lac Vieux Desert. He remembered the times he had come this way with Old John. A smile crept across his face when he thought of the first time the old man had let him drive the team. He had been so anxious to grow up then; now he longed for the simpler life of boyhood. Those summers learning the ways of the Chippewa had been crowded out by the complications of the white man's world, far too complicated, he thought. He was a white boy, born of an Italian father and an English mother and the Indian side of his youth was rapidly disappearing. Suddenly he felt a great loss.

"I don't know what it is ya gotta be leavin' now for," Dominic said. "Frank and Stanley came back this morning and Papa says I gotta go get the sheriff to arrest them."

"I know," Jotham answered. "Papa gave his word and Papa never goes back on his word."

"Well, why you wanna go off and act like an Indian? Sheriff's gonna take 'em to jail. What they need now is some good lawyerin'."

"I can't be a lawyer 'til I pass the exams and that won't be for nearly another year. What I need now is some time to think."

"Well, another year's gonna be too late."

"It's already too late to keep them out of jail, Dominic. What I have figure out is how we get 'em out after Sheriff Michaels arrests 'em. I need some answers and I can't seem to find them here. I've got to do this, Dominic. I can't explain it; it's just something I've got to do. You get the sheriff, like Pa says. When I come back I'll see if there's some way to get them out."

"Okay," Dominic agreed, "but I'd sure feel a lot better if you were comin' with me."

Dominic left. Jotham continued to put things in his pack: a change of clothes, some beef jerky. He rolled a blanket and tied it to the knapsack. He added some of his boyhood treasures, things he had made back in the days when he and Johnny Bearheart worked on Chippewa handcrafts together. Johnny Bearheart, that would be his first stop.

He would ask Johnny Bearheart to go with him. It was Chippewa custom to have a friend go along on a quest, and Johnny Bearheart was his best friend among the Chippewa. He filled his canteen with water, slipped quietly out the door and started down the trail to the Indian village.

When Jotham reached the village Johnny Bearheart came out to meet him. He thought Johnny Bearheart must be a lot like his grandfather, Old Eagle Feather, who always seemed to know that Jotham was coming even before Jotham was sure of it himself. He told his young Indian friend what had happened. Then he asked Johnny to accompany him on his search for wisdom.

A part of him, the white man part, doubted that anything would come of this attempt to obtain answers the Indian way, but he was determined not to let that logic shake his faith. He had tried white rationality and had found no answers. Now he would go back to his childhood, to the stories Eagle Feather told him about how the *anishnabeg*, before they had schools in which to gain knowledge, looked to their dreams for both wisdom and power.

Jotham had studied the Bible when he was living with Aunt Sarah; not that he had wanted to, but Aunt Sarah would have it no other way. He saw similarities between the spiritual life of the Christian and the spiritual life of the Chippewa where his aunt had seen only differences. The Bible called for fasting, and though he couldn't remember the Protestants he knew actually fasting, it was a common element to both cultures. He also remembered reading, way back when he was in high school, that Hindus, Muslims and a lot of others made fasting a part of their religion and he thought if there were so many different folks who believed in fasting, there must be something to it. Jotham had never been a big churchgoing believer, and after he left Aunt Sarah's, he spent more Sunday mornings with his law books than in the Bible. Nonetheless, he had never lost his strong sense of the spiritual, though he wasn't sure how much of that came from Aunt Sarah and how much from Eagle Feather.

Johnny Bearheart led Jotham into the woods. He said

it was the same place where his father's brother, Smooth Water, had dreamed his vision many years before. Johnny brought a pipe carved of stone and a pouch of tobacco for Jotham. He gave them to his friend. Jotham found a place to sit, crossed his legs, and waited. Johnny filled the pipe and they smoked. After a while Jotham dozed off. In what must have been only a few minutes of sleep, Jotham dreamed of Rebecca, of Sheriff Michaels and of Frank and Stanley, but what little he could remember about any of these random dreams yielded nothing that seemed significant. For several hours he drank water from his canteen, but took no food. When it became dark, he and Johnny placed their blankets against the ground and slept.

"Stay close to the ground," Johnny had said, "It is from our mother, the earth, that our dreams get their power."

When the two men woke up the next morning Jotham could not remember dreaming.

"Sometimes it takes days to find your dream," Johnny observed. "Some men go home without ever getting a vision."

"I don't know. I'm not sure how I can tell whether I've had a vision or if it's just my imagination."

Johnny smiled. "I have not yet found a vision, but the old ones tell me you will know." The young Indian handed Jotham some of the beef jerky. They both ate. Jotham took only enough food to take the edge off his hunger. Throughout the day Jotham sat in meditation. Occasionally he would talk to Johnny, but most of the time both remained silent. The day passed and still Jotham observed no significant dream. When night came they again spread their blankets on the earth and slept.

The third day, after several puffs of Johnny's pipe, no food and only a few sips of water from the canteen, Jotham's dream came, but it was a bitter disappointment. This time he did not doze off. In fact his eyes remained open, but the dream vision in front of him was as real as that found in deep sleep. In it he saw a lake, quiet at first, then whipped by the winds of a violent storm. When the storm subsided, he saw something on the waves. At first it looked like a large blue fish, but as it washed closer to shore he saw that it was a large piece of blue cloth. There was an indistinguishable image in the center folds and below that there were what looked to Jotham like the numbers one-eight-four-eight. While he watched the cloth roll over and over as the waves brushed the shore, he saw an eagle overhead. It swooped down and, as it floated above him, a single feather drifted down and landed on the cloth.

Jotham was disappointed because he had no idea what these images could mean. The whole experience seemed so strange, so different, that he had no doubt it was the vision he had journeyed for, but he saw no connection to the power dam conflict nor the arrest of Stanley and Frank. He was confident it was his vision because of the inner calm that washed over him. Besides, he was sure he had remained awake so it wasn't a normal dream.

"You saw it," Johnny said as Jotham shook his head to clear a sense of unreality.

"I'm not sure."

"You saw it. I could tell by the look in your eyes. Though you did not sleep, your eyes were following something."

"Yes, I saw something, but I don't know what it was or what it means. It doesn't answer my questions or solve any of my problems."

"But you feel better about your troubles?"

"Yes," Jotham admitted, "and that's really odd, Johnny, 'cause I don't know why."

"It is as the old ones say," Johnny answered. "Sometimes the vision is given, but its powers are not known for years."

Years will be too late, Jotham thought, but there was nothing more to do but to gather their things and return to camp. Johnny Bearheart did not ask about the dream. It was Jotham's dream and it was his to reveal when the time was right. That was the Chippewa way.

Chapter 24

Jotham thanked his friend for going with him and turned south toward the logging camp. He walked quietly along the path that followed the west side of the lake. As he walked, he listened to the waves lapping the shore. He looked out over the water and imagined the blue cloth washed by the waves and the eagle swooping down over it. The image was still sharp in his mind, but no matter how hard he tried, he couldn't make sense out of it. *It must be an Indian thing,* he thought, then he laughed lightly as he remembered how he used to use that phrase when he couldn't understand all the things Old Eagle Feather seemed to know. He came to the grove of pines between their house and the lake that his father had left standing when they logged the area.

Jotham was still more than a hundred yards from the dam when he heard another sound louder than the waves. It was a familiar voice, but more forceful, angry perhaps, than he had ever heard. It was the voice of Buck Michaels, but at that distance he could not determine what the Sheriff was saying. He didn't have to hear. What was happening became all to obvious when he saw Marty Frederickson and a large contingent of rifle-toting loggers. He scanned the river bank. There must have been close to one hundred lumberjacks forming a picket line on the east bank of the river. Separate from the group and some distance behind the line, he spotted his older brother, watching.

"Dominic," he called out, "What's going on?"

"Jotham. Gosh, I'm glad your back."

"What happened?"

"Well, I went to get the sheriff like Pa said. Some of the guys from the other camps asked where I was going and by the time I got back, they had Stanley and the Frenchman hid away in one of the smaller camps and had this army of lumberjacks lined up on the river bank ready fer a fight."

"Why? I don't understand."

"They think Pa's makin' a mistake, lettin' the sheriff know Frank and Stanley came back," Dominic continued. "They got pretty mad about it. Said Pa wasn't bein' loyal to his men. Then Marty got the other jobbers together and stopped Buck and his deputies on their way in."

"Where's Pa?"

"Back at camp. He tried talkin' to the loggers, but right now neither side will listen to him. The loggers are still mad 'cause I went for the sheriff and Buck's mad cause he thinks Pa got the loggers all riled up and sent 'em out here."

"Tell Pa I'm back. I'll go try to talk to the sheriff."

Jotham ran down to the river headwaters and walked across the dam to the west side. The sheriff met him.

"Marichetti," Michaels called, "ya gotta talk some sense into these damn hooligans. The power company's filed a complaint and I gotta take those two in. I ain't got no choice in the matter."

"I'll try sheriff, but they're a mad bunch. I just got back here so I don't know who's behind it yet. Can't you talk the dam people into dropping the charges?"

"I tried, but they figure they gotta make an example of somebody. Said they're still hearin' a lot of talk about rippin' dams out and if they don't stand up to the loggers now, there's no tellin' what's gonna happen next. Hell, I'll tell ya whose behind it," Michaels continued. "It's that damn Frederickson. He's got a whole army of loggers against us. I only got five deputies. Those power company people ain't good for anything, but they won't give an inch and as long as they got a warrant, I gotta stay here til' I make an arrest."

"Well, don't let any of your men do anything to start a fight. I'll try to talk to Marty."

"No chance of that." Michaels responded. "I got all I can do to keep 'em from takin' off and goin' home, but sooner or later I got to do something. Trouble is I ain't got no idea what it's gonna be."

Jotham went back to the east bank. He'd heard talk about tearing out the dam, too, but that was just from people like Smiley Bartle and he hadn't taken it seriously. He couldn't believe Marty Frederickson would be behind anything like that. Now he thought maybe he should have been more concerned. The power company people were looking for Frank and Stanley, but that fuss was over the dam at Eagle River. The Lac Vieux Desert dam didn't belong to the power company. It was put in by the Wisconsin Valley Improvement Company and that was an arm of the State of Wisconsin. If the loggers did anything as dumb as ripping out this dam it wouldn't be Sheriff Michaels, it would be state troops coming in and it would be a long time before anyone would be logging at Lac Vieux Desert again.

As he crossed the dam he saw more men filtering into positions along a picket line. Some of the older loggers were civil war veterans and they knew how to establish a line of defense. One of them, Red Erik Erickson had served in the Grand Army of the Republic with Colonel Hans Heg and he claimed to have been a drill master. Red Erik, as he was called, had set up a command post and appointed himself chief officer below Marty Frederickson. His hair was grey now, but he sported a long red beard and bushy red eyebrows that seemed to join his facial hair over the bridge of his nose. In his sixties, Red Erik was a man of frail body but husky voice. Jotham found this both frightening and comforting. It was frightening to see an old man who envisioned himself somewhat of a military strategist in control of such a volatile armed mob. At the same time his commanding voice provided a measure of discipline that Jotham hoped would keep the guns silent until something could be worked out.

"This is no good, Marty," Jotham began. "The loggers can get into fist fights with the power people or the millers, but Buck Michaels represents the law. You can't fight the law."

"We listened to you and your pa before, Jotham, and we ended up with a dam across this river. We gotta take care of our own or they'll run us all out of the county."

"Look, Marty. The sheriff says that the hydro people filed a complaint and he's got no choice but to make an arrest."

"He tries and him and his deputies are gonna be eatin' lead."

"That's no good. Any deputies get killed and they'll have an army out here to put you and all the rest of these guys behind bars. They don't hang you in the state of Wisconsin anymore, but people spend the rest of their life in jail for killin'."

"Then you tell 'em to back off."

"He can't do that if the power company filed a complaint."

"Then you go back there and get them power company people to call it off, get 'em to withdraw their complaint."

"Okay, Marty. I'll try, but you make sure nobody fires a shot and starts a war."

"Don't worry," Marty answered. "My men won't fire the first shot, but you can bet they'll return fire if the sheriff or any of his scraggly crew starts shootin'."

Jotham did go back to talk to Brooks, but he knew it was just a stall for time, to keep Marty and the loggers from starting a gun battle. The response, of course, hadn't changed and Jotham wasn't sure he disagreed with the power company representative. Brooks called Frank and Stanley renegade loggers and said if they let them get away with what they had done, if there was no punishment, more lumbermen would start "wrecking dams". The owners would have to hire private guards and pretty soon there'd be a war going on like the range wars in Texas and Oklahoma.

"We've had our problems in Wisconsin," Brooks said, "but so far it's just been a few good fistfights. Nothin' like down there." He turned to Sheriff Michaels. "Hell, I read the other day about a gunfight on the Texas Panhandle where some homesteaders were tryin' to put a fence up across range land. Before it was over, there were more then a dozen people shot dead, most of them homesteaders."

"That's not what we got here," Buck Michaels answered.

"And we don't want to have it either," Brooks responded. "That's why we've got to make an example of those two."

"They were drunk, Mr. Brooks," Jotham offered. "They're not likely to do anything like that again. Pa will see to that."

"Hell, young man, they all get drunk. As for your pa, well, if it was you and your pa, that might be different, but it's gone way beyond the Marichettis' now and no matter what you or Enrico try to do, it's more than you can stop. We got to throw your friends in jail for a while or we're going to have property vandalized all over Northern Wisconsin. Maybe they won't try anything again, but a lot of lumbermen think they did the right thing and they'll be tryin' to do something like it themselves."

Jotham continued to protest, but it was a useless gesture. It seemed that either Stanley and Frank were going to jail or the loggers and the dam operators were going to war. Try as he may, he couldn't think a way to stop it. Stanley and Frank deserved a little time in jail. He'd come to that conclusion himself, but now they had become a *cause célèbre*, an excuse for all the loggers to relieve the frustrations that had been building since the first logjam hit the first wing dam on the Wisconsin. And who knew how long ago that might have been?

As he slowly walked back across the trickle of river below the dam, he wondered what he was supposed to do. He took his time returning to Frederickson so he could think, but no solution came. He had felt so satisfied, so relaxed after his fast, and so sure things would be all right. He thought about his dream, but though he could remember it in minute detail, it meant no more to him now than it had in the woods with Johnny Bearheart.

Frederickson was not disappointed. He hadn't really expected Brooks to relent. He promised to keep the men on the riverbank quiet as long as the sheriff did the same, and Jotham started to walk back to his father's camp. His anxiety about the situation at the lake was overtaken by his hunger after three days of fasting and it was just about time for the clang of the bell that called the men to the cook's shanty. Just into the grove of pines he heard a sound. It was like the whistle of the whippoorwill, but it was still daylight and there would be no whippoorwill sound for hours.

"Johnny?" Jotham called.

"The smiling young Indian stepped onto the path.

"Ahmeek," Johnny answered. "You have come from the river. Why are the lumberjacks standing with their rifles? Are they again fighting about the dam?"

"No. Not about this dam."

"But these are not the dam builders," Johnny offered. "I saw them before when the flow of the river stopped."

"They're not the same ones. These men come from the Eagle River dam."

Johnny Bearheart nodded, then after a long pause continued. "The Council of Elders made mistake. They should have helped you stop the building of this dam. It is not right to stop a river. Look at it. It once ran wide. Now it is but a small tear drop flowing from the eye of our mother earth."

"You are wise, Johnny Bearheart. But that time is gone. The dam has been built. They come now to take two of our men to jail for opening another dam down at Eagle River."

"Opening the dam," Johnny asked. "How do they do this?"

"They opened the valves." Jotham stopped. He realized that Johnny Bearheart understood none of what he was saying. "It's like a gate, a gate that holds the water. They opened the gate and let the water through."

"Oh. Is there a gate on this dam?"

"No," Jotham answered. "This dam has no gate. It's built like a fence without any place to open or close."

Johnny Bearheart looked for a long time at the dam where the Wisconsin River left Lac Vieux Desert. "Then our lake is like an animal, held in a cage with no door. It is not right, Ahmeek." He looked back at Jotham. "Your friends will go to jail?"

"I guess so. I keep trying to think of some way to stop it, but I can't."

"Your dream..."

"The dream hasn't helped. I can't even figure out what it means. Johnny, maybe dreams only work for the *anishnabeg.* Maybe dreams can't help a white man."

"My old grandfather, Eagle Feather said white men think too much. If you stop thinking so much and let the spirits talk to you, then the dream will help you too."

"I've tried, Johnny, but it just doesn't work for me."

"Did you dream of things?"

"Things?"

"Things. You know, rocks, trees, animals, feather..."

"Feather!" Jotham exclaimed. "Yes, there was a feather." Jotham didn't tell Johnny any more about the dream. He wasn't sure why. He knew that many of the old Indians who had dreams kept them to themselves, but he also knew there was no taboo about telling. For him it was a little bit like a birthday wish. When he was a child he was told that if you tell the wish it will not come true. He chuckled a little inside at the thought of that cultural similarity.

"Do you have it?" Johnny asked.

"What do you mean, 'do I have it?' It was a dream."

"Yes, you dreamed of a feather," Johnny explained, "but the old ones believe that for your dream to have power, you need to get the things you dreamed about."

"Really? I didn't remember that."

"Yes." Johnny got very serious. "Get a feather, as much like the one in your dream as you can find or paint a picture of it on the door to your house, then the power of the dream will come to you."

"I'll do that, Johnny. First thing tomorrow morning I'll look for a feather like the one in my dream."

Johnny Bearheart smiled and nodded, then turned and disappeared into the woods. Jotham continued on his way home. He smiled to himself. He had been absent from the Indian ways too long not to feel that maybe he was being a little bit silly, but having committed himself to trying *ina'bandumo'win,* the dream vision, he was determined to go through with it. The other object in his dream, the blue cloth with the lettering on it presented a greater problem. There was no way he could get that. He didn't have the slightest idea what it was.

Chapter 25

Sheriff Michaels' small contingent of deputies was no match for the army of loggers Marty Frederickson had assembled, but fortunately neither side was willing to fire the first shot. Unfortunately, neither side was willing to give ground either. Three days went by with no change in the battle lines. Buck Michaels was patient. Marty Frederickson commented on his patience. Red Erik commented on his patience. The loggers discovered the reason for Buck Michaels' patience when Kalle Kuukinnen came running to the command post Red Erik Erickson had set up.

"Soldiers!" he yelled. "Looks like more'n a hundred of 'em comin' in south of the river."

Everybody turned at once to see the company of trained militiamen, the Bayfield Rifles of the Wisconsin National Guard, under the command of Major Cyrus Reeves, taking up positions on the shallow rise that bordered the river's south bank. Jotham momentarily froze at the sight, but not because of the company of soldiers marching into this remote part of the state. It was something else. Wisconsin's militia had been made a part of the National Guard almost thirty years earlier, and as a company of that militia the Bayfield Rifles were led by color guard and flag bearers flying the forty-six star flag of the Union. Jotham's eyes, however, were drawn to the flag flying to its left, a blue banner, "Wisconsin" emblazoned across the top, a code of arms with the motto "Forward" in the middle, and the year of statehood, 1848, across the bottom. He took the eagle feather from his hatband, the one he had found after Johnny Bearheart told him how the old ones believed the power of a dream could be secured. He had decorated the feather with tufts of blue cord. He stared at the feather for a moment, then looked again at the flag waving in the late summer breeze. *It has to be an omen*, he thought, but he still didn't know what it meant.

With the Bayfield Rifles present, the odds were changed. The numbers were now about the same on either side of the river, but the guardsmen were well-trained soldiers, equipped with accurate, high-powered military rifles. The loggers had no training for combat and a hodgepodge of artillery ranging from a Winchester 73 to a double-barreled shot gun, and even a few muzzle loaders. One carried a Hopkins Allen Kentucky squirrel rifle, highly accurate, but only good for one shot. They were all agitated, and instead of having a quieting effect, the presence of the guard moved them closer to the edge. Jotham knew it was just a matter of time until orders were given for the guard to move and he knew that neither he nor Marty Frederickson, or anyone else would be able to still the weapons of the loggers' army.

Jotham nudged his brother Dominic. "Go get Pa," he whispered.

Sheriff Michaels waded across the shallow river about a hundred yards downstream of the dam and approached Frederickson. Six months earlier that would not have been possible, but with the dam in place, the water that escaped from the ever-growing lake was barely enough to cover the surface of the old streambed.

"Damn it, Buck," Marty began before the sheriff had quite reached him. "What the hell did'ja do that for, bringin' in state troops? Now somebody's gonna get hurt fer sure!"

"I didn't bring 'em, Marty. Brooks did. Those power fellas got clout in Madison."

"Well, what we gonna do now?"

"Just turn those two lumberjacks over to me and it'll all be over, Marty."

"Well, Buck," Marty answered, "I'd like to do that, but I can't. The men ain't gonna listen to me. That Old Red Erik has them thinkin' they're some sort of real army. They ain't gonna do nothin' lessen Red tells 'em to."

"You know this Red, Jotham?" Buck asked.

"Not well, he's not from our camp. I don't think you'll have much luck with old Red. Our men tell me he's not quite right. You know, a bit senile."

"Well, we gotta do somethin'. You two come along and we'll see if we can talk some sense into somebody."

Michaels led the way while Marty Frederickson and Jotham followed him to the makeshift command center.

"Halt! Who goes there?" It was the voice of Smiley Bartle standing guard in front of the doeskin lean-to.

"Smiley, would you quit playin' soldier? You know damn well who we are."

"Well, yeah, Jotham, but Colonel Erickson said..."

"Bartle," Marty Frederickson broke in, "Red Erik ain't no more colonel than you are cowboy. Now where is the old coot? Sheriff Buck here wants to talk to 'im."

"Well now, I can't let you do that, Marty."

"And why not?" Marty asked.

"Well... " Smiley shifted his weight from one foot to the other, sneaking a sideways glance at the sheriff as he did. "The colonel, I mean Red Erik, said I wasn't supposed to let anybody by. He told me to say all that stuff, you know, halt and all that."

"Do you know who I am, Smiley?" Jotham asked.

"Why, sure. You're Jotham Marichetti. I know that but Red said..."

"That's right. Now I'm telling you to take your rifle and go back to camp. Is Old Red in there?"

"Well sure he is... but Jotham," Smiley Bartle protested.

"Smiley," Jotham continued, "you can go back to camp now and go to work tomorrow morning — or you can go back when all this is over and pick up the last pay you're ever going to get from the Marichettis, okay?"

Smiley's jaw dropped as he realized not only had Jotham threatened to fire him, but he wasn't that little boy in the camp anymore and he could do it if he wanted to. Before he could answer, Red Erik appeared in the opening.

"What's goin' on, Smiley?" Red asked.

"These fellas want to talk to ya, Red," Smiley answered as he quickly moved away from the doorway, "and I gotta go back to camp. Sorry, Red."

"Desertin'?" Red Erik responded.

"Ain't nothin' to desert, Red. G'by." Smiley hurried to the trail that led back to the Marichetti camp.

"Damn deserters. Same thing happened back in '62. Soon as the fightin' started the young'ns started runnin' off. Bunch a lily-livered babies, that's what they were. I'm Colonel Erickson. What can I do for you gents?"

"Red," Marty began, "this here's the sheriff. He wants to talk."

"Okay, but make it quick. I got my troops to command."

"Mr. Erickson..." Buck Michaels began.

"That's Colonel Erickson," Red Erik retorted.

"No. It's Mr. Erickson," the sheriff persisted. "There ain't no war goin' on. Your commission's expired."

"How can that be? I got an army," Red Erik answered, "and there's an army on t'other side of the creek. Now, if there ain't no war, what are two armies doin' out here?"

"Colonel," Jotham interjected, trying to humor the older man. "What you've got is a bunch of half-drunk loggers with rifles. Now those fellas on the other side, they're trained soldiers. A bunch of lumberjacks wouldn't have a chance against them."

Red Erik blinked his eyes twice. "Who you?

"I'm Jotham Marichetti."

"Marichetti." Red Erik paused for a long time. "Your pa runs that big camp on the west side, doesn't he?"

"That's right."

"Those two fellas that got in trouble work for you, right?"

"Yeah. They did."

"Then what you doin' with him? You oughta be with us. Git yerself a rifle, boy."

Jotham shook his head. Sheriff Michaels moved in for another try.

"Mr. Erickson," he said. "Tell your men to put down their rifles. You ain't got a chance against a trained army."

Red Erik's eyes danced from one side to the other, then centered in an icy stare at Buck Michaels. "They got the trainin', but we got the high ground."

"Red," Marty broke in, "there ain't no high ground. One side o' this stream ain't more'n six inches higher than the other and I ain't sure which side that is."

"You ain't got a chance," Sheriff Michaels insisted. "Tell the men to put down their rifles and go home."

"They said we didn't have a chance at Vicksburg, but we showed 'em. You tell those soldiers to stay put. You talk to their commander and tell 'em the first one to cross that river's a goner. Now that's all the time I got for jawin' here with you, I got to talk to my troops." Red Erik Erickson turned on his heels and went back inside. Marty Frederickson, Sheriff Michaels and Jotham walked back to the river. Buck waded across to the side where Major Reeves was waiting.

"Marty," Jotham said, "you talk to the loggers. I can't believe they'll listen to Old Red and not to you."

"These men ain't educated lawyers, Jotham. Old Red don't look so crazy to them. Besides, they don't all talk to him. He passes his orders down through some of the fellas they trust."

"You don't want them to call it off, do you, Marty?" Jotham asked,

"I don't know, Jotham. When it was just Buck Michaels and his deputies I was all in favor of comin' out here to stop 'em. Hell, I s'pose I was one of the guys that got it all started. Now it's all different, with the National Guard. I mean, I'm all for not turnin' Frank and Stanley over to Buck and Dan Brooks, but I don't want to see a gunfight where some folks are going to get killed. That wasn't my idea."

Marty and Jotham went up and down the line of loggers talking to as many as they could. Jotham explained that what Frank and Stanley had done wasn't a serious offense as far as the law was concerned and they would probably have no more than a month or so to spend in jail.

"They're my friends too," Jotham said, "but it's not worth getting killed over."

Marty supported Jotham's argument. He said he had been wrong to encourage them at the start and now they should all go back to their camps. A few did, but only a few. Some, like Michael Thomas McMannus, just wanted a good fight. Others were taken under the spell of the pseudo-military status of "Colonel Red Erik" and could not be dissuaded.

"It's a matter of pride and bein' loyal to yer friends," Kalle Kuukinnen said. "The way I figure it, when you give up pride and loyalty, life's not so good no more. If ya got nothin' worth dyin' for, ya probably got nothin' worth livin' for neither."

Jotham could understand that position. It was what drove Indian nations to fight insurmountable odds, believing that death was better than giving up their way of life, but somehow it didn't apply here. No matter how much he argued, however, Kalle, like more than a hundred other loggers, refused to leave his post.

By the time Enrico Marichetti and Dominic returned, tension was at a peak. Most of the loggers were dug in and ready for a fight.

"What happened, Marty?" the elder Marichetti asked.

"It just got out of hand, Enrico," came the response.

"Well it's gotta stop. Tell 'em to take their rifles and go home. Tell 'em to go get the Polack and the Frenchman."

"We tried, Enrico, but they won't listen to me no more."

"Then you go to my camp, get a couple a good men and go find 'em. Bring 'em back here."

"Go Marty," Jotham added. "Pa and I will go talk to the officer in charge of the guard."

"Won't do no good to talk to the other side," Marty protested.

"We gotta talk on that side," Marichetti asserted, "'cause nobody's got brains to talk to on this side."

Buck Michaels was glad to see Jotham and his father crossing the river and took them immediately to Major Reeves. Jotham told the major that Marty was on his way to get Frank and Stanley and asked that the guard hold its position until they got back. Reeves was skeptical. He had been briefed by the sheriff after his first trip across the river and couldn't believe the Marichettis' could have changed the situation so quickly.

"How'd you get that old Yankee soldier to back down?" the major asked.

"We didn't," Jotham confessed, "but Frederickson's taking some other loggers and going after the two men the sheriff wants."

"Sheriff says Frederickson's lost control."

"That's true where the men over there are concerned," Jotham admitted, pointing at the picket line, "but Marty's taking some of our men to look for Frank and Stanley. He can bring them while Old Red Erik is still preparing his battle lines. Then you can pull out without a fight and Buck can take the two of 'em back to town."

"How do I know you'll bring them to me?" Buck Michaels asked. "How do I know you aren't just stallin' for time while you slip those men out of the county?"

"You know us better than that, Sheriff," Jotham answered. "Just give Marty time to get back with Stanley and the Frenchman."

Major Reeves had been listening carefully. He didn't want a fight that was going to cause death for no reason, but he wanted to do the job he was sent to do and get back home.

"I'll give you one hour," the major said. "If you don't have the fugitives here by then, I give the order to attack."

Marty, accompanied by, Ben Wigghers and the Swede, hurried to the camp where the loggers had been hiding Frank and Stanley. Most of the men were at the river, but two or three remained to watch the bunkhouse. Marty explained what was happening at the river and asked where he could find the two troublemakers.

"We got to turn 'em in," he said, "or there's gonna be a real battle out there and some of yer friends are gonna get killed."

"They ain't here, Marty," came the answer. "Ole Red Erik sent word back to keep 'em on the move, from one camp to another so nobody'd be able to find 'em."

"We gotta find 'em," Ben Wigghers urged. "Ya got any idea where they went?"

"Last I heard they were headed over to the old Johnson camp. Johnson brothers pulled out after the dam was built, but they left the buildings and such."

The Johnson camp was more than a mile through the woods. Marty didn't know about the deadline, but he was hurrying just the same. When they arrived at the camp they found not one but several buildings standing. The three of them split up and went from door to door calling for Frank or Stanley. Fifteen precious minutes passed, but at last they found them in one of the smaller bunkhouses.

"You gotta turn yourselves in," Ben Wigghers said. "They got the army there now and it's gonna be a shootin' war if ya don't."

Frank objected, but with Stanley's help they quickly convinced him. Marty was glad to have Stanley's common sense prevail because he knew even the Swede would be no match for Frank if he refused to come. A few minutes more and they were all on their way back to the dam prepared to surrender to Sheriff Buck Michaels.

"What's taking Frederickson so long?" Jotham asked, looking up at the sun. "It must be getting close to an hour since he left."

"They'll get here," his father assured him. "Is not that far to the camp."

"They should have been back by now," Dominic observed. "Ya don't suppose the Frenchman put up a fight, do you?"

"Not with Stanley there," Jotham answered. "Stanley'd be able to talk some sense into him."

"Well," Dominic continued, "I sure wish they'd get here. The Major is out talkin' to his soldiers now."

Jotham looked across the river. It was obvious that Major Cyrus Reeves was preparing for an attack. Red Erik was equally aware of the major's movements and passed the word for his men to be ready to repel the soldiers.

"Give the order to fire the minute they get in the water," Erickson said.

Major Reeves drew his saber and yelled, "Move out!"

The line of guardsmen started down the shallow incline that approached the river. Jotham looked toward the lake and saw Stanley and Frank, along with Marty Frederickson coming out of the grove of pines. He turned and was about to start toward them when he saw Red Erik raise his rifle and yell to his army of loggers.

"All right boys. Be ready now. Aim…"

The guardsmen had just reached the south bank of what was left of the river when an explosion, greater than the sound of rifles on both sides could have been, ripped through the air. Bits of concrete from the dam flew into the air and showered down on loggers and soldiers alike. A wild yell arose from the river's edge where soldiers turned and scrambled back toward their lines. Two or three on the upper end, closest to the dam, had to be pulled out of the raging water cascading down the old Wisconsin River bed. Most of the Bayfield Rifle company was soaked to the waist before they scampered to high ground. Major Reeves dispatched a squad that had been far enough back to miss the flood to the dam site to find out what had happened. The lumberjacks, moments before ready to shoot any soldier who got as far as the water, dropped their rifles in shock, then broke into uproarious laughter. Except for injury to their pride, no one was seriously hurt, either by rushing water or the debris from the explosion. The soldiers were cursing so loudly that Jotham could hardly hear Buck Michaels and Dan Brooks shouting back and forth. Major Reeves, professional soldier that he was, calmly walked among his troops to restore order.

As soon as the water had crested and a man could traverse the suddenly wider and deeper Wisconsin River, Sheriff Michaels started wading across. An angry-looking Dan Brooks quickly stepped into the water behind him. Jotham looked back toward the pine grove where he had last seen Stanley and Frank, but they were nowhere in sight.

Chapter 26

When the sheriff and Dan Brooks reached the river's north bank, soaked to the chest, Jotham could see this was not going to be a friendly visit. Michaels squinted until his eyes were thin slits and his hand twitched as though with a mind of its own it wanted to draw his revolver, but Buck knew that would be neither necessary nor appropriate. A voice that Jotham thought rivaled the sound of the explosion came booming out while the sheriff was still ten to twelve yards away.

"What the hell is this, Marichetti? You tell us you're bringin' them renegade lumberjacks to us to stall for time while your men blow up the dam, huh?"

"You'll pay for this, Marichetti," Brooks added, "you and yer whole damn bunch of loggers out here."

"It's not the loggers," Enrico Marichetti protested. "We didn't blow up yer dam."

"No, not you," Brooks answered, "but some of your men. Sheriff, I want these men arrested."

"Us?" the elder Marichetti father asked in amazement. "You got no reason to arrest us!"

"The hell we ain't! You've got the biggest camp out here and the loggers do what you tell them to. Buck?"

"Wait a minute," Jotham protested. "You don't have a reason to believe that, much less any evidence to support an arrest. We didn't do anything. Whatever the other loggers might have done, and I'm not saying they did anything either, doesn't involve us."

"Well, I say it does," Brooks continued. "What are ya waitin' for, Sheriff? These two are the leaders. Those hellions that broke my dam in Eagle River work for them."

"That makes no difference," Jotham responded. "There's a supreme court ruling that no man can be held responsible for the act of another over whom he doesn't have a master's control." He remembered that from someplace. He thought it had to do with libel law, but it sounded legal and he figured the sheriff might be impressed.

"That's a bunch of gibberish, Marichetti," Brooks snapped back. "You two got plenty of control over these loggers no matter what camp they come from and you know it. Sheriff, you gonna arrest 'em or not?"

"Well, I dunno Mr. Brooks. Seems to me they got a point there. Unless we find the loggers that set off that explosion, there ain't nobody to arrest."

"It won't take long," Brooks asserted. "Soon as the major catches the culprit, you'll have plenty of reason for an arrest."

"I don't think so, Mr. Brooks," Jotham asserted. "Sheriff Michaels," he continued, "I think if you check, you'll find the Lac Vieux Desert dam doesn't belong to the power company, so Brooks isn't the one to make a complaint. His company has no abiding interest in matters involving this dam."

"Is that right, Mr. Brooks?" Michaels asked.

"Well..." Brooks began.

"This dam belongs to the Wisconsin Valley Improvement Company," Jotham broke in. "There isn't any power connected with it so... Well, I have to pass my exams before I'm a real lawyer, but it seems to me the power company, that is Mr. Brooks, can't be the one to lodge a complaint."

"Don't listen to him, Sheriff," Brooks snapped back. "I may not be a representative of the Wisconsin Valley Improvement Company, but it's obvious the law has been broken here and it's pretty damn likely these two had something to do with it."

Sheriff Michaels was beginning to look mighty confused and the argument might have continued for a long time if Major Reeves and an officer of the Bayfield Rifles hadn't come wading across the river. The water was subsiding considerably, but it was still a wide, shallow stream they had to cross, not the little rivulet that had separated the loggers from the militia an hour before. Reeves marched up the incline as though he had just traversed a dry field. The officer with him, tired from an unsuccessful pursuit of the dynamiters, fell several times on the way across and was dripping with Wisconsin River water from the neck down. Jotham had to stifle a laugh, but in spite of his unmilitary appearance, he admired the young officer's attempt to keep up with the major and emulate his professional bearing.

"Didja catch 'em, Major?" Brooks asked.

"No. The Lieutenant here followed them almost to the Michigan border before he lost them."

"Lost them?"

"They was fast, Mister," the junior officer asserted. "Ran through the woods like a herd of deer, they did. My men tried to cut 'em off, but it was no use. They had too much of a start on us."

"Damn loggers," Brooks cursed. He was getting a little more worked-up with each surprising turn of events. "They'll be back though," he continued. "You can bet on it."

"I don't think so," the Lieutenant answered. "They weren't loggers, Mister. They were Indians."

Jotham was as surprised as the rest of them. He too had assumed the dam had been blown up by some of the lumberjacks.

"Indians?" Michaels looked stunned. "You mean it was Indians that blew up the dam?"

"Sure was, Sheriff. War paint and everything. A bunch of young braves, I'd say."

"Ya gotta go after them, Buck," Brooks insisted.

"I can't do that. Dan. I'm just a sheriff. I got no authority outside Vilas county."

"Major Reeves?"

"I was sent over from Bayfield 'cause of them loggers up there. I got nothin' to do with Indians."

"But the dam has been blown up," Brooks protested. "That dam belongs to the state of Wisconsin, Major. You're the state militia. You've got to do something about it."

"Maybe so," Reeves answered, "and if we were dealin' with the lumberjacks, maybe I'd try, but were not dealin' with them anymore. The Lieutenant said they were Indians and they crossed the state line."

"Hell, Major. Out here nobody'd know the difference. Those Indians don't even know where the state line is."

"Well, I do. Mr. Brooks," the Major continued, "this ain't the territories anymore. That's Michigan and this is Wisconsin. We've been a state for more'n fifty years now. These men aren't the U.S. Army. An act of the state legislature back in eighteen seventy-nine made them a part of the National Guard assigned to the State of Wisconsin. That means our jurisdiction ends at the Wisconsin borders."

"Well somebody's got to have jurisdiction," Brooks insisted.

"Even if I did have a right to go after those braves I wouldn't do it," Reeves added. "Hell, that dam is just a few yards of dirt and a few bags of concrete. You could rebuild it in a week. I'm not gonna be the last officer in Wisconsin to precipitate an Indian war."

"Ya mean you're scared of a bunch of Indians?" Brooks bellowed.

"Not scared of 'em," the colonel answered, "just respectful. Wisconsin is about the only state in this part of the country never to have had a major Indian uprising. I don't want to be the officer that breaks that record."

"Okay. I guess maybe you can't go after the Indians," Brooks admitted, "but what am I going to tell them downstate?"

"You've got to tell them the truth," Jotham asserted. "Tell them there's been some resistance to the dams up here and Indians blew up the dam at Lac Vieux Desert."

"Yeah, but..." Brooks muttered, totally confused by the turn of events.

"What about the loggers, Sheriff?" the Major asked. "I kinda hate to see any of those boys get hurt over a prank like that."

"What about it Dan?" Buck Michaels asked. "You still set on goin' after them two?"

"Ah, fellas," Jotham broke in. "I might point out that if this is still a war between the loggers and the army, you're all standing on the wrong side of the river."

Brooks looked up and for the first time was aware of all

the armed lumberjacks only a short distance away. Most of all he was aware of Red Erik, staring his way with a sinister smile peeking through his bushy red beard.

"What about it, Dan?" Michaels asked again.

"Forget it," Brooks answered. "I'm going to have enough trouble without dealing with this rabble. Besides, they're probably across the state line by now too."

Both Jotham and Dominic heaved a sigh of relief.

"I think that's a good decision, Dan," the sheriff offered.

"Well, I don't like it," Brooks answered. "I don't like it a damn bit, but I guess I'm going to have to live with it."

Brooks turned angrily and started back across the river.

"Well Buck," Major Reeves said, "looks like you won't be needin' me any more. Me and my men got a long march ahead of us."

"Thanks Major."

Reeves turned to Jotham. "You're going to make a good lawyer, boy. I'm glad things turned out this way, nobody gettin' hurt." He smiled and shot a glance at Red Erik. Red returned a big toothless smile and winked, then turned to the loggers and started barking orders to pack up.

It took a while for Major Reeves to get back to his side of the river and mobilize his troops for the march back to Bayfield. When the color guard took their place at the head of the line, the major called back to Jotham. That's our state flag, son," he shouted, pointing at the blue banner unfurled in front of him. "When you're a lawyer, it'll be your job to uphold it."

"I know that sir," Jotham called back. "Thanks."

Once Reeves and his troops started to pull out, the line of loggers began to break up and return to their respective camps. After most of them were gone, Jotham and Dominic walked over to the dike that bordered the north side of what had been the Lac Vieux Desert dam. Dominic looked at the muddy water still pouring out of the lake.

"Ya reckon that really was Indians, Jotham?"

"Johnny Bearheart."

"Johnny Bearheart? Really?"

"Yeah. I saw him here a few days ago. He was talking about the dam and said it caged the lake like an animal, but I didn't know he was planning to do this."

"Them Indians is funny," Dominic said. "It took them a long time to decide it was the dams, not the loggers that was causin' them trouble and ruinin' the rice harvest, but once they decided they didn't wait. They learn slow, but they act fast."

"No," Jotham responded. "That's not it."

"No?

"No. They've always had wild rice. Wild rice is very important and they believe the Manitou will always provide the red man with wild rice no matter what we do. It's the same thing with fish. It's a big lake. The dam makes it even bigger so they're sure the fish will be okay."

"Then why'd he do it?"

"Because for the Indian all of nature has a purpose, rivers included, and a river has to be allowed to do what nature intended it to do."

"Huh?"

"Rivers must run, Dominic. That's all there is to it. Rivers must run."

Epilogue

Johnny Bearheart's gesture was symbolic. The dam at Lac Vieux Desert was small and quickly rebuilt. In fact, it was one of twenty-two dams completed by the Wisconsin Valley Improvement Company on headwaters of streams feeding the Wisconsin by 1910. After that, four additional dams were built, but those were large hydroelectric dams constructed far downstream from the logging area to feed the growing paper industry's appetite for electric power.

Shortly after the Lac Vieux Desert dam was reconstructed, the federal government initiated licensing requirements. The power to license dams was first given to the War Department. A 1920 act of Congress created the Federal Power Commission, which held licensing authority for the next fifty-seven years. While that did not end the controversy, battles from that time on were more often waged in the courts than in saloons. Most of the virgin pine had been harvested by 1910. The loggers turned to hardwood for paper pulp. Railroads proved more efficient than rivers for transporting pulp wood. By the 1920's only a few pockets of forest provided enough pine for a real logjam. Interestingly enough though, when the Federal Power Commission was challenged in the 1943 Jersey Dam case, the Supreme Court of the United States reverted back to the days of the lumber barons of the Wisconsin logging era. They ruled that any stream large enough to float a log was navigable water and thus came under federal jurisdiction. Enrico Marichetti and Marty Frederickson would have been pleased with that rationale had they still been alive.

The Chippewa ceremonial ground still stands on the west side of the lake, but the Lac Vieux Desert Band has moved to a tribal center in Watersmeet, Michigan. Eagle Feather, of course, is no longer wtih then. Johnny Bearheart too has gone to be with his fathers, but the son of one of those who went with him to blow up the first Lac Vieux Desert dam still lives as of this writing. He is reluctant to talk about the event to a white person, but his daughter and other tribal members willingly pass the story along. As for the old Indian, born about the time of the dam's distruction, he prefers stories about the lake and the forest, the fish and the deer. The Lac Vieux Desert Band still harvests rice in the lake's shallow northern bays, but he says, the fish are gone. The old man tells of the days when the walleye were big and plentiful. "You could go out any morning and catch your dinner," he says. The loggers didn't clear cut then as they do now and he talks about how easy it was to find game in the woods. His voice, weak to begin with, saddens and softens. "Now they are all gone," he says.

Much of the timber has grown back. Though not the original endless stands of virgin pine, the lake is surrounded by forest. The pines are second growth and not plentiful enough for commercial logging, but large enough to provide a vague image of what must have been there at the turn of the century.

The dam, rebuilt, still stands. Like its predecessor it generates no power. It serves only to hold back the lake in the wet season so that the Wisconsin River will provide a steady source of power in the dry season.

Those who travel to Northern Wisconsin can still see the dam and the small rivulet that a few short miles downstream becomes the mighty Wisconsin. It lies about sixteen miles north of Eagle River via U.S. Highway 45, and two-and-one-half miles east on County Highway E. From that point a blacktop road leads a short distance to the headwaters of the river. There is a parking area and signs that point to a narrow dirt path. It's a walk of perhaps two hundred yards to the dam, but worth every step. The trail, sheltered by tall pines that have had nearly a century of regrowth, follows the river where Jotham played as a child. The traveler will discover why he found it so enchanting. Jotham, Johnny Bearheart and old Eagle Feather are all gone, of course, but a lucky visitor can still see the osprey diving out of the sky and scooping his dinner out of the cool, clear, waters of Lac Vieux Desert.